I0818599

Little Mocos

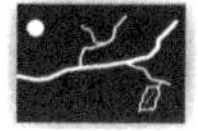

Also by John Paul Jaramillo

The House of Order

Little Mocos

john paul jaramillo

a novel in stories

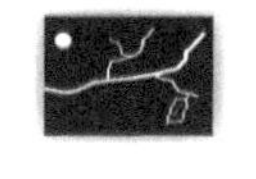

Twelve Winters Press

Published by Twelve Winters Press, a literary publisher.

P. O. Box 414 • Sherman, Illinois 62684-0414 • twelvewinters.
com/contact

Little Mocos was first published by Twelve Winters Press in 2017 and is also available in a digital edition.

Cover and interior page design by TWP Design.

ISBN
978-0-99987057-1-2

Printed in the United States of America

Acknowledgments

“Arkansas Flood 1964” has appeared in *Pilgrimage Magazine*; “Trip Home” online at *Fogged Clarity Arts Journal*; “Laundromat Story” online at *Crash Literary Journal*; “Descansos” has appeared in *Paraphilia Magazine*; and “Little Mocos” online at *Duende*.

Contents

Part One — Huerfano County
1. Animales | 5
2. Relles' Boys | 12
3. Little Mocos | 20
4. Cornbread | 32

Part Two — The Old Folks
5. Birthdays | 47
6. Bear and Peaches | 55
7. Burma | 62
8. Dog Track | 65
9. Korea | 71
10. The Crew | 73
11. Arkansas Flood | 84
12. Chingazos | 91

Part Three — Bruna and Neto
13. Drive | 109
14. Retreat | 113
15. Yesteryear | 118
16. Backyard Marriage | 133
17. Wrecks | 143

Part Four — Pinche Murder Mysteries
18. Rudy Martinez | 153
19. Cornbread in the Attic | 161
20. Lunch | 166
21. Beer and Milk | 171
22. Hamburgers | 176
23. Descansos | 186
24. Laundromat | 193
25. House of Order | 202

Contents continued

Part Five — Half Adult
26. Dead Jefita | 215
27. State Hospital | 218
28. Segundos | 229
29. Apartment in Oregon | 239
30. Long Distance | 245

Part Six — San Luis Valley
31. Trip Home | 257

For my Deborah. For my Family.
Special thank you to Jennifer C. Cornell.

Little Mocos

Part One

Huerfano County

I

Animales

My Tio Neto sat on the bed shirtless and hungover, shaking his balding head at the reality of missing his father's funeral service. He raised both arms to smell his pits and started digging into his jeans for a comb.

"There's a lot of the old folks waiting on you upstairs," I told him.

When he saw who it was, Neto stood up and kicked off his sneakers, coughed blood and spat at the basement's concrete floor. He dropped his soiled pants and rolled up in the sheets.

"You the only Ortiz worth a damn left alive in this neighborhood," Neto said. His clothes were in two great big garbage bags, and he stayed still a minute as I dragged his only collared shirt out from under his stash of nudie magazines and fungus-looking weed.

Later, I put Neto's clothes down deep in the washing machine and asked out loud about the whereabouts of my own father.

"Listen to what I say. I can tell you this, boy," Neto lectured before collapsing back down. "A man is born alone and dies alone. Family will leave you. Women will leave you. All you have is your own damned self."

In the afternoon Tia Viola, honestly the roundest and sloppiest woman in the county, talked to me while everyone sat tristeando after the funeral services. We both ached for the dead grandfather, but it was pretty much invisible. One of the relatives from San Luis that nobody liked very much came through the front door asking for Neto.

"Sleeping," the fat Tia Viola said.

"Sleeping again?"

"No," she said. "Still."

"Didn't see him at the service. What's he been doing with himself? Where's he been?"

"I told you," Viola said. "Sleeping."

Next, Abuela Ortiz went down to the basement with her cold-as-ice looks. She had her apron over her fine black dress and stood on the basement stairs peering down at Neto's face and bloodshot green eyes. "You been drinking?"

I held a plate of rice and beans for Neto, and she stormed halfway down and ripped it from my hands. "I brought him food," I said.

"No talking to these payasos. Get him some clothes."

"There you go, Ma," Neto said. "Arguing and yelling at me and my boy like we're damned dogs. Look I'm putting on clean underwear."

Viola shuffled down and soon had the man standing and pulling on borrowed socks and inching towards dress pants she'd ironed.

"No respect for the dead. The least you can do is honor your dead father and his people by showing your face."

Neto argued, "They should've visited when the viejo was up and around. Those people just want food."

The Abuela peeked farther down and thought on the situation: her fat sister—Viola—and her abandoned grandson—me—and her drunk good-for-nothing son—Neto—all now under her roof and talking shit when her house was filled with family and guests. "What the hell have I done to deserve such sinvergüenzas?" she said.

—

NETO GATHERED TIA VIOLA and me around him and confessed the whole incident. Without anyone around to witness, Neto's oldest compadre, Ray Vigil, had confronted him over some owed dollar bills. He whipped Tio Neto with a rusted, old-fashioned cowboy gun and drank alongside him all night, forcing him to promise payment. Then he dropped Neto off to the front yard on Spruce Street.

"Who is that man?" Tia Viola asked. "What does he want with you?"

"I need money and I need a car, Viola."

"You mean my Imperial?" she said.

"Do you have another, mujer?"

I was quick to add, "I can drive, Tio."

"For Christ's sake," he said. "You're the littlest of mocos."

He ordered me to grab car keys from the Tia's coat, but after making my way through the house filled with old folks, I couldn't resist checking all the pockets sprawled out over the bed.

Viola could be heard in the living room revealing the entire situation to the Abuelo's people and Father Cassady who had also showed in time to eat.

The old folks whispered in speculation how Neto lost his work and money, his home and a string of wives. I overheard the names the old folks had for the man: Neto the loser. The cabrón. The safao of the neighborhood.

"All his life," one went out of the way to comment, "worthless. Never like his father."

I searched the Abuela's dresser, studying the pictures of her and her dead husband along with all of the Abuelo's possessions. I tried to keep the old man alive through his tobacco pouch and collection of pipes, his worn leather boots still thrown in the corner and waiting for him.

"What in the hell is taking you so damned long," Neto's

voice carried through the walls. “Did you get the keys or what?”

“Can’t see’ em,” I said.

After a while Viola ran in and took over. “Right here, stupid. Open both of your eyes.”

It took twenty minutes to start the ancient and primer-colored Chrysler Imperial. We raised the hood and removed the air cleaner to pour gasoline into the carburetor. All in Sunday dress clothes.

“This is a classic,” Viola said. The engine cranked and cranked and refused to fire right off.

“Classic to who?” Neto said.

Viola crushed the springs beneath her seat. “There’s nothing wrong with my car. Just haven’t started it up for a while is all.”

It turned out Neto turned the payments over to Viola years and years ago back when her second husband had work and dollar bills coming in. He still saw it as his own.

The car smelled of cigarettes and pine, and Neto complained about the driving while Viola sat behind the wheel reciting directions. At one point along the way they rolled down all the windows to keep the windshield from fogging over.

“Damned defroster,” Viola complained.

Over by the west side rails, down by the 4th Street Bridge, they got lost and circled around for twenty minutes.

Neto started to curse and complain, worry really. “What the hell we doing?”

“My old man’s hiding place was out here. When he worked for the railroads.”

“Way in the hell out here?” Neto pointed to a group of abandoned looking cars and buildings and said, “Which one, mujer?"

"I'll know when I see it."

Viola threw the car into reverse and zigzagged back towards the most tagged and spray painted, most ancient looking mechanic's shack. She slammed her foot down and nearly jumped out the door before she had the car in park and the door wide open. She and Neto tripped over to the cinder block building and disappeared inside. A second passed and wild dogs were howling and I smelled burning tires. My breath filled the air.

The train cars opposite the shack sat in a locomotive graveyard, two rusted engines standing wrecked out and sideswiped. I climbed free of the Imperial and ran up the set of burnt-up stairs into the cab.

Inside, someone had stripped the seats and tagged crew signs, stickered and spray-painted the floor and ceiling, along with all the walls. The panels of decaying controls had been removed and the broken glass crunched underneath my feet. In one place I could see straight through to the earth below.

First, I whistled and made the destination calls. I thought of the Abuelo, wishing the old man and the train could somehow wake and howl towards California. Next, I leaned and ran my hands over the locomotive's rust before smashing and kicking out glass panels.

Outside Tio Neto started up the Imperial and cranked the heater. When I got back to the car I noticed he was grinning and holding a rat. "No, not a rat, Manito," he told me. He had the brown body by the tail. "Caught myself a mole. For Christ's sake what do they teach you in school?"

I dropped back inside, and Viola was quick to joke, "Damned fools out searching in all this snow and oblivion with no coats."

"Never been able to catch one. I hoped to take it alive."

"And would you look at your clothes," Viola said. "All messed. Your Grandmother Ortiz's going to kick hell out of you."

"They still look good," I said leaning back. "It's just a little dirt, Tia."

"Little dirt!" she said holding my arm. She pushed her finger through the gaping tear in my sweater and pointed out all the mud on my chinos and loafers. "And where's this blood from?"

"Don't know," I said wiping at the stains.

Later, Viola finally revealed the contents of the paper sack. There were stuffed animals, candy that looked like money and cheap carnival ride prizes.

"No problems at all," Neto said with the dead beast cradled in his lap. He rifled through the sack, and one at a time Neto slid a roll of bills and silver dollars into his shirt.

"You gonna hold on to that thing?" Viola said.

"Poor damned little guy. I must've hit it with the shovel. Goddamnit."

"I never seen one close up," I said staring from over the bench seat.

The road to get back to 4th Street seemed to cut straight through the middle of all the snowfall. We drove over train tracks again and again, circling to the darkest parts of the dead end.

Viola said, "This car has no headlights. I forgot to tell you, Neto."

Wearing a Stetson hat and greasy canvas coveralls, Ray Vigil sat at the dinner table and consoled the Abuela Ortiz. He drained cups of coffee and munched pan dulce, the gun safely locked away in his car. He spoke respectfully through his salt and pepper mustache and admitted how Neto ran out on his wife and bills. How he left her with a mortgage and car payment and zero dollar bills. He apologized for all sinners. He apologized for the fraternity of all men and for my Tio.

"You don't know such things because you're still young," Tia Viola told me while I swept and collected beer bottle empties. "It doesn't matter if these men have sympathies for animales or not. Vigil could've come in and shot Neto right through the damned head for what he'd done. Nobody on the block would've blamed him."

Out in the backyard Neto handed Vigil the borrowed dollar bills and silver coins. And as the two men buried the mole's carcass, my Tio cried and made the sign of the cross across his chest.

2

Relles' Boy

One Sunday the compadres dealt cards and told stories of Tio Neto murdering my father over a junker Packard Cavalier. "Didn't kill him, boy," the mustached Tia Viola corrected. "Just fucked him up real bad."

It was some kind of holiday, the Feast of the Body and Blood of Christ it might've been, while the old folks were trying to win dollar bills for lottery tickets or more beers.

"Who the hell knows why those pendejos were going at it," Tio Jake said, his eyes hidden behind hipster sunglasses. He admitted the cops had the two shirtless men pleading and weeping like children out on Spruce Street. "We all heard the sirens, Manito."

I looked down the long card table they had set up on the concrete porch. "There's always some cabrón from the block yelling for blood. You know how it is," Jake said.

"As kids they rode on snow sleds down Spruce and that time they wanted to bash one another's brains," Old Man Hernandez told me shifting his cigarette from underneath his harelip. "And it wasn't just about a damned car. I can tell you that much."

I imagined young faces. Coveralls and dark skin stained with one another's mucus and blood. Hands bruised from teeth and ribs.

"No, not coveralls," Tia Viola recalled after throwing down a losing hand of two pair. "Jeans and ripped-to-hell undershirts."

Hernandez said, "Are we gonna play cards or bullshit?"

"Calmate," Jake ordered.

"I came to play poker."

Jake shot Hernandez a look and puffed at his cigarillo. "I'm telling you they both looked pretty goddamned bad. Knees dirtied with soil from the Vega's garden and oil stains from the cars, you know. Shouting all loud like you hear at the fairgrounds."

"They looked all savage and shit," Viola said. "In their eyes. We thought they'd kill one another for sure. That's really the story."

Old Lady Norrick stopped by and sipped from a bottle hidden away in a paper sack. She frowned and said she had no idea why they fought that afternoon. She only knew the brothers borrowed her husband's tools. "They scarred one another something awful. You could tell by all the blood," she said.

Tia Viola sold it as the boys fighting on the porch until they crashed the Abuela Cordelia's La Virgen de Guadalupe shrine. Though she couldn't testify to any of it, I kept at her until she described the blood on the floor and the walls.

"This porch, Tia? Here on Spruce Street?"

"What the hell you think we been talking about this whole time, boy?"

Downtown the next morning Neto told me Anthony Quinn was born in Chihuahua, Mexico, and also that the man spoke fluent Spanish and French. He jabbed a plastic siphon down my mouth. He assured me: "It's only flammable in gas form."

I choked and spat stolen gasoline all over blacktop. "For real?"

"Hell yeah, kid." He lit a match and burned the tip of

his black cigarillo. "I saw it in a trailer for *The Children of Sanchez*. Down at the dollar movies on Abriendo."

"I'm talking about the gas, Neto."

"Oh, I've seen men throw cigarette butt after cigarette butt into barrels to put them out." Neto howled with laughter and slapped at his jeans. "Let's light one up for you and we'll see."

Next, he read the sign COLDEST BEER IN TOWN and ran across for one, giving the excuse, "I've got these damned pinche nerves."

My lips sweated gasoline, and grit coated my tongue. I spilled more down my chinos and onto the sidewalk.

When Neto finally returned he was buzzed and agitated. "Did you take a bath in the shit? The hose, cabrón. Got my hose? I'm going to shit all over you if my tool box is light."

"I must've left it."

"Well grab it. You gotta learn to finish work, Manito."

While I ran, Neto tuned to Mexican waltzes and oldies on the AM radio.

"Man's got to have gasoline for his vehicle and they don't make it easy," he yelled from the driver's side.

On the east side of town, he bought more cigarettes and a quick drink at a dive bar called The Senate. He retrieved gambling winnings from his compadre nicknamed Freddie Fender and he bought me a cheeseburger. He told me more about the dead grandfather's younger days. "That man was a bastard like no other," Neto insisted. "You never knew your Abuelo like I knew the man. Wouldn't stand for not producing."

Outside in the parking lot Neto tamped another cigarette and rested behind the wheel. At his insistence I stood and blotted puddles of spilled gasoline from inside the trunk. That's when the police cruiser rolled up. Neto spat and cursed to himself. "Cabrónes."

The Crown Vic stayed behind and Neto searched the glove box for his New Mexico driver's license.

The cop kept one hand on his service revolver and ordered me to sit on the curb. His teeth held a toothpick and the whole sad afternoon reflected off his sunglasses. He asked Neto, "Been damn near twenty years and your old man's Packard still fires up, huh?"

"Chauncy?"

"Officer Sandoval, Neto. No one calls me Chauncy no more."

I didn't say a word. I had fumes deep in my nose.

"Listen, Chauncy," Neto said. "I'm looking for work and the kid here was taking me around."

"You been drinking?"

Neto sucked at his teeth and stared at the cracks in the windshield. "No beer, sir. And I wasn't driving anyhow. We're parked."

The Officer's cough nearly turned into a laugh. "Jesus. Why do you make it so easy, Neto?"

The next Sunday Tia Viola shuffled and flicked cards with a flourish. She smoked, using her drained beer bottle as an ashtray. She said she remembered the Grandmother on hands and knees with a bucket scrubbing bloodstains from the concrete stoop. "That woman loved Neto and Relles. Loved her boys," Tia said. "But they were strays even though they had her and this house, you know? Like dogs, I mean. I love that woman but those boys of hers. I don't know what else to tell you, boy. Don't know what you want to hear."

The compadres admitted finding beer bottles littering the garage. "They were working on your Abuelo Ortiz's Packard and that old worthless transmission."

Viola made it known, "I'm gonna tell you straight out,

kid, that bitch-of-the-world mother of yours, Bruna Montoya, was probably the reason."

Later, between bets and them throwing down poor cards, Neto himself appeared after an afternoon nap, wearing a sweaty t-shirt over his greasy jeans and with his hair wetted down and pushed back. Ever since the wife put him out and the Abuelo Santiago died, he'd been living in the man's room and wearing his clothes.

He pulled the cigarette from behind his ear and slapped down on my shoulders. "A man has to learn poker, mi'jo."

"We're talking about when you were eighteen," Viola said. "Remember that shit? When you were fixing up your old man's car with Relles and brought the cops down on you."

"Who the hell knows?" Neto said, rubbing at his neck. And before he ignored them all for liquor store neon lights down on Northern or maybe 29th Street, he giggled mindlessly, "It will all be fucking yesteryear soon."

Neto said I should walk with him to Pedro Mendoza's and roof houses. The man was bowlegged and once when Pedro had been drinking and working on his truck alongside Neto, he punched me in the gut with his oily, leathered hands.

"For Christ's sake," Neto lectured as we walked. "That's all done with. You got to learn to forgive, no? Can't you leave it at that?"

Hours into the first day, afternoon clouds saved us from the scorching sun, and I was the one kneeling, knees burning through my jeans.

Neto lit a cigarette and directed me to clear old nails and tar paper. "A man needs to learn how to put in a day's work."

Mostly Pedro ordered us up and down ladders and

pointed out mistakes as they scraped off rotting roof paper from carports. I noticed Pedro's name scratched into half of the tools we used and red paint marking the handles of the other half. "It's so we don't steal them, Manito," Neto explained.

After a shared lunch of bologna and RC Cola, the old man's eyes looked tired. "You know I was a steel worker," Pedro told us. "Like your Grandfather. And when I was laid off and needed for my own, these side-jobs saved my ass. Kept my mortgage paid, you know?"

Neto scraped off his t-shirt to sun his chest. "A man works to pay his bills."

"I remember this one time I told the foreman I knew this one compadre who should be hired on. So I pick up my phone one night and give him a call and tell him to meet me at 7 a.m. *Bring your tools*, I tell him."

"That's exactly what I told this one, Pedro," Neto offered, pointing his thumb in my general direction.

"He's still in school, no?"

"It's summer," I said.

"Anyhow," the old man finally continued, "this man showed up late. So I told him *thanks but no thanks* and I'll be damned if he wasn't upset as all hell. Punching the air and kicking at the concrete beneath him when he finally showed. Telling me he's got a new wife and baby on the way and needs rent money."

"Ay, que cabrón," Neto said.

"I remember I watched him walk across the road bawling and carrying on. Said he didn't have a car that was reliable and had to walk."

"No shit."

"I tell you I felt sorry. And you know who that was?" Pedro said as Neto stared. "It was your brother. Years and years back. You don't remember?"

Neto finally offered, "This is Relles' boy here."

"Who?"

"This one here," he said thumbing over at me.

"Oh, that's right, ain't it?" He laughed out loud, pulling the hat from his head and nearly falling off his balance.

Neto told him that my father was dead and that my mother Bruna was a whore and ran off.

"Didn't mean nothing by laughing," Pedro apologized.

Neto blew smoke from a cigarette. "So he never got the job?"

"Shit. The foreman was playing with him. Said if he was Army, if he worked half as hard as me, he'd be a damned fool not to hire him. Called him back across the street and offered him work on the spot."

Neto had to ask, "Why and the hell didn't you call me that time, Pedro?"

On the last Sunday of the month I held a handful of earned quarters and dollar bills and Old Man Hernandez dealt me into the game. "Your father was legit in those days," he continued as he replaced cards. "Out of the service. Thin and handsome. No debts and no enemies. Nothing like your cabrón Tio Neto out there."

"Relles had a wife and a baby on the way," Viola agreed. "To this day I have to say it's not right for one brother to be jealous."

"It's like biblical and shit," Hernandez said.

"What the hell do you know about the Bible, old man?" Viola demanded.

"Shit, those brothers were all the same," Jake finally corrected.

They agreed the boys would get into it sooner or later.

"They'd been at each other's throats for years. Since they were boys. I hate to say it," Viola told me, "but they weren't angels. You're fooling yourself if you think they were. The folks used to say chingazos and fighting was all they knew."

"Naces pendejo, mueres pendejo," Jake said. "Born stupid, die stupid."

When the old folks had drunk all they could, and around the time the sunlight drained from the neighborhood, I complained and cried.

"For Christ's sake. Give the kid back his money," Viola said, nearly pleading. "He doesn't understand the kind of game you men are playing out here."

3

Little Mocos

The little dirt-faced Beatrisa and I would slip out after midnight down to the blacktop of 21st Lane past cottonwood and locust trees. This was back in the day when the Abuelo was still alive and had us working onion fields near Española, New Mexico.

On bare feet stained from running along ridges and furrows, we crouched and dug with sticks, collected rocks and targeted road signs. We avoided barbed wire fences and leaped into blossoms of cactus stems with our feet and heels. One night I tripped up and fell the farthest down, every grasp for balance spiked with pain while Bea pulled me level.

Outside our shared bedroom window, I boosted Bea up and then whispered, scratched at the window and growled and cried like a dog until she strained to pull me inside. In bed, we arranged ourselves and carefully removed barbed spines from arms and legs. We kissed one another's skin with sympathy and stayed awake as long as we could, listening to mutual breathing and staring into the colorless walls.

When the sun finally filled the space, the Abuelo Santiago, our Grandfather, washed our dirtied feet and faces and warned us about what would happen if dogs were to ever catch us.

"Not scared of no dogs," we answered back.

The Abuelo had hauled padlocks and metal for the back

door and laid the locks out on the kitchen table. The job of securing the house was what he meant to do, but we ran him ragged most days. He didn't have the eyes to match locks and keys.

Before the summer ended, my shady Tio Neto showed up and sprayed gravel when he slammed on the brakes. He often drove by and brought fresh corn and vegetables from the fields, brought cigarettes and a bottle. He slid out from the ride and handed the supplies over and gave word about some government check the family was waiting on.

He walked right in and sat and yelled for brewed coffee. He squinted and sniffed the air and then he complained about the general condition of the compadre's workhouse and yard.

"Why the hell don't you set these kids to work?" he asked. He pointed to the piles of laundry and dirtied bedding that lined the hallway. "Don't you ever clean around here?"

As the two men talked and smoked, and then later after the Abuelo and Neto drove off for who-knows-where, we hung out in the side yard and kicked at dirt clods and rocks. We held hands, drank cool water from the hose and stroked one another's hair. We chased frogs around what used to be the flower garden and then crawled under the porch and discovered snakes.

WEEKS LATER while warm in that ancient metal-framed bed, I listened to the Abuelo stoking the woodstove for breakfast. The old man toasted tortillas on the stovetop and brewed strong smelling coffee and could be heard lecturing Neto who had returned after days of drunken partying. I shot up and stood beside the kitchen door, peering around the corner to see the men draining coffee mugs and smoking.

"What's up, little man?" Neto said to me. He jabbed his cigarette into the ashtray and slapped my hands and sparred with me. He gave a fake left to the jaw, and I gave him a fake uppercut. I could see scratches on his face, his eye bruised and blackened. I smelled cigarettes on his clothes before I heard him speak.

"You're strong, huh? One day you'll kick some ass, boy. Fists of cement, uh," Neto said.

"I'm trying to teach respect and work," the Abuelo told him. "And you teach him to be a goddamn disgraciado. Don't want him to be no punk, no juevon. He even runs off at night like his damned uncle."

"Little man can do what he wants, viejo."

"He's not your boy," the Abuelo said. He rose slowly, wearing only boxer shorts and scratching at his immense hairy back.

"Get down, protect your head, dodge and slip around my punches. Protect yourself, Manito," Neto continued, jabbing at my face.

"Jesus, Neto," the old man snapped, crossing his arms. "Can't you go a day without trouble? Go clean yourself up. We got field jobs today. Both of you."

As I dressed Neto came into the shared bedroom and wrapped medicine strings around my wrists. He slipped a bag of sage around my neck while Bea sat and sniffed the leather and root. "For evil spirits," he told me.

Soon, we were in the Abuelo Ortiz's Dodge in an onion field parked side-by-side with rows of ranch trucks and battered old cars. The smell of grasslands and morning dew drifted on the wind. The Abuelo sat on the truck tailgate talking with a mix of other workers guzzling from metal thermos tops. He watched Neto and me, along with Bea, slip on gloves and choose our shears and sacks. Just then a row of headlights, the sheriff's and two others, jolted down the old highway toward the collection of men readying to start work.

"Looks like it's all caught up with you, no?" the Abuelo yelled. He laughed and slapped Neto on the back as hard as he could.

Neto's reaction was to sprint. I kept up with him for a while, but then eventually slowed and watched as two deputies held my Tio's arms and another pushed at his head, cuffed him and crumpled his body into the ground.

For the rest of the afternoon the Abuelo kept looking over and warning us. "There's right and there's wrong, mi'jos," he told us. "You understand me what I'm trying to tell you?"

We came inside from another night of wandering around the fields and found the Abuelo sitting in the kitchen drinking coffee and suffering from chest pains. We stood with muddied feet and pant legs asking for breakfast, and then the man yelled for Bea to do the work of peeling potatoes and frying eggs.

He took the opportunity to tell Bea her mother planned on returning for her soon. He told me to get ready to leave for his home in Colorado. "When will my mama come?" I asked only to be ignored.

"The fieldwork is over and done," the man explained. "No more summer in New Mexico for you. Hear me? So no more running off. That means you, boy."

I shook my head and felt the tears burning.

"Children don't run around them fields. You don't want your cousin killed do you?" he said to Bea. "You'll fall in a damn irrigation ditch and never be heard of again."

"Do we have to go?" we complained.

"Can't stay on around here." The man sat in the kitchen and set down the rules of behavior for us, how his wife, the Abuela Cordelia, would expect absolute obedience in Colorado. Then he walked into a backroom of the ancient workhouse and found the sofa, and we could hear him snoring and coughing in pain well into the afternoon.

The mustached Tia Viola who was also making the move came by later. She had a bag filled with some new clothes from the K-Mart, a dress for Bea and a stiff dress shirt and slacks for me. We were making painful faces as we were forced into our baths and then our clothes, our nicest and most slippery pair of dress shoes for church.

Next, we loaded our boxes and suitcases leaving the dirty laundry behind. We first stopped at St Francis of Assisi for Mass, and Bea and I whispered and giggled through the act of consecration to the Immaculate Heart of Mary prayer. The Abuelo was the one to grab our arms and twist and pinch at our skin. Out in the lot, in between parked cars, he was the one to slap at our bottoms and legs.

"You'll learn to be respectful in the house of your Lord," the Abuelo announced.

Later, we moved into our home on Spruce Street in Huerfano County, Colorado. That night during the chores of scraping dishes and sweeping the kitchen floor, we noticed welded bars to all the windows and the security door, double locks to both sides with no way in or out.

THE DAY BEFORE Bea's mother, Cynthia Otero, made her way down Spruce Street to introduce the girl to her father, the woman had smoked meth for the first time. Her boyfriend of a few weeks nearly choked her out over some kind of check she couldn't cash.

"It makes me sick as a goddamned dog I have to come here," Cynthia began. She kept her daughter in the running car as the morning rain pattered around them. "You know she's yours, Ray."

Ray "Cornbread" Vigil had come to his door shirtless, with his myriad of tattoos exposed. He wore a razor thin mustache and his belly popped out over his belt buckle. "Jesus Christ, Cynthia," he said.

"I was thinking maybe you have something for us." For a long aching minute there was nothing.

Cornbread stared and snuffed.

"Well," Cynthia continued, "don't worry. I ain't leaving her with you. If that's what you think. But I hope you'll do right by her, Ray. She's with my Tia and you should watch out for her is all I am saying to you."

She paced back to her Plymouth confused. She lit a cigarette and nearly cried over the steering wheel.

"Who is that man, Mama? What house is this?"

"Be quiet, girl. He's nobody to you."

Cynthia showed up at Ray Vigil's many mornings after that first visit, for money or a place to sleep. According to Tio Neto and the neighborhood, only two people knew the truth of those morning arguments between Cynthia and Cornbread Vigil.

The papers reported the woman was finally shot right through the front door of that old basement apartment. The police say that Vigil held a .380 caliber handgun below the peephole and emptied the weapon. A bullet slammed into her spine. The papers said Cynthia passed on after a week in a coma.

Tio Neto had a clip from *The Huerfano Chieftain*:

> *Vigil has been charged with second-degree murder in the March 26, 1983, shooting death of 28-year-old Cynthia Otero. He is accused of shooting Otero as she entered his East Side apartment. A Denver District Court trial in the shooting ended in mistrial last Nov. 1 after Otero family members were spotted outside*

the courtroom showing an 8-by-10 photo of Miss Otero to jurors. Jurors reported they had been discussing the photo in private. Huerfano public defenders Doug Wilson and Victor Reyes asked for a mistrial because of the victim's family's misconduct.

Vigil stood with his front door open while the mother of his child was on the floor in front of him, and he stared down at her bloody face and clothing. Neto swore the man was not the cold-blooded killer they made him out to be. He assured people Vigil screamed and wailed for forgiveness.

According to *The Huerfano Chieftain*:

Vigil told the 911 operator, "She's lying in the hallway." When asked to look closer, he added, "I recognize her now. It's Cynthia." Another key piece of evidence was a security chain lying on the floor of Vigil's front door. The defense suggested it was forced off, causing Vigil to suspect a would-be burglar. "This was an instantaneous, split-second reaction to an apparent breaking and entering," Wilson told the jury.

Tio Neto explained later that if Cynthia had come a day earlier Vigil would have been drunk and asleep. A week earlier, and Vigil would not have had several unregistered weapons in his possession.

"I DON'T KNOW how it all could ever be understood to such a young mind," Tia Viola told people not long after the death of Bea's mother. She said the girl's hands were made for sorrow and trouble, broom and mop handles. "Oh, that poor girl. Pobrecita. Like a slave. Like a damned stray dog."

That was how it played out. The young girl's painted fingernails left cracked and bitten from the chores of peeling potatoes and soaking beans to cook. Skin dried and burnt up, prone to hives from cleaning with bleach and cleanser. If I was the Grandmother's eyes and ears, Bea was her hands and legs.

"Your mother calls you or sends money from wherever the hell she happens to be shacked up, but out of all the family Bea is the one with nothing, Manito," Viola explained to me. "Her mother is dead and gone and the father in and out of jail for years. Not a penny."

She said I was lucky to be born a man, lucky to do whatever I wanted, when I wanted.

"That girl has to ask for permission and money to do anything. The Grandmother has them foster kids in control. Especially that one. She has to ask to go out to the backyard. The poor creature," the Tia said. "She has to earn her way. But this one isn't a daughter. She's a slave. Mark how I tell you. She'll go the way of her mother for sure. Pregnant or dead. Dead or pregnant."

LATER DURING her high school years, Beatrisa, the fifteen-year-old whore of Spruce Street, ran out back with her mess of fake crimson hair. She screamed and carried on: "Neto grabbed at me!"

Abuela Cordelia was sweeping up October leaves when it all played out. "The whole damn neighborhood can hear you and your mouth. What is it, cabróna?"

The girl rubbed at fresh bruises. "I was looking in the closet for one of the Abuelo's sweaters and the boys said Neto was dead drunk and wouldn't hear."

"Oy lo!"

Bea, the skinny grasshopper of a girl, rolled her eyes. Her legs shimmered with lotion, and she looked at me and nearly smiled. "I put a mirror to check his breathing."

"For Christ's sake!"

"He pulled at my hair and kicked me in my ass and legs. Locked me up in the closet and wouldn't let me out." She acted out the man's blows, trying to capture every detail and drama of the crime.

"Hey, who taught you to say ass? I'm not one of your friends. Who taught you that kind of talk?" the Abuela Cordelia snapped through her shaky, false teeth. "Didn't I tell you not to mess with those clothes? To mind your own goddamn business."

"He's dead and don't wear 'em no more."

"You don't have to tell me my husband is dead, cabróna," the old woman argued. "I'm the one who buried the man."

"He didn't have to wail on her," I said.

"And who the hell's talking to you?" the Grandmother snapped, shutting me up. "Both of you. Get in the house and get the breakfast going."

Bea bawled and punched at her thighs. "Neto is the one!"

A FEW WEEKS LATER Bea's lip came up busted and scarred, her t-shirt ripped off of her. She found someone with quarters and called from the Mesa Theatre pay phone. I convinced Neto to drive out and the first thing he did was give her his sweatshirt. She begged us not to tell the Abuela.

The next day she wore heavy makeup over a pretty obvious bruise, the makings of a deep scar on her temple, and we bypassed school. We walked over to China Lantern Diner near Santa Fe Avenue to blow dollar bills on egg rolls.

She was particularly striking even with her wound, radiant and fragile, and on the way she gave a 4th Street vagamundo a five-dollar bill.

"If he doesn't use it for anything worse than cigarettes or

booze that will be good with me," she said. "People ought to look out for one another, cousin. That's what religion's for, no?"

All she had to do was speak. I was too young not to love her.

In a booth, under a mural of the Great Wall of China, I asked her why she had dragged me there. I told her the place was greasy and the waitresses were careless.

"It's one of the great works, Relles," she explained, and in my memory she was the only one back then who called me by name.

I didn't say a thing, kept munching on fried rice and draining refills of RC Cola.

"Like those cathedrals in France, Manito." She had just read *The Hunchback of Notre Dame* in school and listed all the places she dreamed of travelling.

I asked why she fucked such cabrónes.

"Who says I fuck guys?"

"Neto says. Brandon Flores and his brother. Derrick Espinoza."

After a few sad bites she answered, "None of Neto's fucking business. The creeper Neto. And what about you? The hediondas you drag home? Come on. Dolores Mendoza?"

"What about her? She gets me into the dog track for free."

"Pancake assed," she said, laughing. "And so now you're a dog player like your pinche good-for-nothing uncle."

We walked around most of the afternoon, and that night stood in the living room listening to Neto's Richard Pryor albums. We repeated the punch lines out on the back stoop, and under a disaster of telephone and electricity wires, we stood and dreamed, made sad promises to one another.

—

One day, at the bus stop after school, Bea stood and smoked weed, another of her sins. She smoked in alleys and in cars, down in Bessemer Park and empty parking lots, sitting on picnic tables and sitting on concrete pylons under interstate overpasses. Those were the usual haunts. Sometimes her friends laughed because she wrapped a flannel shirt around her hair.

"Why do you wrap your head, Bea?" they all asked, laughing.

"Porque the Abuela slaps me if I have the smell on me. The Tio too. Caught me one time because of it. I told him like this, I say, *You ain't my Father*. He pulls me out of a car because he spotted me with a loose smoke behind my ear."

The girls she hung with didn't know the home on Spruce where she came from. But I knew. We were the same.

"*Cabróna, you better not be smoking*," Bea mimicked the Grandmother for the benefit of her crew. "*Your Abuelo Santiago died of the cancer. In his lungs. His tongue and throat completely dead and rotted out*." Bea said, "I hate her and that stupid son of hers. I hate looking at them."

When it was just me walking alongside of her, off of Abriendo Avenue, she put her arm around me. I smelled weed and vanilla perfume.

"These trees are oak," she announced while walking from the bus stop. She held a monstrous pack filled with textbooks and library books. I didn't even carry a notebook to school anymore.

I stared at her brown eyes and her freckled neckline. "What do I need to know about trees, Bea?"

"Because I'm telling you," she said with those full and scarred lips, the same as her murderous father. "Because they're damn beautiful. And because you should study so we can get to college."

Dogs were barking up and down the street and for Bea

it was as simple as that.

"For fucking trees?" I said.

"Biology. Or maybe philosophy or engineering. Mrs. Medina says I got the grades. Says, *The more math you take, the more money you make.*"

"I could go into the army. Like the Abuelo," I said. Then I asked her if she missed the old guy.

"I halfway expect him to be around sometimes to lecture me when I come up to the yard, you know?" In the time it took to drag on her cigarette she put her hand into mine. "I like to go into his closet to smell his clothes. Smells of wood smoke and pipe tobacco."

"Is that when Neto caught you?"

"Now that's the worst of it. Having him around all of the time. Neto the idiot. Neto the loser. Like I say. Well, loser-ish, anyway. I'll tell him to his face if it comes to it."

"You don't think women would want a man like Neto?"

She laughed. "Ask any of his wives. Ask them! Any woman with half a brain threw him out on his broke ass."

So I was cruel to her and called her a whore. That was the way we all treated each other on the block. As I write this I regret owning only one wallet-sized photo of Bea, and in it she is much younger than I remember her. She's on Spruce Street in the backyard with her mother. This was before the hair dye and the lip piercings, before her Goth days when she went and shaved the sides of her head. Before the reputation and the god-awful cheap tattoos that carved her ears and neck and that the Grandmother said made her even more of a whore and disgrace. Before all the self-loathing we were all known for. At this time her mother is still the love of her life. She smiles wide and stands back against the metal clothesline pole where as little mocos we ran blindly through mazes of drying bed sheets and flapping Levi's.

4

Cornbread

Most of the snitches in the neighborhood, the old folks and the old men sipping coffee at the Sinclair Station, told me the same: "What in the hell do you want to know about a man like Cornbread?"

Cornbread's adobe house two blocks over from the Abuela's, the one littered with dead weeds and half-buried and rusted machine parts, was the hangout for a number of the other cabrónes. There were so many men like Cornbread in the old neighborhood. Men like Tio Neto and their endless amount of afternoons and evenings filled with smoke, rum and RC Cola and talk.

"Hey, Cornbread," Neto shouted. "What should we do when the cops pull us over? What's the word?"

He schooled Neto on rolling the windows up and locking it all down and never offering a thing up. He knew.

"Don't say a goddamn thing," he insisted. "They don't care what you say anyways."

Cornbread kicked at the dirt while making most of his positions and claims, and never supported them with more than the words, "I am for goddamned sure" and "Don't tell me, I know, cabrón." Long, slow laments on the status of the American worker and genocide of the Navajo people. Most things Neto never understood.

People remind me this was all around the time of the steel mill collapsing and the times of "sky-high" unemployment. Cornbread's record of felonies alone proved there was some truth to that.

They say he hunted for the opportunity to grab supplies from his girl working at So-Lo Grocery, and pulling a new television out of the K-Mart's emergency exit. They say he pulled comics from Bolinger's Card Shop and ran out on meals at Jorge's Restaurant. Drove off on tanks of gasoline and sold weed with his compadre Mariano who everyone called "Marijuano."

And for those in the neighborhood or in the family who think Tio Neto wasn't innocent, they should be happy to find out Neto only stole from employers he felt abused the working man. So, yes, Neto did steal nails and tools from the old steel mill. Old Man Samora told folks he saw Neto drop nails before the security gate and stuff wrenches and bolts in his lunch pail.

"Is that what your Abuelo taught you in that house?" Old Man Hernandez once asked me.

One morning Neto sat crudo draining mugs of black coffee and explaining his compadre's "incidents." He pulled the frayed bits of newspaper clippings from his billfold:

> *A 1958 burglary conviction . . . A 1970 conviction for assault with intent to kill, which was overturned by the Colorado Supreme Court 2 1/2 years later . . . A 1973 first-degree murder charge, which first ended in mistrial, then resulted in a conviction, for which he was sentenced to life under the habitual criminal statute (which the Legislature changed) . . . And a 1983 aggravated robbery charge for which jurors acquitted him. . . .*

He told me Cornbread was the older of the two men, born sometime in the 1940s, and always in dusty, faded jeans and work boots. He was always loitering and honking his horn for neighborhood daughters, his foot on the gas to keep the old beater from dying.

"Well, if I had to say. When he was young I think he looked like a rail thin Lon Chaney, Jr., you know?" Neto told me. "Since he was 18 the cabrón was tough-looking. From that one movie with Randolph Scott? You know the one I mean?"

"Which, Tio? *Albuquerque*?"

"Holy shit, Manito! I was gonna say *Albuquerque*. You seen that one?"

"I seen it with you. At the dollar movies."

Later Neto scraped at burnt toast and told me, "This one time on Carter Avenue, the landlord was coming around looking for Vigil's rent."

"I didn't know those houses on Carter Avenue are apartments."

"I said they were apartments, Manito," Neto said. "Listen up. So this landlord, Montelongo, lets himself in to the house and threatens Vigil. Right in front of his girlfriend and her friends. Calls him a deadbeat."

"So he killed him, Neto?"

"No. Another time Vigil went down to where Montelongo's mother was living. On a thought he might be there, right? Well, happens they were out in the back patio, right? Vigil walks into the backyard and puts his hand in his coat to give Montelongo the rent. Montelongo jumps and runs into the garage and the mother she's all screaming for her son's life, you know? My hijo! Oh my hijo! That Montelongo is so nervous and scared he comes out with a gun and gets off a shot. It misses Vigil but nails his own mother right in the goddamn chest."

"What did Cornbread do?"

And that's when Neto lectured me. "You don't know

him like that so you call him Vigil. You got it? If you don't know a man you have to earn the right to call them something they don't normally want to be called. I mean a man has got to have respect."

"Neto, the story!"

"So Montelongo is screaming: Mama, oh Mama! I mean he's screaming his lungs out. I was blocks away and we all heard it. I was on the Abuela's porch or maybe I was at The Donahue having a few. We all heard it."

"What happened to Montelongo?"

"Vigil had to move, you know. But the mother ain't dead. She talks to me all the time, Manito. I saw her last month at the Stations of the Cross. She was cutting out headlines like for scrapbooks and shit."

"Did the cops get him?"

"No, they couldn't get him, you know," Neto said. "They didn't have no witnesses other than Montelongo and he's the one that owned the gun. The cops were more than happy to make a case against Montelongo wanting to shoot his mother. All Vigil was doing was holding an envelope."

"If you knew back then what you know now, would you have been scared of him?"

"Probably not," Neto said.

"Really? No?" I said. "They say he killed those people, Neto."

"Who said?"

"The newspapers and the TV."

"Why the hell are you believing what you read in those papers, Manito? I told you the papers ain't nowhere near the truth of these stories."

CORNBREAD DROVE ALL NIGHT out to Albuquerque. That's Neto's next story. To the suburbs east of the city to a high-rent apartment complex where his sister lived with Leroy

Romero. Cornbread found the underfurnished rooms smelling of ashtrays and the sister with blood filling her mouth.

Standing by the toilet in the apartment's large bathroom, the sister worked on the cuts to her eye. She pulled up her shirt gently with her thumbs and showed Cornbread the black and blue scrapes to her back and what she worried might be a cracked rib.

When the sister called her brother hours earlier, the round, suspender-wearing Leroy was wrestling the phone from her thinking she was calling the police. Said he owned her the way he owned the apartment or the truck.

"Shit," she complained. "He beats me and leaves. Is that how it works? For God's sake, Raymond, that man did this out in front of the whole street. The whole fucking neighborhood. I'm forty years old, brother, and went and got myself beat down by another man."

With her brother near she was quiet and somber. She wiped tears and mascara from her eyes.

"I'll find him and I'll kill him," Cornbread offered. "Why not? Tell me, sister, why not?"

His sister dropped the washcloth and hydrogen peroxide bottle. She chuckled nervously and searched for cigarettes. She packed the rest of her clothes. "I'm moving my shit the hell out of here and you ain't gonna do a thing, brother."

Later the two referred to the night as "The Beating" and the whole thing needed no other context. When they talked of the Youth Offender System they referred to one incident as "The Rape" and their mother running out as "The Boyfriend" and their father dying at the steel mill as "The Accident."

Vigil convinced her to drive his car and leave him behind to retrieve her car keys, her purse and driver's license.

Next he fixed himself a sandwich and drained some of Leroy's beer. He went through all their cabinets and drawers and squatted down in a closet with a tire iron.

Victor Reyes, the neighborhood lawyer who represented Vigil, told Tio Neto the weapon allegedly used by Vigil in the "beating" death was never found.

"I DON'T KNOW if I could hurt nobody, bro," Neto said that afternoon Ray Vigil placed a gun in his hand and pulled bullets from behind his truckito's bench seat.

Ray and his brother Alex picked Neto up at the corner of 4th and Broadway at 9 in the morning. He was holding a brown paper bag filled with his disguise: a black winter's cap and his thickest winter coat folded around his last carton of cigarettes.

"You can't do this with just a knife, Neto," Ray Vigil answered.

"I know that Ray," Neto said.

"Then shut up and get into this, Neto," Ray said. "Everybody has to be into this if we want a chance."

The two-door truckito Ray drove was Alex's so it was not quite stolen. Alex Vigil hadn't worked in months and needed the money for his mortgage and for his girlfriend and two daughters.

"Let Neto drive," Alex said. "If he don't want no gun let him drive."

"You drive, Alex, and we all get a gun, cabrón," Ray said. "Don't you hear me? We all gotta be into this or we make nothing."

Neto finally sat in the middle between the two brothers with his legs straddling the transmission box. Alex had brought his own paper sack and Neto had to carry both bags while they drove. Neto could see Alex's bag contained prescription sunglasses, a clip-on moustache from someone's old Halloween costume and a ridiculously wide, grey beard.

"This stuff all looks real fake," Neto said.

"It doesn't matter, Neto," Ray said. "The gun will give you away so you just need something to cover your face."

"I'll be in the car so I won't need it, right?" Alex said.

Ray didn't respond or say one word as the men drove. Their thoughts were all signs of failure in his mind. He stayed cool though and efficient as they passed intersection after intersection, as they passed the KFC and then the Yellow Front.

"I gotta smoke, Ray," Alex said.

"You can smoke when we stop," Ray said.

"I don't have nothing to smoke."

"I have a carton," Neto said. "My old man gets them by the carton and keeps them in the Frigidaire."

"That don't keep them fresh," Alex said.

"Sure it do," Neto said.

"No, no, no," Alex said. "Freezes up the tobacco. They would deliver them in refrigerated trucks like beer if that was the truth."

"Shut up," Ray said. "I'm gonna say this one last time. We all gotta be into this. I wouldn't have brought you, brother, if I knew you were gonna be like this."

"Like what?" Alex said.

"Like all distracted and shit," Ray said. "Because you gotta be calm, man. You'll be scared and nervous but you can't move. Jesus, don't you know where we're going? You have to sit in the car and leave it running and stay motionless."

"I know, Ray," Alex said. "I'm telling you I know."

The men stopped in an alley three blocks from the neighborhood branch of what used to be called Minnequa Bank and Trust. Ray placed a twenty-gauge shotgun in his lap and the barrel reached over Neto's lap almost keeping him from throwing on his winter coat. He placed the moustache over his moustache before trading it for the beard. He gave the glasses to Neto.

When Alex switched places with Ray, he immediately started jabbing at the push button radio under the dash, rapidly pressing and pushing to change the stations.

Rosalie Arguello later testified she saw the men arguing in the street that morning while she watered her tomato plants. She testified to watching two of the men running off and leaving Vigil alone. Later she testified to knowing Vigil's mother and how the woman would be rolling in her grave to know about the men's actions that day. She never met Neto's mother but she was sure the woman would feel the same if she were a Christian.

The Huerfano Chieftain reported:

> *Public Defender Victor Reyes argued that the photo identification lineup of six individuals by the bank teller and a local homeowner, who saw a man running and getting in his vehicle, should not be allowed at trial. Reyes said both people had told police the man they saw was dark-skinned, but Reyes said it was obvious that Vigil stood out as the darkest-skinned person in the six photos.*

When he was much younger Cornbread was after an eighteen-year-old dancer who was living with a man who claimed to be her high school sweetheart. Cornbread rode down to Aguilar County for her all the time.

He came to the screened door one night to confront the couple. The boyfriend was at his gas station job and so the dancer let Cornbread sleep on the floor. That was the story. The boyfriend returned after his shift, and asked, "What the hell you got here, Cynthia?"

"He's been following me around for weeks," Cynthia Otero said with a half cigarette burning on her lips.

"Ain't I seen you around?" the boyfriend asked.

"No," Cornbread said.

"I've seen you at the Sinclair Station."

"I've been in California."

"I helped you out with some money, right? Dollar bills. For gas."

"It was just a few quarters."

"She ain't worth any of this shit," the boyfriend finally cursed.

"Baby, I was just giving him a place to sleep."

"Jesus," he said to her. Soon the boyfriend moved out his couch and books and she was pregnant with Cornbread's baby. This is all according to Tio Neto who visited the trailer to drink or play cards.

When Cornbread watched the naked Cynthia dancing for the very first time, in full make-up on stage and beneath the red and blue lights, it was his twenty-sixth birthday, and Neto told the story of how the man nearly cried and decided to spend all of his dollar bills. It wasn't the drinks or the weed that moved him. He said he saw the future of his family and spirit that day. Neto said, "I swear I ain't never in my whole life seen a man that tore down over no woman."

Cynthia's mother and father came around to deliver the Holy Bible and to drive Cynthia out to doctor appointments because all Cornbread had in those days was a motorcycle.

"We'll get on," Cynthia said. It was all she had for her mother's worries.

"How will you live and eat? What will you do for money, cabróna?"

"I guess we'll have to eat the goddamn baby."

"Cynthia!" the father yelled.

"Well, Jesus. What the hell do you think we'll do? We'll work. I work."

Vigil at first stayed outside with his bike. When he heard the arguing he reached down and threw away his cigarette and walked back inside. Neto said he might've gotten the father around by the necktie, or he might've dragged the mother out by the hair. At this point nothing can be certain but the legend of the man. What was clear to Neto was the fact the parents never came back and the following week Vigil began payments on an orange Chevy Nova.

After the baby came, later that next spring, Cornbread became obsessed with hearing the words "I love you" from Cynthia. He was sitting on the bed with his hands in his pockets. Cynthia stood across from him and held the baby they named Beatrisa in her arms. "I tell you," she said to him. "I tell you all the damn time."

Cornbread looked at her. His big forehead looking thoughtful and needy. "Well," he said. "I can't remember the last. It's like you just want the kid."

The future of the baby stayed above their heads and had them dizzy in their arguments. By then Cynthia was tired of his stinking, greasy jeans and how money never stuck to him. She told him that as much as she could.

"You've got to have something you want to do in Colorado," she snapped back at him causing the baby in her arms to spit and cry. "Can't sit all day and expect me to say the words. You got to work and get out there sometimes. You gotta earn it."

"It'll all be fine."

"You know? How the hell do you know?"

"You were a fucking stripper when I met you. At fucking Aloha Gloria's."

"I had work and I had money. People taking care of me."

"Your men were taking care of you."

Out on the highway the traffic was relentless, but happy hour over at The Spanish Peaks Inn allowed them two beers and tomato juice for the price of one, at least for two hours during the day.

Later that same year Cynthia left Cornbread permanently for a junk dealer named Delacruz. She pulled Cornbread's clothes and photographs from the dresser mirror and had them for him on the porch. She pointed her ex's double barrel shotgun towards him to get him to finally drive off. This was after the winter ended and Neto remembered Cornbread calling Cynthia a killer and a traitor. Neto also remembered Cornbread planned this Delacruz' murder and had the knife he wanted to do it with. Neto said he talked the man down and took him out drinking whenever he could. He introduced him to the latest girlfriend. And even after Cornbread married that girlfriend and moved in to a rented house on Spruce Street just down a few blocks from Neto, Cornbread confided to people he paid Cynthia's phone bill until she and the new boyfriend finally moved south to New Mexico.

WHAT FOLKS CALLED "THE ARREST" began as a traffic stop for an illegal tag or taillight or some other cabrón thing. "Jesus-fucking-Christ," Cornbread called out. He left the Chevy in the middle of the street with the door open and gasoline still burning.

I was in the backseat behind Cornbread's daughter, Beatrisa, and could smell her vanilla perfume. Too many years have passed and I can only get a sense of the afternoon, the green lawns and red brick buildings and driveways. I remember the old folks coming to their front doors at the sound of sirens.

They had Vigil down and had pushed the side of his face into the grass of the Abuela's front yard. They laid their guns to the back of his skull. Cornbread's daughter yelled to him as it all escalated and his shirt was ripped from his shoulders.

The men hog-tied Cornbread, his arms behind his back tied to his feet with leg irons. "He was like a beast with those cops," Old Man Hernandez told me later on. "The cabrón had been asking for it, if you ask me. A man needs to answer for his crimes."

That afternoon the sun was turning the sky towards the steel mill a quiet, bruised pink, and when I rounded the car I found Bea crying with the shame of it all. She looked up from the narrow street as the junker was chained and finally towed.

"I don't know how that girl could still love a man after all his crimes," the Abuela Ortiz once told me.

THAT SISTER OF HIS and Bea would put him in a kitchen chair down in the basement and wrap a towel around his shoulders. They would trim his neckline and his eyebrows grown thick since his thirtieth birthday.

"Those women did everything for Cornbread," Neto liked to say.

"Like what, Tio?"

"Cut his hair and washed his teeth," Neto said. "Like the Fats Domino song, no?

"Which, Tio?"

"Pinche 'Sick and Tired'. Ah, these kids nowadays don't know a thing about music. What do they teach you in that school?"

Neto admitted Cornbread got an awful bicep tattoo after his last stay in the Youth Offender System in Huerfano County that read "Cornbread". The nickname came from his sister who he used to call "Mop" because of her uncontrollable hair that would grow out instead of long.

"They all had nicknames back in those days," Neto explained. "Don't know the proper Christian names of half the neighborhood, you know?"

The nickname came from the kitchens of his youth. The sister, who was more of a mother to the boys and especially to the youngest, did all the cooking. Neto insisted the family ate cornbread and milk most mornings. It was about saving dollar bills.

Years later in the Kansas City slaughterhouses, Cornbread packed coffee cakes and donuts. The gabacho workers teased him.

"Cornbread," they laughed and sneered. "Where's your cornbread, boy?" At lunch while he ate his bologna and mustard sandwich and his raw onion, they hounded and berated him with laughs.

"He didn't know no better," Neto said. "Like I say, the world made him tough." All morning long Neto told me smiling stories about Cornbread. About Cornbread's mother running off and how the boy was abandoned, about how the whole family's happiness depended on the sister. "The family and the stories were all split up and splintered, Manito," Neto explained. "Astillarse. All smashed up like pieces of an exploded tree. Like the one near the alley that got hit by lightning. You remember that one, boy?"

"Mis nalgas," the Abuela answered back, all while she cleared Neto's crumbs and breakfast dishes. "Don't you feel sorry for that one or his people. I don't know how an animal that evil could walk around in his own damned skin."

Part Two

The Old Folks

5

Birthdays

With scissors and two towels behind her, Cordelia Ortiz, little Neto's Jefita, stood in the bathroom waiting for her crew to come with long hair and dirty necks. She heard protests from Neto like, "Oh, Mama," and "Don't need no trimming."

"Estoy listo!" the Jefita said. "So get your ass moving." She wiped her hands on the apron over her housecoat. "Do you want to look all vagamundo? Like your Tio Emeterio?"

"Yes," the boys all agreed.

"Ah," the Jefita said. "You'll never be men with that attitude. Look your best. You can't steal the girlfriends with hair in your eyes and down your neck."

The woman looked after those boys so closely, clothed them, patched their socks and mended the holes in their pants and canvas sneaks. She wiped and put lotion on their elbows and knees. She tended their wounds.

"In my day," the boys' Jefe, Santiago Ortiz, explained as he ate his breakfast of tortillas and butter, "the Abuelo took a bowl and put it on your head and cut around and that was that, mujer."

"They have to look presentable for the people," she answered. "What will the family think of boys looking like this? And don't you go wandering, viejo. The same goes for you."

—

"CUT THOSE WEEDS and clean the grass, boys," the Jefe ordered late in the afternoon. "Your family is coming from all over Colorado and New Mexico to be with you."

The boys moved piles of branches and litter to the wheelbarrow. Old picnic tables with butcher paper coverings were brought side-by-side and the blessings of candles placed near ashtrays and dishes of candy. The comadres placed decorations on fences and clotheslines, transforming the little backyard into a gathering place with Christmas lights and colored paper.

"Just like that, boys," the Jefe said. "Vata bonita."

Later on, in their Sunday dress pants, slippery shoes, and button-up shirts, the boys witnessed the neighbors and family drop off washbasins of beer and RC Colas, bottles of rum and jugs of wine. The boys hovered over the sodas and the Jefita warned: "Stay clear, boys. Wait until the party."

Around five or six in the evening the relatives and neighbors appeared, adult faces that the boys could not recognize. To the boys there were at least three funerals worth of warm food displayed on the kitchen table: bowls of menudo and posole, along with plates of fried beef, lamb and chicken, and Tia Ida's sweet empanadas and tamales.

"Ay, mujer. I married you for your food," the Jefe commented. He drained his beer and smoked his cigarillo in the backyard and the glowing light.

I've heard that in the twilight time of the party, the men and women all looked so happy coming together to eat and tell stories. And there had to be music too. Tio Ben's makeshift crew included Alejandro's guitar, Ben's bass and Jeri Valesquez' accordion.

"What's the matter, Benito?" the Jefe yelled. "You forget how to play or what?"

"I haven't played in a year," the man answered. "A man's

memory goes."

Bobbi came from across town with his drum set to produce the beat. The screen-less window from above the sink brought the noise of men tuning and banging on their instruments.

The neighbor's dog yelped and barked along, and littlest Neto and the rest of the crew of fosters stared as the men argued and slapped hands. They collected their music and of course drained their glasses, their RC Cola and rum. The people finally applauded as Tio Ben collected ideas and selections.

Those men drank and wailed so many tunes out to the backyard, the dance floor in the driveway and the alleyway.

"You know 'Wheel of Fortune'?" the Jefe hollered.

"Yeah," someone followed and the men began the tune, struggling at first for the chords and the introduction before the sound rose and found the beat.

EVENTUALLY SOMEONE became drunk, drained one too many rum and RC Colas. Sometimes it was Emeterio or Julian. Maybe Tio Ben or even the great grandfather.

"Goddamn it, Mano," the man would say. "You don't respect me."

"Fuck you," the other would say, and on and on until they professed their frustration and their true affection for family and life.

"Take that shit out to the street," someone yelled.

Later, little Neto witnessed Tio Emeterio's woman, the one with the grandote tetas, push her way through and confront her ex.

"You bastard of a man," she said.

"What, mujer?" Emeterio said innocently. "I'm drinking and standing here."

"I've seen all of what you done. I seen."

It was a matter of time before some family threw chingazos or argued over money lost or owed. Terrible crimes held deep inside until that moment. It happened nearly every year.

Daisy and her boyfriend Benito tussled over him dancing with old lady Hernandez. We've heard the old woman couldn't resist dancing with him after sitting in Benito's lap the entire night. Junior fought over the lack of respect for his mother and father after someone cracked a joke about ranch people.

"You faggots don't respect me," Junior said drunkenly into the alleyway. "My family wants the best for you, and in my whole life you never respect me."

"Yo! Cálmate!" the Jefe yelled. "This is a party and not a trial. Calm down."

ALL THE WHILE the old folks, the Jefe and the Jefita, told and listened to their people's stories from New Mexico. The women complained about the men, and the men complained about their steel mill. Comadres and compadres argued and laughed under the night sky.

"No, Cordelia," some neighbor explained. "My mother was born in Chama."

Someone corrected, "No, the town she came from was Questa."

"No. Seven Mile Plaza."

Later, Tio Archuleta from Aguilar and Tia Viola from Denver argued over which song to sing as a whole group for the tribute, which song to best capture the family gathering and reuniting.

The Jefita and her comadres quickly drained their rum punch to sing:

De colores, de colores se visten los campos en la primavera

De colores, de colores son los pajaritos que vienen de afuera
De colores, de colores es el arco iris que vemos lucir.

The Jefe interrupted and grabbed the attention of everyone and made his birthday announcement, his statement of respect and honor for the Ortiz family and all the relatives and friends from the neighborhood and the steel mill.

"I am so happy to have all of you here for another year! Please drink and eat and let me enjoy you all!"

LATE INTO THE EVENING the band invited each guest and kid out playing in the alleyway to dance. Neto hated the broom dance game, hated to be the one stuck swaying with the broom, so he bent and jumped along with the beat. He also hated to be the one who danced with his Tia Jordine who stunk of perfume and sweat, or with Melda Quinones and her scratchy, hairy arms.

"Oh, I haven't seen you in so long," the women said. They swept him up and danced around the yard. "You such a tiny framed thing."

"The runt of the litter," some compadre drunkenly added.

After the singing and before the desserts were served, little Neto might've punched one of the foster kids. Maybe he crashed over a lawn chair or pulled his brother's shirt, nearly ripping the seams. Maybe he stole his foster brother's glasses or he knocked one of the other boys into the alley or down to scraped knees.

"I swear," the Jefita said. "Not on this day. Wait till no one's around. I'll give you such a bruising like you won't believe if you keep on."

The boy wept, abandoned in the house and away from the adults and the crowd of children all laughing and having their sodas and the Jefita's rice pudding. He slammed at cabinets and kicked at kitchen table legs.

"You'll reap what you make, boy," the Jefe drunkenly lectured. He dragged the boy by his elbow and paddled him in front of the kitchen window, in sight of the entire family and guests as they drained their drinks and laughed. "Birthday or no day. You goddamn hear me?"

Banned from the party Neto dared to tour the parents' bedroom to find the bed unmade with the Jefe's work clothes piled on. He pulled the man's work knife from the leather sheath and read the words: Western Knife Co. Boulder Co. 997.

He tested the blade with his thumb and took the knife and cut at the Jefita's dresser. He failed to carve the wood though he tried. With the knife swinging from his hand and the sheath under his arm, the boy found his mother's Spanish to English Bible. He rested full length on his stomach with the Bible in one hand and the knife in the other. He found a stash of dollar bills between the pages and counted it up. He smiled and fought the urge to carve out the leather cover.

He read the following lines his mother had underlined:

> *Love is never boastful, nor conceited, nor rude;*
> *never selfish, not quick to take offense.*

His thoughts and imagination flowed over the outline of the room, the blankets and dresser, the St Joseph and St Francis of Assisi hanging on the wall behind their glass frames. He felt the silence without the foster boys and parents.

—

Later on, Neto and the rest of the little mocos were encouraged to spend time with their elders. The skeleton of a man, the great grandfather, holed up alone in the living room, all the way from Taos. It was Neto's punishment. "You don't know how long we have the Abuelito so you better soak him up while you have the chance," the Jefita said. "You are lucky. I never had old folks to hear and learn from."

The old man's frail arms balanced Neto along with his drink. "Your birthday and mine are the same month, boy."

The boy first giggled mindlessly and ignored the viejito's words, more interested in the man's wig-like hair and wooden cane, the cracks in his leathered hands and ancient nails.

"I say we are the same," the old man hissed. "This month we were born the same."

Littlest Neto sat silent and stupid.

"Follow the word of sus folks, mi'jo," the ancient man breathed as a whisper, when he believed he was holding the boy's attention. "You hear me? There is good and there is bad. You must do what is good for your mother. For your people and for your life." His thin, strange face should have stood as a creeping symbol to the boy of a man's old and tired life. "Soon I will be dead," the man repeated to each moco he placed on his knee after Neto, "and you will be here at Los Dias without me."

"Yes, Grandpa," Neto reluctantly repeated.

"I'm the last of my age," the old man nearly spat. "You and your brothers are the next."

"Those ain't my brothers," Neto was first to interrupt.

"Oh, Neto," the shaky and sweaty old man answered. "They're all the love and trust you will ever know."

The boy stared back with no words to say in return.

"Do you hear me, boy? This will be all you have one day

so you have to stay close."

The old man trailed off and Neto struggled from the man's grasp. He slipped away from the scene, as the Jefe drank and the Jefita gossiped with her company.

Towards the alley and between parked cars, Neto escaped the company of fosters, cousins and neighbor kids, out to the wide, empty space between the adjoining yard and Hernandez' empty lot. In that moment, alone under flickering street lamps and bugs, where no one could see, he howled with freedom and flew up to steady footing on the chain-link fence. Behind the boy the old folks wept and drank, their arguments and cigarette smoke rising in one immense cloud.

6

Bear and Peaches

The Jefita found the girl out back of Dundee Cleaners, and she had an idea there would be trouble but paid no mind. She brought the skinny and bleach-colored thing smelling of the dumpster out of the afternoon heat.

"You have kids and a yard, Cordelia," her sweaty boss, Krensky, reminded her.

"She's such a sweet thing."

"Take her, Cordelia."

The viejos and kids on the bus riding home fell in love with the girl too. They pressed the Jefita for a name.

"Peaches," she said with a slow smile.

That night her husband, her Jefe Santiago, told her to tie "it" up to the utility pole. Out back the crew of fosters took turns late into the evening petting and giving the dog bits of tortilla and fried potato.

"How are we going to pay to feed a dog, mujer?" the Jefe finally argued as he scraped beans from the plate and drained his beer.

The Jefita didn't say a word. The Jefe spoke louder and louder. "That dog is damn dirty. Goddamn stray," he barked. "We don't need no more pinche dependents."

"Santiago!" the Jefita said. "The boys will hear."

He complained of the smell. He hated the shit in his backyard and he hated the barking.

"She protects the yard, viejo," the Jefita pleaded. "The kids need something to care for."

"They have the rabbits and the chickens out back."

"The kids work so hard for you and the girl is so sweet." The Jefita stood in her kitchen and watched the dog in the back chase and jump up at the kids. Their faces were flushed red with smiles.

"What is this with you and sweet, mujer," the Jefe barked. "Everything is goddamn sweet for you. For Christ's sake the thing licks at culo half the time."

THE FIRST NIGHT the Jefe sat and stared and drained his rum and RC Cola. He kicked at the girl and walked out back and let the gate open. In his drunkenness he tamped at his pack of cigarettes and shooed her out across the alley and out across side streets.

With the sunrise little Neto and the Jefita both cried and carried on.

The Jefita was steady. "No one eats until we find the girl."

"What, mujer?"

They searched in teams and on their bikes and quickly found her in the abandoned lot near the highway. The Jefita found the collar half burnt up in the trash pit. "Ah, this man."

THE JEFITA GATHERED the fosters, little Neto and Relles, some kids from across the street and down the block, enlisting them to protect and watch over the girl. She told them to report on the Jefe.

"Goddamn it," the Jefe said. "You got the whole damn neighborhood turned against me."

"You do it to yourself, viejo."

As the boys drove with their jefe to the onion fields, she poured out bottles of beer and rum. She took his Marlboro Reds stored in the Frigidaire and piled them onto the trash pit.

That night the Jefe found his wife and the girl sleeping in his bed and Peaches licking and wetting down the sheets. She nuzzled in close to the Jefita.

"Put out of my own bed," the Jefe yelled from the doorway.

"She's done nothing to you," the Jefita returned. "This is my dog. Fed with my money and taken care of by my children."

That night the Jefe sat in the garage until the late hours of morning. He smoked and piled the butts onto the grass for his boys to clean. He was quick to curse, "Goddamned woman."

The bear was another story. It came from years earlier, from the Woolworth's downtown, on one of the Jefita's bus rides out to pay on her account at Denver Furniture. A little yellow thing the family said resembled a giraffe, but they joked matched the looks of Tio Emeterio from California.

Instead of plastic machine guns or water balloon hand grenades or even bb's for the Jefe's old rifle, the bear was all the little Neto begged for.

"You're softening that boy into a little girl, mujer," the Jefe declared over the dinner table. "That shit is for babies."

"Jefe! It's a toy."

That night the man snatched the bear from Neto's arms, after the boy nodded off. Neto began to scream and wail before the Jefe made it to the door. The Jefita returned it, to stop the tears and to ensure the boy's sleep. Night after night the Jefe schemed.

It became another of his demands. Like the beer and the frying of onions at almost every meal despite the smell on his breath. The way he demanded the Jefita take "naps" with him every morning after long 11-7 shifts. The way he filled his thermos with orange juice and vodka despite the words of advice from his Compadre Julian, or the warnings from Father Pearce.

The bear became the test for the Jefita. At least a dozen times that month Relles and the crew of fosters saved the bear from burning in the trash pit. By that time the fabric smelled of burnt garbage, so the Jefita washed it and mended the loose threads and stuffing.

"Don't worry, mi'jo," the Jefita promised as she put her boy and his bear to bed. "Now get yourself to sleep."

Before the light of dawn, the Jefe came home early from his graveyard shift to find his wife crying and boiling water for tea.

He noticed the teapot sitting on top of the burner without a flame while his wife sat alongside an empty mug. He cracked a metal can of beer and drained most of it. "What are you doing?"

"Don't you see I have nothing to say to you?"

"Oh, come on now, mujer. We can pick up some wine and some bread and make a lunch for the city park."

"Cabrón, I can't drink," she said, giving him a look, giving him the look. "Stupid. Guess why I can't drink?"

The man ignored his beer and ignored his hunger, and he left his cigarillo to dangle from his lips. He stroked at her back and hair as the Jefita wept softly.

When the bus dropped her from sharing the news of her latest pregnancy with her sister, after a week away, she noticed the dead chickens, neglected and rotting in their pens. The rabbits stolen or escaped, she couldn't tell which.

The late summer heat had risen and the Jefe sat in his truckito enraged after first kicking open the plywood pens out behind the garage with his steel-toes and breaking open the rabbit pens, scarring his knuckles and fingers. He'd dragged the woman out back and commanded his wife to explain, then told her to shut her damned mouth. The entire time she held the growling Peaches in her bare arms.

The crew of fosters cried out, "Mama!"

She told the boys to go inside, to wash up and ready themselves for Saturday Mass. To put their good button-up shirts, their dress pants and shoes.

The backyard absorbed the afternoon noise of crickets and car backfires and left a silence until the church bells from Saint Francis chimed. The plastic figure of La Virgen de Guadalupe stood with her, the place where she once tried to grow roses and other perennials but the Jefe insisted they grow cucumbers and corn. She looked down the fence line where her flowers had been changed out for tomato plants. She kicked at the dirt with her slippers.

"Can you tell me why in the name of Christ you left the goddamn chickens to be stolen, mujer?" the Jefe put to his wife, his voice carrying beyond the alley. "What the fuck were you thinking? Where the fuck was you?"

The Jefita stood sullenly, the resentment so clear in her face. She said, "I went to see Viola."

"Denver?"

The Jefita didn't answer immediately. She felt the eye of judgment. "I can go where I want. We are married but you don't own me."

"Goddamn it, mujer. I'm out working and bringing in dollar bills and you do this."

"I want a house and family. Not a goddamn work crew."

The Jefe's head wagged and he stuck his hands out in to the air with each thought and rebuttal. "Leave the house and your job for a week and leave the chickens to die and you calling me out."

"So what if I went?" the Jefita said. "And I swear I'll go again and I won't come back."

"Jesus. You bitch."

The tears came hot from his eyes. He didn't have it in him to thrash the mother, to hurt the woman. He looked at his wife's expressionless face, down at his bleeding knuckles and threw his dark looks towards the earth and grass of the yard. He threw his body down at the woman's feet. "I'm doing for the boys. What the fuck else do you want from me, mujer?"

The Jefita stroked the Jefe's sweaty hair and forehead. She spoke softly. She pawed at his neck and shoulders and examined his wounded fists. The girl, Peaches, finally licked at the man too. The mother's smile slowly broadened and then slowly glowered. "It has to be different with this baby coming," the Jefita cried. "You hear me? These boys need a man and not a goddamn monster."

THE LOWLIGHT OF MORNING brought the Jefe's chance. He loaded up the back of his truckito, filled the bed with barrel after barrel of tree limbs from the many side-jobs. He picked the Vecina lady's garbage along with whatever he could think to throw out, the endless amount of clanking beer cans and rum bottles. He pulled the old bear from his coverall pocket and pushed the brown thing down to the darkest reaches of the load.

He pointed the truckito out west towards the mountains of Beulah and towards the landfill. He stopped once for sweet rolls, gas and coffee to sober up for the twelve-mile drive.

"Goddamned woman," the Jefe huffed at the crisp air and his cigarillo had him reconsidering, the dark smoke spilling from the driver side window. Having dumped out the cans he was sweeping the back of the old Dodge when he caught sight of the bear falling, covered by dirt and branches, egg shells and chicken bones.

"No, he needs this," the Jefe said aloud. "I'm doing right by my boy."

7

Burma

Neto labeled the war story "the Jefe Ortiz's 'first' death." From before mortgaging a home on Spruce Street, and before he met my Grandmother and had little Neto, Relles or foster children to watch over.

In 1944, during his great war, the Jefe trained as a machine gunner with the Army sent to the great China-India-Burma Theatre. Back when his arms and legs held power and strength, and when the Jefe had bright eyes for the world. Under the lavender moon of Burma, he took on several child workers, fed them and gave them cigarettes. In return, they washed his laundry, shined his shoes and kept his pants pressed.

The boys there liked the Jefe because his skin was dark like the Chinese and like the rest of the Burmese children. The Jefe liked the boys he found in Hukawng and Mogaung Valleys of North Burma around the units and encampments for exactly the same reason, because they reminded him of New Mexico and the dark-haired boys the Jefe called brother and cousin.

And before the city of Myitkyina fell to Allied Forces, before August of 1944, the Jefe and his favorite worker he called "Than" worked the airfields and the diesel electric plant running the whole city and practically the entire island. In those days the Jefe was in the throes of the worst illness of his life, worse than la gripe that killed his first wife and worse than the stomach and throat illness that struck him as he crossed the great ocean on the Queen Mary. The illness made him sweat and hallucinate Cocos and monsters around his bunk. Than brought water to the Jefe, wiped the man's forehead with a washcloth and with alcohol to soothe his burning fever. The medics thought he had malaria and something called hookworm, fever and vomit and the worst of diarrhea, abdominal pain and cramping that led him to prayer. For the first time in the Jefe's life he dragged his body out of bed and knelt down to pray to La Virgen de Guadalupe. He made the sign of the cross at his chest and held his crucifix tightly to his palm.

Neto told me that for days his Jefe imagined death in the latrine or from dehydration. A sad, dishonorable death far different from the romanticized service he had dreamed about, so far from the stories of his father and Tios from the Mexican Revolution and the battlefields of Juarez. For days, he hallucinated his mother and her soft words to attend school instead of the Army, instead of military duty. The mama whispered and pleaded to the Jefe, but his cousins and friends had all gone and so he volunteered before the draft.

"The pinche government will never want you as much as your people," the Jefe's mother lectured the boy in those sad dreams.

The Army had simple plans for her boy: stand behind a machine gun and pull the trigger. First clean floors and peel potatoes. Mop up after güero officers.

In those days there was only Than to bring food and water, buckets of fruit and packs of cigarettes. The boy tried to learn Spanish and the Jefe tried to learn the language of Bamar, to learn about Buddhism and teach the boy about La Virgen de Guadalupe and her beauty, how she worked to save the Jefe from his fever and his disease of the latrine. Mostly Than only smiled and nodded, asked the man for money.

The day Than stopped bringing water and his shine box, the Jefe found his senses. Found his stomach able to handle food and water. The medics put him back with his unit and his thoughts went back to cleaning duties and preparing his unit's weapons and his own supplies, ammo boxes filled, stacked and distributed to gunners.

And after weeks of that work he travelled with his friend Millburger to search for Than.

"Is that your boy?" Millburger asked.

"What kind of shit is that to ask me?" the Jefe replied. "I need him to work."

Than's mother lived in a shantytown of shacks where her people starved and followed the soldiers for work. The mother spoke very little English and lived in a filth and squalor the Jefe had never known. As they stood in the woman's shack no bigger than a few square yards, the woman told the Jefe that his little Than had died in the depths of a mine field. Than's body too far gone to be collected. The translation was exactly that: "to be collected."

Years removed from the war, in the backyard of that old house on Spruce, the Jefe drunkenly slipped from time to time, calling out: "You little shit, Than. Get the hell out of the road. Stay away from those roads. Get the hell back inside with su Mama."

8

Dog Track

"If I'm going to be staying here, hijos," Emeterio said, watching the crew of boys, their shabby clothes, bare feet and stained t-shirts, "then we need to get the ground rules straight, no?" The boys marched through the living room to their beloved uncle and laughed at his wide, bald scalp, how he flattened across the last remaining hairs. "And, sabes que, mi'jos," he said, "the rules are we must attend the dog track in the morning and earn enough money to attend the Mexican movies. Those are the rules."

The boys, Relles and Neto and even the crew of fosters, yelled and agreed. He told them their parents had abandoned them for the week. He did not explain that their Abuela in New Mexico turned up dead-meat and buried. Instead he pulled a bottle from his coverall pocket and took a long, passionate kiss. He called for the youngest Ortiz boy.

"What, Tio?"

"Are you getting smaller and smaller?"

"I'm growing, Tio," little Neto said, and the boy held his arms up to show the tiny mounds that would one day be biceps.

THE NEXT MORNING the boys ate a breakfast of fried bologna and fried potatoes before climbing into the bed of the Ranchero. They headed for dollar bills owed from Joey Aguilar's house. He wasn't home, but a fat, ancient hand served the cash through a window.

Next, the crew drove out to the fairgrounds and the swap meet, and Emeterio had a conversation with a woman, her long, black hair parted down the center and her eyebrows drawn in an arc. She stared and shook her head, threw her hand onto a corduroy hip. "Jesus. What you doing, Emeterio? You stealing kids now?"

"My brother's kids."

She asked, "Your mama?"

"Dead."

"What happened? I'm sorry, Emeterio."

"She's just dead."

"You see, mi'jos," Emeterio explained from behind the wheel, "at a casino you bet against the house. And, when you bet against the house, the odds are pretty bad. You know that? Any man has to know that."

"Yes, Tio."

"It's all French. You know French? 'Pari-mutuel', hijos," Emeterio explained. "It's French. It's a wager and not a bet. What do they teach you in that school?"

The boys said nothing. Their mouths were open wide until the oldest, Relles, finally asked, "What does that mean?"

"Mean?" Emeterio said. "Well, it means you win better. It means you are not playing the house, but you are playing the betters. Los Agents. That's what it means."

"Es eso Agents?"

"Agents. You know agents. Here you make your own luck. Here a man can know his numbers and know his runners and win. And we're men who win, no?"

"The Jefe says you can't win gambling. He says you should focus on a paycheck and earn your way."

"Oh, mi'jo!" Emeterio said, grinning. "Your father has

mouths to feed and cannot bet. But we have no children. Neto, do we have children?"

Neto shook his head, dumbly.

"We have no children, Relles. And that means we can take our risks," Emeterio answered. "We can go to the daily double with our ten dollars and triple our money. If we know the runners. I don't have a house to take care of. I am independent and free from all of those, mi'jo. Once a man has a paycheck and a job he loses all his freedoms."

"But a man needs to work, right? Tio?" Relles insisted. "It's not right to do this in the middle of the week."

"Oh, hijo," Emeterio answered.

THE DAILY DOUBLE started promptly at noon, and Emeterio and the crew were the first in line. Children must be supervised at all times, was what the ticket agent told Emeterio as he talked and talked. He purchased candy bars and sat to study his race program.

Emeterio explained: "Gotta find a runner, mi'jos. Gotta find the right one for us."

It took him nearly five minutes of study, but he found a runner called "Juanita's Boy." He decided to pass on another called "Short Nothing."

"He's won at this time slot every day last week," Emeterio said. "This is the time for him. This is the time." He grinned and ran to the betting agent with the boys. He waited and staggered across the betting lines, and he threw down all of his dollar bills, saving absolutely nothing for the day or for any amount of *in-cases* or *what-ifs*.

"The start don't matter," Emeterio instructed, gathering the boys around. "It's the stretch, hijos, that matters. The stretch call is what matters. That's when we'll see if 'Juanita's Boy' is the closer we're looking for. The last stretch."

"I don't think you picked the right dog, Tio."

"Shut it, Relles. You're just like your old man. You gotta trust the handicap. You gotta trust it. It's about following the numbers, boy. It's about watching the dogs and the races closely. Whether the dog is a closer or a breaker. It's about watching positions and the first three dogs that cross. That's all it is. Goddamn it. I'm wasting my words."

The boys got the Tio's buzz. They began whooping and hollering. They screamed out the dog's name.

"What's the stretch, Tio?"

"Shut it, Neto," Emeterio said. "Shut the hell up when a man is concentrating and thinking. Go, son! Go! Now's the time, son! Go, son!"

A couple of minutes later, even after he drained his beers and spit at his own feet, Emeterio did not confess to the crew of boys that he chose "Juanita's Boy" because the mother's middle name was Juanita, and so he had to put the money down on this day of her funeral. That was his duty as a son.

"What happened, Emeterio? What happened?" the boys said in another minute after the booming voice announced a "no-race."

"It seems," Emeterio said, "the dog has done up and died, hijos. Ran into the pinche rabbit and then the fence and had to be put down. That's what it looks like. Sometimes it happens. The races are not for soft dogs."

One of the fosters began crying over the dog, crying for lost Juanita's Boy.

"Don't cry, hijos," Emeterio pleaded. "No-race means our dollar bills will be returned to us. It means we'll get our money and we'll go to the Mexican movies. First, though, we'll put more money down. A man always puts more money down so quit your damn crying. You want the money out there, don't you? For the movies?"

"But what about our dog, Tio?"

—

AFTER THE THIRD RACE the crew miraculously had money for the Mexican movies over on 4th Street. Emeterio weighed his bets more carefully, saving dollar bills for admission, hot dogs and RC Colas.

Emeterio liked the Riverside Drive-In or the Mesa Drive-In, but mostly he liked "the 96" downtown because they allowed little mocos in the truck bed.

Emeterio directed Relles to place the speaker on the driver side window and control the volume, and the crew was jealous.

"Why does he get the front?" Neto and the fosters asked.

"Because I say," Emeterio answered, "and because he is the oldest. Now, pay attention, boys. They show your people's movies. You have to learn your language. Español? Tu sabes? It's a damn shame in the garage you boys speak such shitty Spanish. Your Great Grandfather would be rolling in his grave to know his people couldn't follow what he said."

And that was how Emeterio saw the Mexican movies, as school for the boys.

"These movies are about life, hijos," Emeterio lectured. "You watch them close and you'll learn a lesson about your lives."

Mostly they liked the classics, puro classicos, the westerns of Pedro Infante with his singing and his womanizing, his charro crooning. The crew couldn't follow the plot, but they liked the action of Los Hijos de Maria Morales. Emeterio liked the cornball jokes.

"You know I met him in California," Emeterio said before he downed his hot dog and drained his rum and RC Cola.

Relles asked, "Who, Tio?"

"Pedro Infante."

"You never met him."

"I swear I met him," Emeterio claimed. "In California. I swear. I was with my Tio working in the fields and he came to talk to the workers. We all saw him." Emeterio was in love with those songs and those movies; they reminded him of growing up in New Mexico. They reminded him of his old folks.

The concessions saved the crew of boys, Relles and Neto. The footlongs and the hamburgers. Arms full of RC Cola bottles and hot-buttered popcorn. Soft pretzels, sno-cones and pizza slices. Endless strings of rope licorice alongside boxed candies.

"Rich, flavorful and satisfying," little Neto repeated from the intermission trailers.

After the first feature, just before the end of the second, Emeterio took off his boots and put his stinking feet up on the dash. His body ached like a cavity so he banished Relles to the back of the Ranchero with his brothers. And, finally, when the crew, wrapped up in Emeterio's old horse blankets, had pulled off their sneaks and snuggled up next to the tire wells, Emeterio could finally think without bother or question. This was the time Pedro Infante crackled through the speaker and wailed Las Mañanitas, and the time Tio sobbed for Juanita's Boy. He held the speaker and turned up the volume to maximum, until the warm voices were all the boys heard.

9

Korea

Emeterio stepped onto the gravel tarmac of the old airport in Huerfano County just blocks away from the old neighborhood and his brother's house. He had spent two-and-a-half years as a prisoner of war in a Chinese POW camp and his sister-in-law wiped away his tears as she hugged and helped the man walk to the Jefe's truck. The year was 1954 and he was barely twenty-two years old.

"I had no idea where Korea even was, hijos," Tio Emeterio told his boys. "I had wanted to join the Air Force but couldn't make the scores."

He had enlisted in February of 1950 and he was only eighteen when the war broke out; by the end of July he was on the front lines with the 15th Field Artillery Battalion. The first thing he remembers on his eighteenth birthday was seeing dead Korean civilians, a man and a woman lying on the side of the road.

"I heard somebody saying we were heading north, hijos. North like a big flying owl. We all thought we'd be heading home soon."

"That was the longest and hottest summer of my life, hijo," Emeterio would say. "In Pusan we were the first to fire on the North Koreans."

"Were you scared, Tio?" they asked him.

"The North Koreans shot people in the back," Tio explained. "We saw pictures in the newspapers of them binding GIs' hands with wire and shooting them right in the back. So hell yeah I was scared, hijos."

"The Chinese took the high ground. They came in and changed everything. They were only like a football field away. They were right on us."

"What did you do, Tio?"

"I fell asleep in the back of a jeep. A grenade hit my stomach. Hit my chest and I ran, hijo. In war all you can do is run."

"Did the grenade go off, Tio?"

"Yes, and we returned fire."

"Like in *The Longest Day*, Tio?"

"Fuck *The Longest Day*, hijos. I returned fire with my carbine and I ran. I ran until I fell and until everything fell. I thought we were safe. They were shooting and we were running."

"Did they shoot you, Tio?"

"No, hijos. No shots could touch me. I crawled and I pretended I was dead. I played dead."

"Were you dead?"

"No, just playing. Somebody stole my watch and somebody checked my wrist again and again for more watches."

"What did you do?"

"I sat there and played dead. It was all I could do. In war that is all you can do. Finally some North Korean soldier turned me over and shined a flashlight in my face. They took my weapon. They took my coat. They took my pinche boots."

"What came next, Tio?"

"Hunger and pain, hijos. Praying and listening. Mostly hunger and pain."

10

The Crew

The summer and the beginning of the Jefe's side-jobs took the boys out of town to work the fields of Avondale, Colorado. With his nasty black cigarillos and his thermoses of coffee, the balding Emeterio came along as an extra hand.

After sunset they loaded onion shears and buckets, and Emeterio warned, "Run, little Neto! Run before the Coco gets you!"

During the long ride home, whenever a poor squirrel or rabbit was found bloodied and dead-meat along the road, Tio Emeterio blamed it on the Coco.

"That's from a car on the highway, Tio," Relles said. Relles was oldest and less afraid of the spirits Tio Emeterio sold.

"Oh, no. The Coco doesn't eat animals, Relles. One bite to taste the blood."

"What does he eat?" little Neto asked. The rest of the crew listened intently with open mouths.

"The Coco eats little boys, Neto," Tio Emeterio taught. "Their bones and clothes. Every bit off of them. So I hope your little legs and your sneakers can carry you."

At home, the boys learned the Coco lived in the garage and inside cabinets. They learned he came out at night, as the wind howled during violent thunderstorms or hailstorms. When the crew of boys fetched lawn tools and dragged the Jefe's trash bins, the boys learned the Coco rested in the basement and near the furnace, and in any dark and dank place. When the boys took down bags of potatoes or beans and the light switch seemed yards away from the stairs, the Tio yelled warnings for the boys.

WITH KITCHEN WINDOWS opened wide and the whole crew waiting for the Jefe and the Jefita to return from nights out at The Donahue with their compadres, or from the endless number of festivals and dances at St Francis of Assisi, the stories came while they sat and played cards.

"A man has to learn poker," Tio Emeterio instructed. "Your Jefe don't teach you nothing you need in this world, mi'jos." As they played they learned the Coco lived everywhere, outside of the house and down the street from Old Man Hernandez'. Down from the Vigil family house and even in the darkness of Minnequa School's playground.

The boys were thankful for the advice. They jumped on Emeterio's back as he ran up and down the stairs to the basement yelling, "Climb aboard, little mocos. I'll save you. I'll ride you out of town."

The Tio drained his beer and smoked the Jefe's cigarettes, never worrying about the consequence, and advised how to avoid any of the Cocos that existed in the world.

"Where do these Cocos come from, Tio?"

Emeterio paused solemnly before answering: "The fields of New Mexico, boys. They come from old haunts in Española and in Belen. Your Jefe has seen them. Your father has fought them and won."

"The Jefe?" little Neto asked.

"Yes, your Jefe defeated them. We all ran from the lettuce fields but your Jefe burned them all down with the eyes. The looks that could kill. He tore them down with those dirty, awful looks of his."

The boys all nodded and agreed. The Jefe did have masterful dirty looks.

"Tell us more, Tio," they demanded, pulling the Jefita's kitchen chairs and stools around the man.

"You see your Jefe was working the fields with the Abuelo, that was your Great Grandfather Ortiz. Well, you see that old man was a cabrón. You never knew him like I knew him, but I'll tell you he was as mean as a damn ghost himself. He left his boys out in the fields all alone with no lanterns or lights or nothing. Left them in the moonlight to work and fight with whatever Cocos happened upon them."

"Tell us more, Tio."

"Well, su Jefe was scared. I was there and I know. I was afraid too but your Jefe called out to them. And it was a big voice for a little moco. He was no bigger than you, Neto."

He stood up on his chair and re-created for the boys: "Cocos!" he says. "I am Santiago F. Ortiz and I fear no Cocos. I am a man and I have to work! So let me work!"

"Is that what he said, Tio?"

"I'm no liar," the Tio reminded them. He sat to drain his beer and smoke. "Those Cocos threw down their tree branches and threw down their leaves. You see they look like trees and shadows. Oh, those Cocos are sneaky. They look like a damn night sky, but they were so afraid of the little Jefe they ran and never came back."

"Whoa!" the crew of fosters said.

"Yeah. They let us get work done until your Abuelo came and turned on the truckito's headlights. Until the workers returned with their lanterns."

"Were you scared, Tio?" little Neto asked and all the foster boys nodded.

"No such thing as ghosts or monsters," Relles answered.

"Ah, Relles. I was scared. You should be scared too. Those Cocos will go after the littlest of men. They like non-believers best. About your size. They know little mocos like you usually don't put up much of a fight."

"I won't let them get me, Tio," little Neto answered. "I can run."

THAT SEASON WITH TIO EMETERIO the boys imagined baseball games and championship marble matches. Handball to the garage, stolen bases and line drives. Massive climbs and military maneuvers over the back concrete wall and the Abuelo's shed. The Jefe's tools made the best lances and weapons, machine guns from the wrenches and climbing tools from the hammers.

The Jefe paid no mind. He had the business of the Ford and the old truckito to deal with. He had the grind of changing oil, checking and changing the spark plugs, finding the right size wrench for oil filters. Keeping his vehicles moving for the work in the fields.

Even in Neto's day, there were Tios to distract. Older men who hung out while the Jefe worked, men who filled the alley with smoke and drained beer cans. Men like Emeterio and his lazy way of treating the day. He stole smokes and shots of rum or whatever he could get his hands on.

Emeterio and his hipster dark glasses and white t-shirts. Sometimes a guayabera or a short-sleeved bowling shirt, cigarette behind his ear and a pack in the pocket over his heart. The Tio felt for the kids who had nothing but the alley. He brought them bags of marbles and bags of green army men, remembering back to his childhood days. He brought them RC Colas and sometimes he brought candy or gum, and if the kids were real lucky he had handfuls of baseball cards or bottle caps from the liquor store. Whatever change he held in his pockets was given up to the boys, quarters and dimes the boys saved for comics down at Bollinger's Newsstand.

In his Ranchero, Emeterio brought cardboard boxes and empty buckets from job sites and from his work. For a time he worked as a plumber's assistant for the State Hospital, and sometimes he had the remains of a day's work and let Neto and the fosters turn the cardboard into pirate or rocket ships.

"Why do you encourage them, Emeterio?" the Jefe complained.

They used his knife and wire cutters to turn small nail buckets into armored helmets and masks. The kids drew their own crests and family names with grease pencils. Neto drew a horse and made three lines that he said represented the llano of New Mexico where his Abuelos lived.

They dressed up Emeterio in a suit of cardboard and bucket armor. They transformed him into a robotic Frankenstein's monster and the kids all screamed and ran around him. They dueled for what seemed like hours until he collapsed under the back tree to energetic blows and angry lashes.

"You have vanquished me, mi'jos. I have no more fight for you."

The boys wore the scars. Neto found he had skinned his knees and ripped up his jeans. No-named Lucero ripped his lip, had blood down his already stained white t-shirt and was crying with laughter.

"Don't cry," Emeterio said. "It happens to the best of us. But don't ever let them see you defeated, boys. Keep that shit deep inside."

The Jefe ranted for his tools and for his wrenches, for some sort of basin he needed for his oil change. Poor Ricky was unlucky and wore the bucket as his backside armor. Emeterio had clipped a hole to tie the makeshift armor around and over the boy's shoulders.

Jefe screamed at the kids and at his brother and ripped

the bucket from Ricky's back, called him names and paddled the boy's butt.

"I need them tools to finish up," the Jefe said. "I don't want to be under this hood all damned day."

It only took a mention of it. Every person in that house knew it.

"Pick up these clothes, hijo," the Jefita said. "Or your father will get the belt. You don't want him to get the belt, do you?"

Thoughts of the belt kept the boys up at night and kept them running and hiding, worrying on how he drank and worked his side-jobs many nights of the month. They knew how it all made him quick to pull the belt, wrapping it around his hand and doubling the layers over his fist and knuckles scared the boys more than Principal Roberts at Minnequa School and the old paddles over his desk.

"No, Mama," the boys answered.

The belt was used for minor things, unjust things, like when Neto burned the beans when cooking for the old man, or when Relles dropped the masa for tortillas the Jefita prepared.

The belt was used for rare occasions of mischief, like the time Neto jammed toothpicks into the locks of Jefe's truckito. The time Neto piled too much paper into the toilet and flooded the bathroom and hallway. The night Relles stayed out in Bessemer Park field with the daughter of Joe Valejo. The time Neto dropped the Jefe's hammer off the roof and cracked Emeterio's windshield.

Neto swore the worst instance was when Relles was caught with marijuana cigarettes. Somehow the oldest boy found himself "holding" for a friend but he got the shit from his friend Mariano.

"I didn't raise you for this," the Jefe said in his most official telephone voice. "I didn't raise you for any of this. I may not always be the best of fathers to you and your brother but I didn't raise you for this."

Neto was surprised at the sympathy, and maybe it was all for the benefit of the Principal, as if the Principal listened and not Neto. As if the Principal rated the mistakes of the son as the mistakes of the father.

"I want to know who gives you these things?" the Jefe said.

The way he said "things," Neto wondered what there was to those marijuana cigarettes Mariano sold around the neighborhood.

"They say you've brought chaw to school and cigarettes," the Jefe continued. "They found these things on you, boy. Where do you get them? Do you steal them from me?"

"No, Jefe," the boy said.

"Do you even know what you're doing? How this makes the family look?"

That night, while the Jefe lectured away at Relles and as Neto and the fosters did their nightly chores of cleaning dishes and folding the Jefita's loads of laundry, they all giggled as Relles got his. They grew silent as the boy cried and cried, the moans growing louder and more tragic.

Emeterio drove his Ranchero down to Ralph's or sometimes Chet's Market for his supplies, a loaf of bread and bologna. The Tio was a connoisseur of bologna. Of course, the best came from New Mexico but he settled for what they had at JJ's Market.

"If a man is gonna fish," the Tio said, "then the man has got to have his supplies."

The Tio stopped for his beer, either Dogpatch or Loco Liquors on East 8th. He bought Miller High Life or Coors, whatever he could afford. He bought them six-packs of

RC Cola or sometimes, if they were lucky, he bought them chocolate milk and big bags of pork rinds and taffy bars.

He drove over to the Mexican Music Store where he found his 45s of Tejano music. In those days it was Freddy Fender, Little Joe and La Latinaires and the Al Hurricane band, maybe the Stingrays or Ruben Ramos. "Puro classicos, mi'jos," Emeterio instructed. "A man has got to have music."

Later, on the lake, Emeterio spent more time draining beer and sleeping, but eventually he taught them how to fish, to use a lure and bait. He showed how to keep a worm secure on a hook and how to keep a night crawler on a liter rig. How to choose a proper weight and how to respect your neighbor's line as you cast.

"Your Jefe is a good man, but he teaches all wrong. Most things aren't work, hijos."

Inevitably when the boys pushed and shoved one another, the Tio taught them to share soda, not to fight like dogs.

"You must stand up for one another, mi'jos. Because all you got is each other. Take it from me, hijos," the Jefe advised.

He cut his bread and cut his bologna and served up the best sandwiches filled with mustard and cheese for his crew of boys.

When the summer rain poured down, and the boys hid out in the Ranchero away from the water and mud of late afternoons, they studied their Tio closely. They watched as he stood bare-chested, casting his lure over and over, his portable record player becoming soaked. Soon the rain became so complex, the boys had to roll up the Ranchero's windows. Their Tio became a blur on the lake, no way of separating him from the rolling land.

—

ON ONE OCCASION Emeterio took his nephews down a few blocks to Ralph's Corner Store with his winnings from the dog track. He drunkenly joked with the seventeen-year-old girl behind the counter. "I want to speak to Ralph," he said.

She was quick to laugh at first but he wouldn't let it go, wanted to keep talking.

"I'm serious, girly," he said. "I want to talk to Ralph about his sign out there. I don't think Pepsi is best. I like my RC Cola."

The boys sought out their gum and their candy in the distraction, running down through the aisles and grabbing comic books, magnet toys and Match Box cars.

"Go on get your toys," Emeterio said. "Get them while we have the money porque tomorrow it'll all be gone, hijos. Tomorrow you'll be old like me and won't have no time for play. Right, girly?"

Old man Woodbury watched from the back room, and when he put his hands on Neto, Woodbury caught Emeterio's wrath. He flicked his cigarette into the man's face, and the men tussled to the street and into traffic, causing a bus and old man Hernandez' Lincoln to pull off the road. It was as if the entire neighborhood judged. Emeterio crushed the man's face and his crotch. After a few final slaps Woodbury was down on his knees and almost in prayer to Emeterio, spitting blood and snot onto the asphalt.

"Them boys wouldn't have been stealing if I was there with them," the Jefe argued days later after the fight and the police report. "I'll tell you that goddamn much."

THAT NEXT MONTH the Jefe had errands for little Neto, had him around Routt Avenue and East Evans down to Chet's Market for RC Cola. Down to So-Lo's Grocery to peruse the toy section and the air rifles. Across Northern to Bessemer Park and across the immense ball field where he could watch baseball, dreaming of the day when he would have the height to play and catch up to "real" fly balls and line drives.

Down to Bollinger's Newsstand and the yards of comic books and candy, old lady Guzman let him read and sit for hours no matter the warnings listed by the owner's signs.

He rode on to a little bar and billiards room called The Klamm Shell across from the Veteran's Bar.

The story is that after riding his bicycle for blocks and blocks Neto rode into the place and asked for his Tio Emeterio.

Usually Neto found Emeterio drunk and screaming madness into the pay phone or sleeping in his truck. One time he rode the man on the handlebars of his bike.

The men of the bars directed Neto to a woman named Loretta, somewhere blocks down on Routt Avenue. He wanted to find Emeterio, get him home to bed. He worried that the bar types, people so much like Emeterio, would take the man's money from the government check he'd received that month.

Neto rode the neighborhood until he found Emeterio's Ranchero. He found the door to the house wide open and slipped in, finding no one around even when he yelled his Tio's name.

The place was still and cold. An empty bottle of Johnny Walker Red sat on the card table and beer bottles littered the wooden floors and Indian rug, cigarette butts stuffed into ashtrays and thrown along the love seat and chairs. There was no television or radio.

He found the couple in the bathroom, Loretta cradled in his arms and the two sleeping in the bathtub, a needle in the Tio's arm. He finally shook the man, "They want you home, Tio." The man grumbled and could only give a dead look.

"Goddamn disgrace, Emeterio," the Jefe said after little Neto finally tore home and ratted. "I can't trust you to even take care of your damn self. I brought you here for work."

"The fruits of my labor, bro." It was all the man could offer.

"Look at you. You can't even say a word of sense."

His boys washed the man's forehead with a warm cloth and pushed back the man's hair from his eyes. Offered him water and a warm blanket. The smell of coffee filled the air while the Jefe and the Jefita argued. Their voices filled the home and filtered through each thin wall into the bathroom and into the kitchen, wherever the boys and Emeterio managed to hide.

II

Arkansas Flood

Dozens of men lined the sidewalks like spectators for blocks, when the Jefe arrived. He was crudo and tired, with a toothpick between his dark teeth. He had been up most of the night listening to the storms and the radio reports. It had been nearly agony to rise before dawn, wrangling his boys into the truckito's bed for the long day of salvage.

Julian was struggling to get his work coveralls pulled up over his jeans when the Jefe banged at his screen door. "Goddamn river rose five feet at its worst," Julian said.

The Jefe surveyed Julian's mess and felt the damp and humid air. Where there was summer grass and where there had once been garden now looked like an empty lot of truck ruts and bulldozer grooves. He marveled at the deep ruts of mud and wash made from the city trucks weaving in and out of the neighborhoods.

"Basement is damn near lost," Julian said, and his face seemed sincerely worried as he pulled another cigarillo.

"I brought my workers." The Jefe motioned to his truckito and the crew of boys waiting, littlest Neto, Relles and the rest of the crew of fosters.

Julian stood still on his porch and slowly motioned for those who had not seen the water's rise and eventual fall, those who had not lived through the night. "It ain't even hardly a street no more," he complained.

A young girl in cut-off shorts ran from the house to

cross the street with shoes in one hand and what looked like her money for Chet's Market. Her legs glistened in the morning sunlight and her feet looked caked in mud. Jefe's crew yelled and laughed out loud as she slopped through the center of the street.

Julian spat and nearly wept. "Never thought the damn water would stop rising, compadre. I thought I was gonna have to jump up on the roof. Nearly made the decision but that cabrón rain was coming down."

"Hay que cabrón."

"You see that, Jefe?" the youngest Neto said pointing out towards an abandoned truck. Mud had surrounded a flatbed and covered nearly all sides and every tire up to the ruts.

"The damn current pushed her into the side of the neighbor's house," Julian answered. "We heard it slam into the wall. Damn thing won't fire now, I don't think."

The men of the work crews who had been working all night on the power lines leaned on their state cars cleaning mud from the ruts and from their boots and socks. One in firefighter gear had his socks removed and was rubbing his feet dry.

The Jefe nodded approval to his boys and the work of pumping the basement began. Julian ran to the garage for buckets and the Jefe unloaded his sump pump and his hoses.

"Thank God for you and your boys, no?" Julian repeated mournfully as they worked. And later as they handed buckets of water and filth to the boys to dump out onto the street, he said, "I was sick as a dog all night, compadre. I thought I was dying. I wanted to write my will and get all my last wishes down on paper."

The Jefe grinned. "Why didn't you call?"

"What good would it have done? The rain was falling

and the juice went out and we didn't even have a pinche radio."

"You'll live," the Jefe said, still surveying the scene.

Weeks before the storm, in the infirmary office at CF&I Steel, someone had left an address book, and while he waited, preoccupied with the newly developed buzzing in his ears, the Jefe wrote out his expenses and his budget on a blank page. He had a carpenter's pencil in his coverall pocket and he laid out the month's bills against the month's check.

At first he worked on figures, subtracting his mortgage from his wage, the light bill and the phone bill from what was left. He subtracted the repair of the Frigidaire and the cost of a thermostat and fan belt, then the expense of little Neto breaking his wrists, the new expense of the hospital and the doctor. He added the side-job dollar bills and the money for taking the neighbor's trash out to the landfill. He began putting down numbers and more numbers.

He noted instantly the math couldn't add up, not with the doctor's bill and the expense of the truckito coming together. He compensated by subtracting from the food costs, and from the expense of his cartons of cigarettes and his rum and beer. Still the dollar bills couldn't add up. He leaned forward uncomfortably on the wooden bench and concentrated. He wiped at the sweat of his brow and neck with his handkerchief while his ears popped and buzzed. He felt sick.

Next, he found himself in the doctor's office answering the nurse's questions, raising his hands as he listened for tones, squinting as he focused on the whirring sounds she pumped into his ears, the sounds degenerating into buzz until he heard nothing, no sound or thoughts.

"You have some hearing loss, Ortiz," the doctor told

him. "Temporary. Go home and come back in a month."

"I gotta work, Doc."

"Take this slip and go down to the secretary. Rest yourself and come back in a month."

"You mean disability leave. I don't gotta hear to work, Doc."

"Take the month, Ortiz."

In his truckito he pulled out the address book and scrawled out more numbers. He added the numbers of the side-jobs and fieldwork, subtracted the extra money he usually received for tonnage.

He made a note of those around the neighborhood who owed him money: five dollars from Bobby DeHerrera and his brother, three dollars for an extension cord the neighbor Margaret borrowed for her Christmas lights, and Emeterio down for the biggest amount—the Jefe figured fifty dollars for meals and room.

The Jefe was this way about dollar bills. Ever since he was a small boy the worry over numbers existed in him. Perhaps it began with his father, with the number of side-jobs that man worked along with his boys, the Jefe alongside Emeterio out in the fields of New Mexico.

"Know your business," the father told him as a young boy. The man kept his money wrapped up with a string and deep inside a wrapped handkerchief. Business meant work and watching those dollar bills. The Jefe took the words to heart and never finished high school, never got out of the ninth grade, choosing work and the family's income. They all pitched in at that time, the time of the Depression and the time of the great dust storms.

The Jefe thought of summers in the lettuce and onion fields of northern New Mexico, his father pushing him to work and bring in money. He remembered the father waiting on the front porch, waiting for his son's pay. The boy gladly turning it over. Everyone contributing to the home, everyone working. He borrowed money to visit his novia over the border in Colorado, drives to find work in the mines or in the steel mill. Everyone said there would be work in Huerfano County, dollar bills to be earned and homes to mortgage. The Jefe borrowed money to visit and when he returned the father waited on the steps. "Take care of your business," the old man advised.

Sitting in his truckito, the Jefe added his bills, his eyes straining with the agony in his ears and his head, until his large hands stabbed and punched at the rearview mirror, cutting the metal and glass free from the roof liner.

After the work at Julian's, when the Jefe finally telephoned the wife from a Sinclair Station, he made the mistake of mentioning it all, forgetting that it was a kind of kick to his wife's religious sensibilities.

"Where's the girlfriend?" the Jefita asked with quickened interest.

"I didn't see nobody but Julian."

"What about his brothers? His people?"

He shook his head and shrugged and gave no answer into the receiver.

"How's the house?"

"The basement has water. Sewer line busted."

"Does he have food?"

"I saw the basement."

She asked about the girlfriend and the miscarriage and the reasons for the girlfriend leaving.

"I don't know such things, vieja," he answered.

"Poor sweet Adeline. She was months along the last time I talked to the poor girl. Invite him over if he needs a meal."

"I pumped his basement."

"Offer him one of the boy's beds in the basement if you

have to!"

"I finished the job, vieja! I have the dollar bills. He's got a pantry filled."

"You took that poor man's money!"

The Jefe decided that he wouldn't tell his wife, but ten minutes later after he bought his boys a dinner of potato chips and ice cream out of the station's great freezer, he decided he better tell. He left the receiver dangling and went into the truckito and found his last cigarillo and returned and sat down at the edge of a concrete driveway and told her about Adeline and the baby.

"What did he say?" the woman asked.

"He told me the baby died after four months. Happened in the night. They took her to the hospital in the night and that was that. Ya se acabó."

"Oh, God in heaven, that poor girl," she said.

"The girl was hurting and so they called and asked what to do."

"And what did the doctor say?"

"I don't know what the doctor said, cabróna. I'm telling you what the man told me."

"Oh, how awful."

"It had been three weeks and he hadn't told nobody nothing."

"We're all in God's hands."

"The kid's dead, mujer. No more than that."

As soon as he hung up he watched the boys and their muddy, filthy pant legs and sneaks. The dark smoke from the cigarillo filled his lungs and he thought of what he never told his wife. What he could never tell: How Julian had no money for kids and how he had no money for doctors and baby clothes. How the dollar bills drain from you. How Julian couldn't understand how the Jefe could do it, working and raising the four boys. How the man had sobbed and told him the death of the baby was for the best as far as he was concerned.

The Jefe called for his boys and pulled what was left of the dollar bills paid to him from his coverall pocket. He placed them inside of his father's wallet, the leather reminding him of the ancient skin from the old man who taught him to cook and clean as a child.

And as he watched his boys through the side view mirror pile onto the bed, and as the engine began to fire, neon lights buzzing offered the only reassurance.

12

Chingazos

A half hour to 5 p.m. the Jefe and the Jefita along with the crew of boys sat for a while with Jorge's Diner all to themselves. Early evening air gusted down Northern Avenue and through the rectangular building, over the propped door and the six butcher-papered tabletops.

In the sharp lime taste of the salsa left on each tabletop, the Jefe found a concentrated memory of cooking he experienced as a boy in New Mexico, back in his mother's kitchen after a long afternoon of work in the campos and after a long ride home.

"I never should have left New Mexico," the Jefe said to his wife.

From fifteen feet away the music bleated from the jukebox. The Jefita wanted Connie Francis and so the Jefe searched his coverall pockets for his change wallet and for his lighter, finally dropping dimes and nickels. The Jefe waved them towards the player.

He smiled. "Go put on something for your mother, boys."

The crew of boys ran across the restaurant and smiled. The boys called out the selections and the cost.

The Jefe called back to them, "Pick one, boys!"

Shaking her head, the Jefita smiled and drank a sip of her milk, put her hand out and placed the Jefe's hand into her own. She began stroking his palm and his wrist softly.

—

Nelson Avellanos was a short and stocky steel worker, full of energy. He wore no shirt and greasy jeans that afternoon, and he walked with a cocky smile. He reminded the Jefe of any number of countless steel workers.

Nelson had come from smoking around the corner and trying the pay phone without much luck. He had ordered three and then a fourth plate of tamales, and the two women running the dinner shift had an uneasy feeling. It was the way he put his arm around the waitress with a boyish smile, or the way he blew kisses. It was his essential look of desperation and loser-ness that had the women on edge. The way he mashed the newspaper to smooth the classifieds and how he drunkenly cursed the ink on his hands.

"Ay que la chingada!" Avellanos yelled over the music.

Poor little Neto jumped and cupped his ears and Avellanos smiled and waved at the boys. It forced the Jefe to stare, noticing all of the beer bottles and cleaned plates of food.

What the Jefe could never have known was that Nelson Avellanos was sitting in the middle of a twelve-hour drunk. He drank to mourn his mother's passing, drank to forget the missed court dates and certain jail time he faced in El Paso County. He spent the day waiting to be found. What the Jefe could never have known was that Avellanos kept a three-inch straight razor in his boot.

"Bring me another plate," Nelson blurted at the women behind the long counter. "And beer. More long necks, my sister."

The Jefe said, "Keep it down, cabrón. There are people eating here."

"Don't," the Jefita whispered, reminding the Jefe. "Please. The boys."

"I'm not doing anything, mujer," the Jefe argued. "Tell

that fool."

Avellanos wagged his head and then nodded. "What you say?" He leaned back on two legs of his chair and laughed. The man rocked back and forth on his chair. "Do something," the man Avellanos ordered.

The Jefe licked and wiped at the taste of salsa on his lips and he giggled. Called Avellanos a boy and told him to make a move.

The woman behind the counter yelled out, "Hey." She warned the men first in Spanish and in a broken, high-pitched English. "Not here," she repeated. "Not here. To the street."

Avellanos cocked his thumb and finger and pointed it at his head and then at the family. The Jefita held on tightly to her husband's arm as he lurched in his chair. Nelson pulled the razor.

The Jefe lurched and knocked their table to its side. A man had to fight but he had things to think of, the pregnant Jefita and the young boys. There was hard and there was reckless, like Emeterio, he thought. "Let's get," the Jefe said. "We'll eat at home."

On the street Nelson blew kisses and called the Jefe out. "You fucking faggot," Nelson yelled. The words degenerated into drunken syllables.

The waitress from inside of Jorge's screeched, "Sangre!" The Jefe backed up with his palms up and searched for the wound on his back. The blood turned up on his suit pants and on his dress shirt. The red started to flow over forearms and on to stomach as the man Nelson waved the razor wildly.

The Jefe taught the boys how to hurt a man that afternoon. He taught them how to take blows from a knife.

"Goddamn it," the boys' Jefe snarled, and he stepped forward and drove his fist into the jaw of Nelson Avellanos.

His temple and his forehead. The man's ear and chest. The crack of punches reverberated bluntly down the concrete and into the early afternoon air of Northern Avenue.

The Jefita began to scream. The sidewalk exploded with voices and with the boys yelping and crying.

The Jefe's punches staggered the man to the ground and his boots stomped arms and fingers, crushing limbs into the concrete.

A man from across the street pulled the Jefe off of Avellanos, and someone kicked the razor out into traffic. The Jefita pulled off her shawl and wrapped the Jefe's arm.

Little Neto pushed and kicked at the men holding the Jefe's arms. Another man grabbed Neto, and after breaking away, the Jefe pulled his son away and family back into the truckito.

The Jefita cried, "Oh my Lord!"

When he found his keys and first gear, the Jefe shoved a cigarillo in his mouth. He muttered: "They'll call the sheriff for sure."

He shifted and shot out from his parking slot in front of the restaurant and fishtailed down the gutter. Relles and the crew of fosters slid in the truck's bed while Neto sat close to the Jefita, holding her arm and her leg. She asked the boy if he had any cuts.

"I got blood on me, Mama."

THE DAYS FOLLOWING THE INCIDENT were filled with compromises and time away from side-jobs, long days that left the Jefe in his stocking feet and in bed for hours. Phone calls came from compadre Julian about fields of onions left undone.

"The working man can't make it in this damn country anymore," the Jefe confessed to the household. He strained from the wounds to his back and his arms.

The Jefita worried so much for her husband that she took no account of the fact that she had no license. In all her years of marriage and having children, she had never learned to drive. But on that afternoon the Jefe's pain grew, the wounds leaked and turned an awful color.

"Get in the truckito, viejo, and I'll get Mr. Hernandez to drive you," she said and the Jefe didn't argue.

Later she wrote notes and kept a brief anecdotal record of all the warnings given by Doctor Bartechi and the nurse. The Jefe made note of the expense, and after they returned home and the man found himself resting and moaning for his bottle, he immediately began to figure his numbers on the slip of paper that prescribed the pain killer. The Jefe knew he couldn't afford the pills so he drank.

"Goddamn it, mujer," the Jefe's thick, painful voice grunted. "Am I going to eat or am I going to starve to death?"

In those days following "The Fight," she took care with the man. She took his words and actions in silence. The Jefita cooked summer soup and brought the man his bottle.

"Where are those goddamn boys?" he said with a voice thick like glue and worry.

"They're in the back, viejo," the Jefita directed. "They are cutting your lawn and bagging your grass."

"They're probably just standing around," the Jefe said, throbbing with pain. "Thumbs in their ass. Laziness taking over."

On the day old man Hernandez drove them back to Doctor Bartechi, the two argued in the driveway. They argued down Routt Avenue and all the way out over Jones Street. They argued in the parking lot of St Mary Corwin and the two argued as the man limped up the stairs and down the long hallway to the elevator.

"Jesus Christ, viejo," the Jefita said, "you can't have me

removing stitches. I don't have no clue about stitches."

"I worry about the money, mujer," the Jefe admitted.

"We'll find it, viejo," the Jefita said. "I'm working and the boys work hard. This is all of our worry."

THERE HAD BEEN RAIN ALL NIGHT and would be for days and days that late summer, and to little Neto, it felt as if all the lonely wind from the southeast of Colorado blew through the house. The boy heard it wailing and heard it slashing at the windowpanes. He heard the padded feet of the old folks and the pounding that came to the front door.

In the Jefita's kitchen waiting and drawn by the strong voices, each boy struggled to peer into the living room. The crew of fosters still held their pillows, and Neto was the boy brave enough to enter the room of uniformed men. He watched his parents on the loveseat sitting side-by-side as the uniformed men stood and talked. Little Neto walked straight to the Jefita and stood next to her, drawing the woman's arm around his waist.

"Avellanos' family filed the charges," the mustached officer began. "You left the scene, Mr. Ortiz. The hospital notified us and so we have to see how this will all pan out."

"He came at me with a knife," the Jefe explained.

"You can get this all down as your side of the story."

"County jail, you mean?"

"Yes, sir."

The Jefe stood too quickly and regretted the action immediately.

"Take her easy, Ortiz," the mustached one said. "We didn't come for this and we want you to take her easy."

"Santiago," the Jefita pleaded.

The younger one already had the Jefe's arm and little Neto immediately tensed and began to cry, tears watering down his cheeks and neck. The boys in the kitchen began to wail too and the Jefita held the boy tightly and told the rest to hush up and get downstairs.

The younger man had the cuffs ready, had the Jefe against the wall next to the door. The older mustached one comforted the Jefita and little Neto.

"Don't you move," the young one said.

"Go easy," the mustached man said. "This is a member of the steel union. Ain't that right, Ortiz. We got sympathies for working men but take her easy. You don't want this in front of your boy."

The Jefe loosened his shoulders and allowed the men to wrangle his massive arms behind his back, allowed the men to tighten their grips and work their cuffs onto his wrists.

"You got a shirt for him, ma'am," the mustached one said.

"Go get your father's shirt, Neto," the Jefita ordered.

On his way back he smelled the work shirt wondering if the man would be gone like Emeterio, if that was what happened to men. He handed it off to the officer.

"Thank you, son."

In the front yard there was no more wind, and the Jefe with his work shirt thrown over him walked slowly and awkwardly with the two uniformed men behind. He never turned or looked back as he allowed the men to crumple him down into their car. He sat with bent head and the Jefita began to slowly cry.

She stopped and regarded her boys, and for a moment as the Jefe pulled away from the front stoop, she had no idea who to contact or what to even say.

It was clear to the Jefita, as she dragged the phone and receiver into the closet-sized bathroom, that she did not want her boys or her crew of fosters seeing her cry.

"Warm something for the boys," the Jefita barked at her eldest, Relles. She made her way into the bath and managed to find her shawl and her purse. She stood in the doorway of the bathroom and grabbed the phone from the wall in the hallway and dialed her sister Viola's number. Nothing. She dialed Mrs. Hernandez' number and slammed the door and sat at the toilet.

"Mrs. Hernandez!" the Jefita said.

She felt the panic creep in again. She felt the tears welling in her eyes and creating a headache at the back of her head.

"I wish you would tell me what has you so upset, hija," the old woman Hernandez said.

The Jefita's words, when she found them, were flat and controlled: "I need your husband to drive me out to the bail bondsmen, Mrs. Hernandez. I need your husband's car."

"For Emeterio?" the old woman said.

The Jefita stopped and turned at the boy's face creeping in and she motioned with her eyes for Neto to close the door. "I have to piss, Mama," the boy said.

"Neto!" She cupped the receiver. "I'm in here making calls for your father."

"Mama."

"Neto!" the woman screamed.

There was a long silence and the Jefita's tears were unstoppable and uncontrollable. Old Mrs. Hernandez started, "I'll send him by after his breakfast, Cordelia."

"Mama!"

The Jefita ignored the boy and spoke quickly and bitingly to Mrs. Hernandez: "No, ma'am. I need his car now, Mrs. Hernandez. I'm so sorry to ask you this but I have to get downtown for my husband."

"Mama!"

"Goddamn, Neto," the Jefita screamed and she slapped at the door, leaning hard into the jamb. "Wait until I get outta here, boy, I'm gonna give you such a bruise. Yes, Mrs. Hernandez. I know your husband needs his breakfast but I need him here. I'll walk there, ma'am. Yes, that's right. I'll come down to you."

"Mama!"

"Yes, ma'am. I'll come down. Okay. Bye."

She stopped and slammed open the door and slapped at her son, and for a moment they faced each other. The mother paddled at the son's bottom and at his legs. The Jefita's eyes burned and her entire face glowed red with hurt and impatience.

"Goddamn it, Neto."

The boy's mouth opened, a dark wash of terror and surprise.

"Goddamn it," she repeated. "Do you know what is going on here? Do you!"

The Jefita's hands were clenched and she spoke with her head down, fighting back tears and sobs turned into full gasps.

"Don't you know what's going on here?" she repeated. "Don't you know I have to call down to the Hernandez' and get your Jefe? Don't you know I'm on the phone in there and calling for your father?"

"Don't, Mama," the boy said as his hands blocked her slaps and her fists.

"I wish you would think for once, Neto. Goddamn it. You have to use your little head and think."

She paddled at his tail bone and pant legs. She was frantic until the boy exploded in tears and ran off.

At a certain moment the Jefe looked around his holding cell and was overcome with a feeling of strangeness and near terror. Not even the familiarity of the toilet and the sinks from his army days, and not even the familiarity of the two drunks sleeping around him, could make him quite accept that this was all happening. The thing real to him was the stench of piss like ammonia and the strange silence pierced by the clanging of bars and voices of deputy sheriffs and their barking orders. The other sound was the torturous wind from outside the iron shutters. In that tiled cell he sat silently with his back against the cement walls. It was so hard for the Jefe to believe that a working man could land with the laziest disgraciados like the men snoring around him, men like his brother Emeterio.

Outside the walls, over the few treetops near downtown, he imagined their occasional whirl and slap due to the wind. With the buzzing from his ears and the fear that came from the surroundings, he felt as if he couldn't trust his senses. He felt as if he was losing his hearing and his sense of true sound, but also losing his good thoughts.

Alone and fearful, all he could do was listen and think, feel his own forehead and slap at his pocket for cigarillos. The hands of the institutional clock on the wall showed 8:35 a.m., and he was tempted to sleep, sitting up on his bench and with his back to the wall. His thoughts ran through his head telling him not to trust his surroundings and not to get comfortable. His thoughts told him not to accept this situation. And, minutes later, as his eyes closed and his consciousness faded, the bars gave their immense clank and another man entered the cell, and with him the controlled fright that whoever had entered would recognize him or start something with him. He worried Avellanos would enter and he would have to become some awful violent thought. The cell would again fill with silence and his eyes would rest and the wind and sounds of the cell would again whine around his ears. He needed the sleep that he knew would not come. And when he jammed his hands down into his pockets, he recognized how tentative and how fearful a gesture that was.

His hands fell down to his knees, palms facing up. After a month of tireless work, his hands had grown hard and leathered, dry skin meeting cuts and wounds. He breathed deeply to soothe himself, but the stench of the cell itself was almost too much to stand, like the stench of men in the field for days and for weeks without a wash.

During his sixth hour in county lock-up, after a strip search, a delousing and a washing, they issued Santiago F. Ortiz his uniform. He spoke to the Jefita on the phone and was waiting for arraignment when the Criminal Justice Agent pulled him from his cell and interviewed him.

As he waited in the hall, chained to the floor, he heard Victor Manualle's voice. Soft at first and then stinging in a convulsive panic. A guard unlocked him and dragged him towards the voice.

The Jefe felt weak as he was escorted into the office and again quickly chained to the floor. The Jefe sat near the desk and felt defeated, his stomach bubbling with worry.

"Ortiz?" Victor Manualle said. "You Ortiz?"

The Jefe nodded and decided to stare at his hands.

"Says here you're a steel worker. This your badge number?"

The Jefe nodded.

"And you're going in front of the judge tomorrow? Please don't nod, sir. Answer my questions."

"Yes, sir," the Jefe managed.

"Better," the man said shifting his weight in his seat and shuffling through papers over his desk until he found the right one. "I'm Victor Manualle and I work for the Criminal Justice Agency and I have some questions for you."

"So."

"So?" the man repeated. "Is that how you want to come across to me? You know they could've issued a bench ticket but they say you fought with them. Report says you resisted. What you say about that?"

"Are you a judge?"

"No, I'm the one gonna write you a letter saying you are employed, Ortiz. Now, I already spoke to your wife and she told me about your kids and your house. Now, you a veteran, right? I'm the one gonna tell them you are a foster parent and that you are a family man. So I think I deserve more from you than yes or no. Don't you think?"

"Yes, sir."

"And you own a home?"

"You spoke to my wife? Where's all this going?" the Jefe asked.

"I told you," he said. "I ask you these questions and I make a recommendation to the judge. I let them know of your standing in the community."

"Community?"

"The city and county of Huerfano. Now, you have no prior record?"

"No, sir. Bastard came at me with a goddamn knife."

"I'm not a judge, Ortiz. Save that for him. Now, no prior record and you own a home and you have foster children in the home. Correct?"

"Yes, sir. Will we lose them?"

"The State and the judge make that decision."

"They're good boys."

"You own your own truck?" Victor Manuelle asked.

"They're good boys. They never brought trouble home, you know."

"Ortiz."

"They never fought or brought trouble to the door. Not

like me and my brother done."

"Ortiz."

"My sons are good boys, too," the Jefe repeated.

Victor Manualle began to soften in the face of the Jefe's demeanor and perhaps the tearing of the Jefe's eyes.

"I swear they're good boys and I seen some of them other homes around and I'd hate to lose them to those places, you know. The Youth Offender System. I'd hate to see them hell and gone from my boys. They're almost like real brothers, you know. They look out for one another. I'd hate to see that all turn to shit."

"Like I said, Ortiz," Victor said. "That'll be up to the state and DCFS. Now, tell me about your work. You work full time? In the union, no? Correct?"

"Yes, sir. But I've been out because of my ears."

"Your what?"

"My ears. I have a ringing in them and they want me out for a while. Say I can't hear the alarms."

"But you're in the union?"

"Yes, sir."

To the Jefe it seemed like an hour since he had begun the interview as he answered yes or no. The questions seemed to run on and on.

"Tell me about your brother, Ortiz."

"What about him?"

"It says here your brother is in Colorado State Penitentiary for felony theft."

"He deserves jail," the Jefe explained. "He never even wanted in to the union and I tried like hell, you know, and he didn't even appreciate it. Everything easy for him. You know he owes everyone in the family money. They won't even have him. Can you believe that? In his own mother's house. His mother passed and no one wanted him. I took him in and the bastard attacked my wife. The man's not even divorced and he's living with another woman. More than one."

"You gonna end up like him or what, Ortiz? That's all I'm asking. Yes or no."

"No," the Jefe insisted. "No. Goddamn it. No. I'm here because that damn Avellano had a knife. On my family. On my boys."

Manualle's face was steady at filling in his forms and notes. "Listen, Ortiz," Victor said. "I've been where you are. I got kids and I hear you. If I make this recommendation and you run or get into something else I look bad."

"I have a mortgage, Mr. Manuelle. Sir. I have bills and I need to work or I can't feed my kids or my wife. I can't be in here and I need to work this shit out as quick as I can." The Jefe rested his hands down to the table and brought them together in prayer. "Please, Manualle. Sir. I need to get out of here for my family. They are all I have, sir. I swore to them I would take care of them. I swore to their mother. I swore to myself and to my God."

After days and days of rain the backyard's lawn spotted with dirt and the green turf felt spongy under little Neto's feet. At the edge of the backyard near the alley and near the Jefe's truckito, he stood without shoes, and the mud and earth felt good beneath his feet and in between his toes. He stepped from spotted turf to spotted turf testing the ground and looking at the imprint of his footprint, checking the style of his own track like the Indian trackers from the movies. The air was so fresh, and he nearly sniffed at it the way he smelled the Jefita's pots of beans or her tortillas.

The gutters from the house and from around the neighborhood howled as the water funneled and rang through the metal eaves and poured out onto the green turf and out into the alley. This morning, if only in his head, the footprint appeared a half an inch to an inch longer. His older brother Relles thought he was crazy to run barefoot in the early morning hours of those summer days before work, crazy to stand and waste time with pulling off his sneaks and his socks in order to make his own footprints in the backyard's brown and green turf.

The brother said, "You'll get mud in your socks for the whole day, sonso."

Little Neto felt like nothing could hurt him on this particular morning. He felt as if the large footprint was proof he would soon be his own man with his own side-jobs and his own truckito. He felt immense and growing in weight and height the way a man was supposed to.

The low south sky and the steel mill's raised smoke stacks towered over the yard, and he could make out the tops above the power lines and the rooftops below the immense morning gray skies. His mind played and climbed on those distances across the narrow street and among that skyline.

The dog they called Peaches sat watching with her belly partially exposed. The boy scratched at her ears and her coat and he raced around the backyard as the old dog chased and jumped after him. Little Neto spun and skipped around while the wide-mouthed dog barked and nipped at his muddy feet and at his rolled up jeans.

And when the newly freed Jefe came to the door in his undershirt, yawning and running out to the truckito with the first cigarillo of the day already to his teeth and lips, peering out from tired eyes to see how the weather looked, the boy watched closely.

"Not sure if it will rain all day today or not, boys. Can't go out until it does."

The Jefe yawned again, and blew the dark smoke from his nostrils out into the cool, misty air of the morning. He stayed on the doorstep and scratched at his armpits and at his stomach from under his t-shirt. Across the yard the boys and the dog ran and thrashed at the wet grass.

After that last gaze, he allowed himself to smile and acknowledge his boys, and then he sprinted barefoot across the lawn. He attracted Peaches' attention and scurried one full-sprinted circle around the backyard while she nipped at his bare feet.

"Feed those chickens, boys," the Jefe ordered, scratching at himself and breathing heavily as he limped back indoors.

Part Three

Bruna and Neto

13

Drive

My mother was sixteen years old that summer and had never been behind the wheel a day in her life when Jeri had her drive the thirteen blocks from the White Horse Bar and Grill back to their home on Evans.

Jeri had a '53 Studebaker Coupe in those days, jet black with a two-tone paint job that didn't come standard. Little Jimmy Mestas had taken it upon himself to give the car a canary yellow strip along the bottom half. That made the little car look fast and Jeri cherished the car ever since the day his '50 Chevy Bel Air came up with a cracked block and he traded it. Under normal circumstances he would have never trusted that car to the young Bruna. He loved that car and the tire pressure it sat on.

Initially Bruna resisted but Jeri and Bruna's mother were not speaking to one another and the woman had wanted nothing to do with the White Horse. She didn't care to catch Jeri with his crew of friends down at the place.

"I want you to go down there," Bruna's mother had screamed out the front door and Bruna nodded, "and tell that S.O.B. to get his ass home."

"Okay, Mama," she said.

By then Jeri had been on a drunk for days, and later when she found him, angrily jammed the keys down into Bruna's palms. He looked up and down the block.

"I been here for hours. Calling and calling. Where the hell have you been?" Jeri yelled.

He placed a cigarette between his lips and proceeded to search for matches. He found a nickel on the ground and lost his balance placing the coin in his pocket and almost fell backwards. Bruna caught him with both hands and the two almost chopped each other to the ground. For the first time the two embraced, clasping hands and holding one another for balance.

"I don't know how, Jeri," Bruna said.

"You can drive. Anyone can drive."

For a girl who had never driven a bicycle before Jeri might as well have asked her to steer the city bus home. She sat in the driver's seat outside of the "beer joint" and felt the sweat run down her front lip and down from her armpits, staining her bright blue sweater vest.

Bruna gripped the steering wheel. Her lips that afternoon were coated with a light pink lip gloss from the Woolworth's that she was nervously licking and biting at. Her small, perfect hands ached as she clenched and gripped the metal gearshift.

"Get the clutch down to the floor," Jeri instructed. "Get it down to the floor. And don't make an ass of yourself."

Bruna stared out over the traffic moving north. She had studied Jeri's driving in the past, sitting in between him and her Mama on countless road trips out to west Colorado, San Luis and also Monte Vista and the Montoya's family lettuce farm. Her arms suddenly felt heavy and tired as the engine kicked over and the car began to vibrate with energy.

"Well come on," Jeri said. "Shift. Goddamnit!"

The car started rolling and Jeri had his hand on the steering wheel and the gearshift. The gears strained and moaned as she let the clutch out. The car lurched and died. When the car finally got going, Bruna's eyes were locked on the road. Jeri was screaming and moving his arms and looking in every direction at once. Jeri did not allow Bruna to change lanes or shift out of second gear. That was his instruction. Fear and frustration built in Bruna's eyes and neck. She became aware of road signs and traffic lights. The car passed 4th Street Bridge and downtown near Union Avenue. Each street sign and street corner passed with waves of worry and Jeri's screams.

"Brake," Jeri yelled. "Brake. Brake. Go. Go."

Sweat poured from Bruna's hands and forehead, moistening the curls over her ears.

"Keep away from the curb," Jeri yelled. "The curb. Keep away from the curb. Brake. Brake. Brake. Go. Shift."

"All right," Bruna said with the confidence of eight blocks behind her. "Don't get mad."

Jeri raised an almost reassuring hand and nearly smiled.

"Did you know Father Dwyer drinks?" Bruna asked. She mostly said it to calm herself down. To calm Jeri.

"What you say?"

"I say Father Dwyer drinks. I seen him."

"What's the church come to?" Jeri said. At this he slumped into the door and leaned his forehead against the cold passenger side window.

Bruna's eyes dulled and her hands ached. For a few blocks while Jeri closed his eyes she was free of the sense of impending dents and scratches to Jeri's car. For a second she was excited by the speed of the car and the control of the engine as she stepped lightly on the gas. For a few blocks she felt whole and alive. She passed Centennial and Lincoln Street. Near the Chief Theatre she slowed to read the marquee. Soon her eyes were straining against the late Sunday afternoon sun and the dark shadows hiding out between the rectangular buildings of Junction Street and farther out to Colorado Avenue. Bruna sat up squinting before scraping the parked Mercury.

Jeri jumped up and screamed Bruna's name over and over. The two cars grated together, throwing them off course into oncoming traffic. She closed her eyes and let go of the steering wheel.

Before the Studebaker hit the curbing on Colorado Avenue and the front end popped into the air and jumped up onto a small yard and onto chain link fence that guarded the grass, a buzzing of depression and despair came into Bruna's head, all those scenes of bad luck and family troubles burying her.

Sitting in the crash site, the girl and her red curly hair was in disarray and she clenched her crucifix. She stared at Jeri's closed eyes and aching face. She felt somehow that the family was absolutely lost.

14

Retreat

A carload of nuns and priests departed from Huerfano County in a summer rainstorm. They rode past the steel mill, past the county hospital and past onion and chile farms; past irrigation ditches and cornfields, past horse ranches and cattle ranches. In the back seat, resting between Sister Arlene and Neddie Hernandez, both wearing their best Sunday skirts and hats, sat Bruna. Father Dwyer was driving. Beside him sat Father Holland, a tall, thin man in the passenger seat who was the priest from the old neighborhood.

"We have the whole peaceful trip to look forward to," said Father Holland. "What do you think?"

"I'd say I have to agree."

"We have a car full of youth and faith. You know what I'd like to do some day? I'd like to drive this country and take these girls to every university and parish. Show them California and Oregon. East coast as well. They would appreciate that, I think. When these girls become nuns I'd like to make that drive."

While the two men talked on and on, Bruna and Neddie nodded, laughed and each girl dozed and would jerk awake. In Colorado Springs they had a dinner of burgers, fries and RC Colas.

"This guy doesn't stop talking," whispered Bruna, sitting across from Neddie in the booth. "You know what I mean, cabróna? How you feeling?"

“Hardly wait to get to where we’re gonna get,” said Neddie. Neddie was a year younger than Bruna but they had been friends all through Sunday school and high school. They played on the same softball team and tetherball team. Though not as attractive as Bruna, and though she wore thick dark glasses that were sometimes taped after being damaged at the Woolworth’s Diner where she worked, she had long legs and an awkward lean look to her that the boys took to.

“You may have to keep talking to the guy this whole trip, so don’t knock yourself out too quick, you know?” Bruna said.

“I won’t. I’ll pace myself,” Neddie answered.

“Yeah, you’ll want to pace yourself. Your priest, Holland, has been around so he knows all the tricks. And he’s a boozer, you know how people talk about him.”

Rain kept falling and fog was blowing over the road when they reached Highway 24 and also when they finally reached the Kansas border, near the edge of a sheep ranch, at least fifteen miles from the nearest gas station. Del Monte Greens was near Salinas, Kansas, and served two functions: priests spent time there in solitude and in retreat after seminary, and nuns spent time there before going to their permanent assignments.

Bruna, leaning slightly forward with fatigue, coat unbuttoned, sweater open at the throat, hat back and arms stiff down beside her, led Neddie and the Sister on the way in to the main dormitory and meeting hall. In new shoes her mother bought her special for this trip, Neddie followed, moving nervously around the tentative conversations with new acquaintances and roommates. Both girls stood intimidated in front of Sister Arlene and her many copies. Lightheaded from the drive and hours on the road, Bruna listlessly took off her coat and sweater and lay down on the small twin bed. She shifted about while Neddie looked out the small window they shared and placed her turquoise suitcase on the small bureau of drawers. With care, she opened her case and slowly pulled out her clothes and placed them in drawers. The clothes reminded her of home, and since she planned on becoming homesick, she held the sweaters and the one pressed white blouse tightly in her fingers.

There were many contrasts between the two girls. Neddie's parents had lived in Huerfano their whole lives and they watched Neddie closely. Bruna's parents weren't as strict; they drank and went out pretty regularly. Neddie was a size 6 and rather tall. Bruna was a size 4. For Neddie, this had been her first trip out of Huerfano County and out of Colorado. Bruna had shuffled with her mother and Jeri out to the West Coast on at least two occasions. Neddie pulled her white gloves from her hands, rubbing her hands nervously as she prepared for bed. She crossed the room to Bruna who was now sitting in her blouse and panties on the edge of the bed, her red hair in a high mound on the top of her head.

"I hope we didn't make a mistake coming," Neddie confided. "Don't tell anybody this but I was worrying about this trip all month. I went out last night for a few drinks."

"I was out too. Don't make no difference."

"Who were you with, Bruna?"

"It don't matter if you drink or if you been out, is all I'm saying. You got two hands to pray with, that's all that matters. That's what my mother says," Bruna admitted.

"Who, Bruna? Tell me."

Bruna smiled: "Relles Ortiz."

"Relles Ortiz! You got to want to get out of the house bad to go out with him," Neddie said.

"He's sweet. His brother, too."

"Relles is older," Neddie said. "And he'd be all over you in a second."

"Not too much older. We went out for some food."

"I heard about those boys he runs with. I heard about him."

"Heard what?"

"Well, I heard he took Martha Lucero out to Milton Pacheco's apartment and did the deed."

"What?"

"The deed," Neddie said, bouncing up and down on the bed to illustrate.

"Well, he never took me down there, Neddie. And I hope he never does."

"Hoping never done nothing," Neddie said. "That's what my father says. And you can't be here, you know, out with the Fathers and Sister Arlene if you're out at Milton Pacheco's. I'll tell you that."

"Well, what about the drinking?" Bruna asked.

"What about it?"

"Can you be out here if you be out drinking all the time?" Bruna said. "Because I think you'd be pretty guilty yourself."

"Guilt ain't got nothing to do with it," Neddie answered. "It's all in your head."

A few hours before lights out, another girl came to occupy the third bed in the dorm room. Her name was Manuela Rosales. Neddie was uneasy because Manuela was hard looking and didn't wear any gloves. She was Mexican and came in from Española, New Mexico, in a brilliant red sweater. She jogged into the room and slowed to a prance as she emptied her clothes from her duffel bag into the drawers. The year before, at fourteen, Manuela had lied about her age and jumped on board a bus and come to visit her family in Española. She had been working at the

Santuaro Church cooking and taking odd jobs until she was of age to make this retreat with Father Allen. Tonight she was excited to be out of New Mexico and yet scared to be around pocho girls like Neddie and Bruna. She wanted to know so much about her new roommates. She asked the girls if they lived in houses or duplexes or apartments. Neddie was ashamed that she lived in her own house with her father and mother and all of her siblings. Ashamed that she had a change of clothes in her suitcase for every day of the week and that she was the only one of the girls to have met her biological father.

"Know what makes a good Catholic?" Manuela asked quietly after lights out.

"What's that?" Bruna and Neddie asked.

"You got to want to believe," Manuela said. She pulled a small transistor radio from her purse and extended the antenna. She channeled for Mexican music, and the sounds of accordion and mournful wailing played softly to each girl's inner ear. Manuela smiled. "Know what I say? Why else would we come out here and go without talking for a week?"

Before the three finally closed their eyes and gave in to sleep, the girls clasped their hands tightly and they all prayed to make it through the month. When first light came, they were hit with Catholic solitude, Bible study and lectures without one word allowed between them. Their young female minds were rubbed, patted and kneaded. The decision to join the religious life as a nun, or sister, requires much prayer and counsel, they were advised. They were harangued, reprimanded, and asked not to horseplay while the Fathers and nuns were speaking. They were asked not to listen to anything, no TV, no radio, not even to one another or anything else at all, except for their lessons and their own prayers.

15

Yesteryear

I got the banana," Neto called out to Bruna Montoya, "if you got the splits." Around them güero teenagers were propped against their cars and licking at vanilla cones outside the Jones Avenue Dairy Queen. Neto tried not to feel ashamed of the dirt in his fingers or the sweat stains down his shirt, the broken sink that was his face.

He had seen the young Montoya girl many times around the neighborhood, and once at the St Francis Festival at the Stations of the Cross. He noticed her ears were pierced but without earrings.

"You're as stupid-assed as your brother," Bruna said, struggling with the straw in her milkshake. "Your brother around here?"

Neto shook his head and gave the ground a smile.

"He still have his Ford?" she asked.

Neto glanced between two dancing ice cream bars against a background of a chocolate explosion and Bruna's honey-lotioned legs. "What are you, like a cheerleader or something?"

"Pep squad," Bruna answered, and she bent her knees slightly when she spoke the words. "You know I was writing your brother overseas, Neto? He never wrote me, though."

"Your mother a widow?" He couldn't resist ignoring the brother's name, and as soon as he asked he immediately regretted the words.

Bruna lowered her eyes and squirmed in slow motion.

"I heard that somewhere," Neto said. "I heard it. Maybe I heard it at church or in the rectory. People talk. Around, you know."

"Watch what you say, Neto, because I don't want no one talking bad about me or my Mama."

"I ain't talking bad about you."

When her tears came down, Neto was moved by a sudden sympathy. He chucked his milkshake to the ground and spit. "I could crack my head open."

"What?"

"I feel like beating my head," Neto admitted. "I mean I think the whole thing is sad and I don't know what to say to it, you know. I don't know what to say to any of it."

"You don't have to say nothing," Bruna said.

He stood at a sudden attention and declared to the parking lot: "Well, I won't let anybody talk shit about you anymore. You can count on me. I ain't that kind of Catholic anymore."

"Well, I know you are my friend, Neto," Bruna said. She smiled.

Near the posted wall that read

PAWN
LOANS
GUNS

he thought he might try to put his arm around her. Bruna would have none of that.

IN THE SHADOWS of her people's three-room, second floor apartment on Evans Avenue, Bruna's view was garbage cans and the backyard near the alley. Over the sty that was her people's kitchen sink, she rinsed and stacked plates and lifted the drapes with soapy fingers.

Lena got up from the kitchen table and called to anyone that would listen, "I waited all goddamned night for this good for nothing cabrón."

"Fuck, mujer." He was hungover and tired, now heading for bed. "Shut your fat mouth."

Lena wore her housecoat, no bottoms and no socks. She pinched at the end of her clove cigarette and yelled from the front door, "I want every woman in this goddamned neighborhood to know what a drunk bastard of a man you are."

"You better be careful," the sixteen-year-old Bruna warned, finishing up her chores.

"Careful of that cabrón?" Lena retorted. She was more and more convinced of his unexceptional qualities and his drinking ways, his tendency to stay out all night.

"Stop doing that. He's liable to kill you."

"I want him to hurt me, the bastard, so I have the proof. He's the one that better be careful. The way he talks to me. Like a goddamned dog," Lena said before heading to the bus stop for work. "I want him out of here."

Jeri had phoned the apartment the night before from the VFW or the Arcadia or wherever he happened to be; most bars were on Union Avenue in those days. If Bruna answered he would hang up and keep calling until Lena answered.

"I love you," he had drunkenly said. "I want no one but you. I am the only legit man you know, woman."

THOSE TROUBLES LOST SIGNIFICANCE with the arrival of a brand new Royal typewriter that Bruna was to share with her cousin Connie. Bruna forgave Jeri his crimes or at least forgot about them in the tap-tap-tap of her practicing. The sound of those used, black-and-gray metal-capped keys was how she imagined the sound of work and sophistication. Mainly she pulled the typewriter from its pasteboard case to type up her prayers onto index cards, and later after

Jeri bought her a box of typing paper, she began to type up stories and letters for the church. It was not redemption or praise she wanted but a skill that could lead to work and a way out of her mother's world.

The next month Bruna received a score of sixty words per minute and 96% accuracy in transcription of dictation at Central High, an accomplishment she attributed to the gifted Royal. She walked out to St. Francis and showed Father Dwyer and Father Holland and suggested maybe she could work in the rectory office.

At dinner she jiggled her legs with excitement, and in the middle of conversation she smiled and revealed her love of typing and her accomplishment at school, and how she would become a secretary.

"You're the smartest girl," Jeri complimented.

"Or the most nervous," Lena answered. "Look how you're chewing."

"That's how you get the most out of life," Jeri winked.

Bruna gazed at the horrible couple for long moments as if to gain some understanding or realization. "I don't want work typing," she declared. "I want to work in the church. I'm resolute."

"Oy lo. Muy chingón," Lena said. "Do you hear her? 'Resolute,' she says."

"It means I am serious."

"Get out of here with you 'resoluteness.' And come when I call you to wash dishes."

Bruna Montoya rode in Relles' '56 Ford and asked, "Do you have any idea what it's like to live with that man?"

"How do you mean?"

"I mean he's in jail now but he does go to church. And he buys me things. I mean he doesn't mean to hurt my Mama and I know he don't want to."

Relles glanced at her while steering. Bruna's hairdo and face were near perfect to him and that sometimes left him dumbstruck and unsure of what to say. This was one of those times.

"I mean I don't want to believe anyone could be that way to anyone," Bruna explained. "He's fought with Mama plenty of times but I don't want to believe someone could be that way."

"Someone will bail him out," said Relles.

"I knew he wasn't my real father. Since I was young. A little baby, really. I knew he wasn't my father or any real blood relation. Sure I called him daddy. I did and I shouldn't have. Mama says not to put anything past him. I don't want to believe, you know?"

Relles stared at the windshield and the dead bugs.

"He won't really let her talk on the phone to people. To family or her friends from work. And he'd get so mad at her for talking to Mr. Medina. He works with Mama at the cleaners."

Relles nodded.

"You know Mr. Medina," Bruna continued. "Well, Mama told him this story about this man down at Dundee Cleaners. She told him he perspired right through his shirt and undershirt so much during the summer and through the shifts at the cleaners he would have to shower in the middle of the day. And so Mama tells this to Jeri and he hits her face."

"I know Medina."

"He picked her up and let her have it. I'm ashamed to say that Mama didn't do a thing to deserve it. And she didn't do a thing to stop him neither. She told me that was a part of marriage and I knew right then I would never want to be in one. You know the real shit of it? They ain't married. Never walked down the aisle or nothing."

"It must be love."

"You think that's what love is? Or what family is supposed to be? Watch what you say because I won't stand for insults against the sanctity of marriage. Father Dwyer says that marriage is a special honoring of God. He says it is about a connection between a man and a woman."

With a loud knock he made the brakes squeal in front of Bruna's building. She looked over her shoulder to see if the neighbors or if her Mama were leering. "I've heard about you boys taking girls out to Milton Pacheco's apartment," Bruna said.

"Who told you that?"

"Neddie and the girls around," she said. "No, I was just asking. You mad at me for asking?"

"I'm not mad. I'm worried, that's all."

"Worried about what?"

"Your soul and my soul. You know what they do there?"

Bruna said mockingly, "I know about you. You and Marquita Lucero."

"Well, I'm already done in for," he said. "But you still have a soul to save."

"So why are you worried about my soul?" she said. "We haven't done nothing."

"Well, going out with me means something don't it?" he said. "People say shit all the time, Bruna."

"What would they say, Relles?"

"Well, what they said about Marquita. See, you even heard about it."

"Yeah, Neddie told me."

"The truth is I never done nothing with her."

"Really?"

"Yeah," he said. "People talk."

"Why would they say shit about you and her? I mean I've heard awful things about you and Milton getting her up there."

"I can't understand why people say the things they want to say," Relles argued. And the sudden honesty filled him with panic. He kissed her mouth with an uneasiness. In that moment she looked so exquisite to him, so lovely and graceful with her white gloves and her glow-in-the-dark Rosary beads in her purse. Her feel, her presence and her voice, the feel of her mouth and tongue felt like it would all be soon over so he kissed harder and so did she.

THAT MONTH Neto visited the fat, bowlegged Delacruz girl while her folks worked in the onion fields past Blende, Colorado. He stole kisses or grabbed on her ass, but mostly it was talk, vague plans of the road to Colorado Springs or Denver.

The girl was a quiet, dark-haired daughter with a large face and a short, round body that drove Neto mad. One night he placed a ring box in her hand. He finished by trying to put his hand down the front of her pants.

"What are you planning, Neto, to fuck me or marry me?" the young girl asked.

He gave no answer. Not quite sure what he should do, he placed her hand stupidly on his crotch and kissed at her with a misplaced force. When the Delacruz girl pulled away and stood up, Neto sagged against the cold metal of the truck and he placed the cheap dime store ring back in his pocket.

"My father would shit all over you, Neto."

"I'll tell him I don't care," Neto answered.

"And when he asks you if you have work or a place for us, what will you say?" she asked. "You don't even have work."

"Is that what you think about? I don't think about those things at all."

There was a silence between the two so heavy and cold, the Delacruz girl began to tremble.

She stood at the back of the truck and pulled her arms into her sleeves for warmth. "Answer me, Neto. Do you really care about marrying me?" she finally asked. "Or do you just want to fuck me."

On the day Relles Ortiz and Bruna Montoya came together through the door of The Donahue, a new time of jealous and naïve energy began for the entire crew, especially Neto. He was in a fall, and only his compadre Blacky was working regularly at the mill. Cornbread was part time and doing maintenance. Neto's father and family felt impatience and he could hardly look at them, his eyes at the floor when he came home from The Donahue and a night of drinking.

As he walked home, down Northern Avenue and down Spruce, under bare sycamore and pine trees, the entire neighborhood felt drowned with pungent rain and mist. That night in bed, as he rested in his cot, he listened to the wind and the dripping from the eaves down the ancient wood to the cellar door. He thought of all the good things that had abandoned him. All he wouldn't have. There were days of dense humidity that he fought through for the next week as he crept around the neighborhood.

What the fuck they have to do that for? thought Neto.

One day later he went on a drunk and called Jeri; he called from the phone booth out back of The Donahue. He hadn't spoken to the man since the days before he left overseas.

"Oye, Velasquez," he yelled into the receiver. "I got some good news about one of your girls."

"Who the fuck is this?" Velasquez answered.

Neto heard voices from the background in Jeri's house.

He imagined it was Bruna.

"She ain't ready for the Lord," Neto said. "What do you think about that?"

"Who is this?" Velasquez said.

"You hear what I say. She ain't ready. And she ain't clean."

"Who?"

"She's knocked up, Velasquez." There was silence on the other end. "You hear what I said, Velasquez? She ain't ready for no Lord."

"Who the hell is this?"

"He fucked her," Neto said through the sobs. Coldly he put the receiver down, kneading the skin around his ears and forehead, concentrating on points across his head, rubbing circles into his eyes. His t-shirt sank into damp armpits. "He fucked her. Relles fucked her and knocked her up real good."

The person who brought chile and tamales to my Abuelo Santiago the most that summer was Bruna's Jeri, whose old yellow '53 Studebaker sometimes would overheat in the Abuelo's driveway. He never arrived by appointment or after a phone call. The Abuelo knew of him as one of the San Luis Velasquez brothers who lived on Routt Avenue. He had no idea he was quite nearly Bruna's father. "That bastard showed up anytime day or night," Santiago once complained to Neto.

He would appear at the front door of the house in his hipster apparel, wing tips, dark glasses and long-sleeved guayabera, the pockets heavy with a small notebook and a pouch of Red Man, an eyeglass case and sometimes, if Jeri was ready to play, a small red Hohner accordion case. His long, thin hair, parted at his left ear and combed over a bit, and his awful expressions like "hot enough for ya" and "could fry an egg out here" annoyed my Abuelo, to whom he came as a compadre, a fellow man of the steel mill. Everyone knew he could drink and everyone knew he had spent time in jail.

"Some dinner?" Santiago asked him respectfully in Spanish.

"Mr. Ortiz," he said. "This is very important concerning your son and my daughter Bruna."

Jeri sat at the dinner table and started lighting a second cigarette, placing the first one onto Abuela's lace table cover without seeming to care there was no ashtray.

In a few seconds Santiago was screaming for Neto, screaming his name out towards the kitchen and down to the basement where Neto usually holed up. "Why don't you go get him?" Santiago ordered to his wife.

"I didn't mention any particular son," Jeri said.

"Which boy do you mean, compadre?" Santiago said.

Jeri Velasquez shifted in his chair with a groan and sigh. He could remember a careless time between these two families, the Ortiz family and Velasquez'. I wish I didn't have to be here, Jeri thought. Talking and smoking with old friends after a few swallows of rum helped him keep his wits. He could speak of politics and the steel union with the Abuelo Ortiz, who would not judge or be hurt. Jeri Velasquez wished this to be one of those nights, but the man sensed a storm of jealousy and hurt coming. And when the man learned of his daughter's pregnancy and when he guessed the truth of his compadre's son, he could not help but want to rush to his friend's living room and dining room to question and warn, to hurt the boy in question.

Neto was in the middle of the room before Jeri Velasquez noticed him.

"Where'd you come from?" Velasquez said. "You bring your face over here, boy."

Neto walked over obediently and with a smile, genuinely thinking no wrong from Jeri Velasquez. It was hot and humid that summer night and so Neto's hair was wet and his face sweated because the wood stove was going even in the summer. Neto came through the kitchen to the men's place at the table.

Jeri accepted a drink from one of the women, my Tia Florinda or maybe my Tia Rita. Jeri let the rum touch his lips and he gulped it down in a mix of despair and pleasure. This had been his fifth drink since making the decision to confront Neto, and by this point in the evening, he was increasingly warm and sweaty and anxious to speak. He smelled the odor of cooking beans and garlic from the kitchen. He immediately jumped to his feet and took Neto's immense shoulders in his own hands and stared the boy in the face. The nieces and cousins working on the place settings and the women in the kitchen rolling and preparing tortillas soon stopped and came to watch the two men grappling.

Soon Jeri had Neto up against a window and was pulling Abuela's drapes and her tin crucifix down from the wall. The man held Neto's white tank top undershirt in his fists, and Neto made no move to resist or fight back, out of respect for the older man and his mother's home.

"I know about your phone calls, boy," Jeri kept repeating. Santiago sat still, mostly out of surprise and puzzlement. Santiago had thought Velasquez to be a delicate man with a large round belly and found this new smoldering man to be completely out of order. Neto became aware of Jeri's eyes and the big dark rings of two sleepless nights. Jeri stepped back and drove his fist into Neto's chest and face, getting four or five strong blows in before Neto squirmed away. Jeri Velasquez stood embarrassed as the front room of the house filled with family, by this time Relles and my cousin Kiko.

Jeri had nothing to say and kept his glance downcast to his hands and car keys, sensing himself surrounded and growing quickly tired, drunk. Later Jeri would go through a whole personality of emotions as he drove himself to The Hideaway Bar and Grill out on Northern Ave.

Jeri was drunk when he arrived home that warm evening. He removed his slacks and the new shirt and his wing tips, his straw hat and socks. With a sweat trickling down his biceps, he pulled on his brown robe while Bruna and Lena cleaned the evening dishes. He threw a piss in the small toilet off the bathtub. He wound the leather belt into a firm bandage around his right fist and tested it with blows against his left palm and the mattress.

When Jeri came down the hallway, between the family photos and Lena's crucifixes, his mind was already on leaving. The ache in him felt unending, he wanted to be done with Lena and her disgraceful daughter, and he had the odd sensation that what was to happen next was inevitable. With an economy of movement, hands down by his side, he followed Bruna to the far side of the kitchen, wanting to hurt her for his pride and for his anger, for his family name that Bruna's mother would never take as her own.

Jeri's first slap received no response, and Bruna took the second on her small elfish nose and her cheek, and her left eye. He leaned there over her as Bruna huddled down on the cold laminated tile, and in a single reflex he slapped down at her legs and buttocks.

"Keep away from her," Lena said. Tears streamed down her face as she pounded and smashed the man's shoulders.

Jeri repeated, "She's the fucking whore of the neighborhood."

Bruna covered up through most of the battle and struggled to cover up her stomach.

"Don't you ever touch that girl! Don't you ever touch that girl, you fuckin' pig!" Lena answered. "You pig of a man!"

Jeri dropped the belt suddenly to grab Lena's struggling arms, the broomstick and chair coming at him. He found himself battered and cut, butted twice and pulled around the room by Lena and the smaller Bruna.

The young girl tugged and pushed after losing her weapon and the older Lena retreated, ducking and kicking at the hulk of a man. Lena found herself on her knees where the kitchen table and dinner plates once stood. "You fuck of a man," she repeated. "I'll kill you!"

WEEKS LATER, Jeri was drinking a beer, sitting in his car when my Tio Neto walked up with his crew. Erminia Cruz, Jeri's girlfriend at the time, was pointing the air vents towards her thin face. Jeri had promised her a nice evening out and so he drove her to the Summer Festival at Assumption Parish, the first festival of the summer. They stopped off at the Harbor Inn for some cigarettes and a six pack of Schlitz. She held one of the cans between her lotioned legs as she tried to feel the cool air against her face. Her beers were kicking in when they pulled into one of the last slots.

The rear-view mirror brought Neto's face to Jeri. And because he was drunk, Jeri didn't register anything odd at first. The crew of men approached and joked to Erminia, "A person needs religion for their life and the beer for the world."

"I thought she was family," Neto told him over and over.

Neto's compadre Cornbread came along and pulled the tire iron from behind his back and smashed at the Studebaker's windows to the surprise of Neto.

Ermina screamed and jumped out of the car carrying her shoes in one hand and her beer in the other. She fell back on her tailbone.

"I didn't think anything like that could happen in the parking lot of a church," Erminia told me years later. "I trusted everybody then."

Cornbread's blows were deep and uncontrolled and the glass smashed out onto blacktop. The whole thing seemed strange and unprepared, the three men from the steel mill and the single man from the Army Depot tussling in the church's parking lot.

Neto's thoughts were this: his white undershirt was sticking to his chest. The festival was full of people but the whole thing felt empty. Neto kept hitting at Jeri, who was drunk and couldn't fight back. Jeri acknowledged Neto and Cornbread with a head's up nod. "What the hell?"

Neto tore Jeri from the car, got the man down on his knees and begging for forgiveness.

"Kill that son-of-a-bitch," Cornbread said.

Blacky ran in and held Jeri's massive arms the best he could. The incredible noise of Jeri's moaning owned the brawl over the music and laughter from the festival. Jeri felt the power of Neto's fist smashing at his face and chest, and dizziness set in to his vision.

"Christ Jesus save me," Jeri might've said.

Days later Neto sat in the wooden pews. I like to think Neto's entrance broke Bruna's dread that morning as she kneeled on swollen legs and ankles from her night job out at Newberry's Café and Bakery downtown. I like to imagine the weight of shame she held in those baggy sweaters Lena forced her to wear.

"I never seen you here," she told him.

"They say I have to find religion," Neto said.

"Your mother and father?"

Neto nodded.

“Well, people talk too much, Neto,” she said. She crossed her arms and leaned back into the wood pew, and she rested her arms on her pregnant belly. She put her feet up and stretched her short legs.

“All of the families are a big mess,” Bruna said.

“It don’t bother me.”

Neto put his hand on the woman’s stomach and Bruna put her hand to the top of his.

16

Backyard Marriage

Neto planned a wedding in one afternoon, all while drinking beer. He spoke out loud to a small crowd of chivatos that had formed in the garage.

"Mira, the backyard will be open and we'll keep the guitar players in the garage," Neto explained. He stood in the doorway with a cigarillo in his mouth, and he kept adjusting it underneath his mustache. "We'll move all the cars out and we'll cut all the grass down and the patio and the driveway out from the alley will be the dance floor. We'll make it all look real suave."

"We'll keep the alcohol in the kitchen," Cornbread added.

Cornbread was Neto's best compadre and John Relles' best man. Of the three men he was the skinniest and had the thinnest arms and legs. He was twenty-five and had the general expression and build of an old man.

"No booze until after the wedding, cabrón," Neto said.

"Yeah, yeah," Cornbread said. His face held a child's deep grin. "I'll keep a couple of six packs in my car."

"Are you deaf, cabrón," Neto said. "This is a wedding and I want to save it from all of that. You hear me?"

Cornbread kicked at the Abuelo's dog that had been licking at his pants. The dog yelped in pain and ran out back to his food bowl and blanket out on the concrete.

"Hey, cabrón," Neto said. "Don't be kicking my family's dog."

"Well, tell the motherfucker not to be licking at me."

The men followed the dog out back. "And we'll be sure to have no dogs," Neto said.

"What about the bride, cabrónes," John Relles said. "What will the bride tell me when I tell her all of this?"

"In her mind she'll have to get used to it," said Neto. He had three months growth to his beard, and he wore Levi's and a plain white t-shirt with a pocket over his big heart. In February he was twenty, three years younger than John Relles, the oldest of the entire crew, and he'd been living with the Abuelos since losing his position at the steel mill.

"Without any money, cabrón, what else do you want to do?" Neto said.

While they walked around the yard, gulping from their cans of beer, Neto was buzzed and had to concentrate to light cigarette after cigarette, explaining the whole ceremony to John Relles and their friends. For months he had been hustling ideas from anyone who would bite, imagining the position of tables and borrowed chairs underneath the largest apple tree.

That day he explained the whole situation again to more compadres, his Tia Archuleta and his cousin Kiko, over the back fence. Neto noticed that John Relles had paid little attention to the details of the wedding. Neto assumed that his brother was pissed at the whole disgraceful situation, and that he had been avoiding the wedding project over at the garage where he worked part-time. For two weeks John Relles had lost sleep, turning over and over again on the cot in the basement next to Neto's bed. The dreams would blow John Relles out of bed and scared Neto. "You okay, cabrón?" Neto would scream, but the young groom never answered, could never answer. But I'm sure John Relles' worry softened in the mid-afternoon sun, while Neto stood and made specific plans for the ceremony.

"How much you think this is gonna cost, Neto?" John Relles finally asked.

"I don't know, Manito," Neto answered. "I'll ask the Abuelos for fifty and see if they give me twenty."

"Ask for a hundred," said Cornbread, who had started to chew a fresh wad of Red Man, his front teeth stained with the juice.

"Cabrón," Neto said. "John Relles here has been worrying over this shit for weeks. I don't want to fuck anything up by getting greedy." Neto began to scratch at his beard. "So don't get involved. This ain't even your family."

Cornbread spat and gave an impatient look.

"Do you think they'll give that much?" John Relles asked.

"That's nothing for the Abuelos," said Neto. "And the woman is worth it, no? We should ask for at least fifty."

John Relles didn't say a word but nodded and lit a cigarette.

"So what about her people?" Cornbread asked. "The Montoya family?"

"A hundred," John Relles answered. "Her Uncle already promised."

"Right on!" Neto slapped John Relles' hand. "That's a pile of money."

"Yeah," Cornbread agreed. He was searching for the cigarette tucked behind his ear. "That'll buy a ton of booze."

Neto gave Cornbread a look. "After the wedding. And we'll have to thank her family."

"They're not coming," John Relles said.

"Not coming?"

"You know how it is," John Relles explained. "Her mother won't even allow me in the house. Family is all wrong, you know."

"Well, why don't you talk to him?" Neto asked.

"Yeah, why don't you talk to them?" Cornbread agreed.

"I tried. I told him I am here to talk about my life with their girl. I told him that I swear none of what he has heard is true, but he don't believe me, you know. Man, you know."

The backyard lay in the mid-afternoon shadow and more friends were gravitating to listen to the planning. It was July and the heat seemed more bearable in the shade of the house close to the stucco walls. When Neto and the men finished their scheming and their drinking, they opened the door to the garage to pour sand over the oil stains.

ON THE DAY of the wedding there were a load of relatives and hangers-on in the house and the food was being prepared and displayed on the kitchen table: plates of various rices, tortillas and bowls of menudo and posole, great plates of fried beef, lamb and chicken, and Abuela's sweet empanadas and tamales, Thanksgiving and Christmas dinner rolled into one. Father Dwyer stood and inspected the table carefully, without touching the food.

"What a marvelous celebration," Father Dwyer said. He sought out Neto among the group of people and, fixing his trained Catholic eye on him, said, "Your family, my dear Ernesto, would have been an extraordinary host for the Bishop."

Abuela continued to load the table and almost blushed. She wiped her hands on her apron and swept the hair from her eyes.

"Thank you," Neto said.

"You want a beer?" Cornbread said, picking at some of the tamales.

"What's that?" asked Father Dwyer. He was smooth and fat, almost like a woman. He feathered his hair from his face, and thought for a minute. His voice streamed like a professor's or a Latin-speaking monk's, and his attitude was distant but respectful. "You know the food smells so grand, but I should really wait until after."

"I've got some cold ones in the garage," Cornbread said.

"Thank you so much, Father, for performing the ceremony," Abuela said in Spanish. She said it with such a radiant expression, like nothing Neto had heard or seen in years, not since his return or his brother's return from overseas. There was a similar look in her tired eyes when John Relles arrived from the war. When he arrived in class-A dress uniform, she fell to the ground crying and moaning to La Virgen. She had cried when Neto had arrived but his unit had not seen combat, had not seen anything other than a Frankfurt, Germany, staging area.

"Has John Relles arrived?" Father Dwyer asked.

"He's getting dressed, sir. He lives here."

"Has the bride arrived?" Father Dwyer asked a few awkward minutes later. He looked at his watch.

"She's at her family's house but she should be here pretty soon." He added, "She's walking over."

"I have Mass at 5:30, Ernesto," Father Dwyer said.

"Have you met my Tio Ruben, Father?"

"Ah, no. I don't think I have had the pleasure, Ernesto."

"Sir, he's my uncle from Montebello," Neto explained. "He's playing guitar today. He's a musician."

"Ah, a musician," Father said.

"Yes, Father," Neto explained. "In my family, the music is almost as important as the ceremony."

Father Dwyer nodded.

The two men walked out to the living room, through the main doorway out to the porch where Tio Ruben was sitting. He was out on the old couch that had been dragged through the front door to handle the crowd that would surely pile up later.

"Ruben," Neto shouted. "How are you, Tio?"

Ruben was an old man, obese and hairy. He was a body man by profession and used to work in the same garage with John Relles before moving out west to California. Neto had not seen the man in months, until this moment on the porch. "Father Dwyer, this is Ruben Archuleta," Neto said.

The fat man sat on the couch with his tie already draped around the collar of his shirt. He turned to my uncle and the Father and said, "Qué?"

"Father Dwyer, Uncle. This is Father Dwyer," Neto repeated loudly. The front porch creaked with the weight of the men's arrival. "He's a little deaf, Father."

"I just got here," Ruben finally muttered. His guitar case was thrown to his side, the faded leather cracked and old.

"Ruben!" Neto shouted, his arms falling to his sides. "I want you to meet the Father."

"I'm fucked up, Neto," Ruben said, pathetic with blind drunkenness. He was wearing dark sunglasses and spitting as he talked, not realizing where he was sitting and who he was talking with. His forehead was completely covered with sweat. He kept pushing at his jacket sleeves and scratching nervously at the hair on his forearms.

Father Dwyer could not contain his disgust.

"That's why I don't like to drink at weddings, Neto, because I get fucked up," Ruben said, motionless, without blinking.

Father Dwyer looked down upon him uncertainly. "It's so good to meet you, Mr. Archuleta."

"I'm so sorry, Father," Neto said. He was ashamed. He wished he had stayed in California, wished he had stayed in the Army Ordnance Corps and kept the respect that came with the uniform and the steady paycheck. For the first time in months he wished he didn't drink so much, and he wished he didn't sleep on a cot in his parents' basement. He wished he hadn't lost his job.

"Pinche faggots in the church never respected the working man around here," Ruben blurted and spat.

Father Dwyer closed his eyes and took a step back on the porch, and Neto thought he might have been praying or wishing he had not made the journey the few blocks from St. Mary's over to Spruce Street.

"When the union strikes, where is the pinche church?" Ruben continued.

"I'm so sorry, Father Dwyer," Neto said. "I'm so sorry."

Father Dwyer shrugged his shoulders and smiled nervously. He took another step back.

Neto dried the sweat from Ruben's forehead with his best handkerchief that he had laundered and folded especially for the pocket of his suit. He helped Ruben up, taking his arm under the shoulder and helping the man over to the front door and farther in towards the kitchen.

"Let's get some coffee inside of you, Ruben," Neto said. "We must have music. A wedding must have music, cabrón."

"All fucked up," Ruben repeated. "I'm all fucked up."

The two men struggled over to the door, leaving Father Dwyer alone on the porch.

The Father set himself down on the couch stiffly, avoiding the depression where Ruben's large body had warmed and shaped the cushions. He rested his arm on the guitar case.

Neto finally returned with a glass of water for Father Dwyer and a plate filled with fried meat covered in onion slices. Cornbread was right behind him with a plate of food and a fresh beer under his arm. The two men had left Ruben passed out spread-eagled in the home's bathroom, where he would stay for the remainder of the ceremony.

"I'm so sorry, Father," Neto said again.

"I hope he will be okay as soon as he sobers up," Father said.

"He's never too sober," Cornbread said cracking the tab on his beer, "so I'm sure he'll be all right."

Neto stared him down. "I'm sure the bride will be here in a second, Father," he said. "I'm sure everything will be okay when the bride gets here."

"Ernesto?" Father Dwyer asked.

"Please, Father, call me Neto."

"Neto?"

"Yes, they all call me Neto here in the neighborhood."

"Interesting."

"Yes, Father. All the kids and my family. All the guys in my old unit."

"Your unit? Where did you serve, Ernesto?"

"I was in Frankfurt, Germany. But most recently I spent some time in San Francisco."

"San Francisco."

"Yes, Father."

"I was at UC Berkeley and I went to the University of San Francisco. I studied literature for a while before going to seminary school," Father said without being asked. "Why were you in San Francisco, Ernesto?"

Neto hesitated. He took a long drag and caught the ashes in the palm of his hand.

"He was in jail, Father," Ray said, slouching into his seat.

"Oh," Father Dwyer said.

"Yeah, the cabrón got caught drunk and kicked off of the plane."

"Shut the hell up, cabrón," Neto blurted. He stood up and instinctively the Father stepped away from the trouble. "I'm gonna give you a beating like you won't believe if you don't shut the hell up. Sorry, Father. But I swear I'll fucking do it."

Cornbread started laughing and spitting beer into his hand. "Yeah, Father, the cabrón couldn't stop drinking for an hour."

Neto slapped Cornbread across the top of his head causing his head to jerk violently. Cornbread stood to return the blow when all three men suddenly crowded together. Father Dwyer put his hands in the air repeating, "Please—please." Cornbread had to excuse himself into the house and back to the kitchen. Neto stared him down the whole way and Father Dwyer, again, stood nervously without saying a word.

"I'm sorry, Father," Neto said. "Forgive me but that son-so drives my last nerve sometimes."

Father Dwyer nodded and smiled. "I'm sure the boy is harmless, Ernesto."

"I don't want this day ruined for my brother, Father. I want everything to be good, Father."

"Relax and breathe, Ernesto," Father interrupted. "Please sit and calm down."

"Yes, sir," Neto said, taking one last long drag before throwing his cigarette out towards the street.

"Can I ask you one more thing, Ernesto?"

"Please, Father. Call me Neto."

"Yes, Neto." And in a minute the Father had to ask, "Please tell me why you are so nervous?"

"Well, Father," Neto said, "The old folks told me you had to prove your love in front of God or it won't be any good."

"Oh," Father Dwyer said. "That is a very true thing, Neto."

In that instant my mother, Bruna Montoya, came marching up the front stoop with her picture perfect hair and her crisp new dress, her bruised brow and eye covered with make-up. Her light skin was rouged and her elfin nose red from the sun and the heat of the afternoon, and the walk from the Montoyas' apartment. Neto would later tell me that he thought the pictures taken that day would never reveal the true beauty of that woman on the porch.

After the ceremony, Neto would become drunk as he always would, pass out as the wedding party went on without him, as the dollar dance started and the guitar players began to play las mananitas. He would pass out on the front sidewalk, in the cool early evening shade of early summer, after crying and drinking over the woman he had almost married, crying over the mill and the busted union. Later, after turning down several plates of food, I'm sure Father Dwyer himself would walk past Neto, step over the body on the long walk back to the rectory and his place at five o'clock Mass.

17

Wrecks

Most folks don't know about Bruna Montoya and Relles Ortiz's first date out to the old City Park Zoo. When Relles died it was as if the memory had died; no one would speak of it. I've seen old home movies shot on Abuelo's Instamatic camera. Neto showed me. We used to sit in the basement and set up the projector to watch the two films Abuelo had labeled "The Mummy" and "Dracula starring Bela Lugosi." We happened to load up a roll of film into the projector, and there was a grainy Bruna and Relles up on the screen, him in his full dress uniform standing next to her, both staring down into the bear pit. Bruna wore a red coat with a fake mink collar and her hair was done up, her features tender and pure and her skin fair-colored, smiling shyly at my father and at the camera.

The day of Relles' death my Abuela wouldn't stop screaming. She was in with her laundry and it was one of the few times the woman did not own her temperament. Neto joked she screamed for days before the funeral and before the body was laid in the ground. In my mind this all stood true:

She screamed in Sunday service. She wailed through the night as a steady stream of aunts and cousins and nephews came through the house with their dinner dishes and desserts. She screamed when Father Dwyer came to the house for prayer and for his own personal condolences.

Her muscles shook and strained as she cried and the tears fell large from her eyelids and face. At first the family, including Neto, thought they might lose the woman to grief as no amount of consoling kept her quiet. Later she even screamed as she cooked meal after meal for visiting familia and visiting nuns. As the Abuelo sat and smoked and drank his beer and whiskey from shot glasses, the Abuela screamed the way she did that November morning when she gave birth to her oldest son.

The night came and the Abuela went mad and got it into her head to burn up all his belongings. Every scrap of clothes and every object of memory. As her family slept and while her nieces and nephews dreamed, in just her housecoat she grabbed an old lettuce carton filled with her husband's tools and dumped them onto the front porch. She began with clothes and letters. She piled on strips of paper from grade school and middle school, Christmas ornaments and school photos. An old leather book cover made in high school. She found his wallet among Neto's possessions, under his cot while he slept. She pulled the footlocker and duffle bag with her son's uniforms and every object from his army life. She pulled his tools from the garage and his coveralls off the hook on the side of the garage door.

She found the gas can among the chaos of lawn tools, hand tools and rusted machine parts. She held her Rosary beads and poured the liquid into the footlocker and onto photo albums and the duffle bags of clothes and linens. She sprayed the lighter fluid.

Neto woke to black smoke and ran in bare feet and Levi's to the back door, thinking the worst for his home. "Cabróna," he called out to her, "what are you doing?"

She didn't respond. She sat and wailed. Neto pulled out the footlocker and the boxes of clothes and bedding. He yelled for the garden hose and for his neighbors to bring shovels of dirt.

The Abuela's housecoat was singed and burned. Her skin was red with blood rushing to the surface and her screams reached down the block.

"They all talked of it in Mass," Neto told me later.

The family seemed to scream for their lost son and war hero but they all knew the Abuela Ortiz suffered each hour and each day. The whole family suffered. All except for Neto who spoke plainly and coldly about his brother.

I can speak this way about the accident because this is how Neto has always spoken of it. I can speak this way because I never knew the man. Never spent a day or received a letter from the man, never had one conversation or shared one beer. My relationship existed merely in photos and albums, solitary moments on my knees with the plastic smell of Polaroids and aging plastic sheets covering photos. Mildewed school yearbooks and wedding photos half burned and bruised with smoke. An old driver's license and letters written from a naval station in Guam. Dog tags and one footlocker filled with burnt dress uniforms and old clothes, an old letterman's jacket with paint stains and wallet-sized photos of his Bruna.

The first I ever knew of my father's death was a newspaper clipping I found in Neto's wallet. My stepbrother Romes and I were looking for money for video games and the dollar movies when we came across the faded clipping with the name Relles Ortiz. "That's your father's name," my stepbrother Romes told me.

"Eighth and Abriendo was where your Grandmother placed the descansos," Neto would say but I was too young to understand. "Your old man never drank. Not like that. Not like the family might say. Ain't nothing like it appears,

Manito. I can promise you that."

My father had been driving out to work. He was working at the old state hospital in the x-ray lab. They had him running back and forth between labs cleaning out chemicals or some such thing, Neto would tell me. That was one of about three jobs he was holding on to.

The County Sheriff told me that the official report listed a sanitation truck had pulled out from an alley and the old Chevy broadsided. The driver was dead on impact is how the news articles read.

"You know sometimes the people would say I killed him," Neto said. "They get the fight arrest and the accident mixed up in their heads and say he died because of the fight we had. Can you believe that shit? How fucked up is that. A man killing his brother. People fuck all the stories up."

On that corner I have sat and thought countless times about that afternoon and what he might have thought or seen, a large grey truck coming out of the alley and him with no way to turn. The racing in between jobs with a woman at home and a child about to come into this world. "My poor, poor brother," Neto said. "Found his way out of a war but not the neighborhood."

I HEARD THE RAIN fell all day and night the day after the funeral and Bruna's hair was covered with plastic when she found her way to the Abuela's basement. She pushed her way through the door.

Neto was sleeping one off when Bruna pulled the string on the bare light bulb and had a seat on the mattress. She rested her hands around her stomach and rubbed the belly that was Relles' child. "I can't make rent, Neto," Bruna said.

"Don't worry about that," Neto said.

"What do you mean?" Bruna stared at the concrete floor

and for a long while Neto didn't say a word.

"You didn't come to the funeral, Neto?" she said.

"Been laid up with a cold."

"You weren't here, Neto. I asked your mama and she said you weren't around."

"Went out for work," Neto said. "Man's got to work."

"Your daddy says you haven't worked in weeks. Your mama says she hasn't seen you eat in days. Are you having pains?" She patted Neto's cheeks and put her cool hand to his warm forehead. "You don't feel too warm. Where is the pain? Is it your stomach or your back?"

Finally Neto told her straight: "Lost my brother."

"We all lost him. We're all sick, Neto, but you got to come and grieve with the family. You know? I mean don't you think I'm not sick? You don't think I got to be sick over this too?"

"Needed some days," Neto said. "I don't have a thing to do with you anyhow. You my brother's girl and I have nothing to do with you."

"Listen, Neto," Bruna said. "I got no more work. I can't work at Newberry's. I mean I can't waitress."

"They fire you?"

"I'm pregnant, Neto," Bruna said. "I have to have the baby and need my own place. I can't live with my mama and Jeri no more."

"My mother will take you in," Neto said. "You can live here."

"I need to live on my own," Bruna said. "To show them."

"Show'em what?"

"That I am doing for myself, you know? I'm sick over all of this too." Bruna put her face in her hands and she wept.

Bruna kept the studio apartment and cooked for Neto, the fake husband who slept on the hardwood floor. He woke in the middle of the night hurting for his brother, breathing hard with guilt and staring at his new surroundings.

One night he sat up in his bed thrashing while the young, naked woman showered and hummed. When he finally woke he knocked the foldout over and across the room. He staggered over to the window and looked at parked cars. His t-shirt and pants were wet with sweat and his lips hurt from thirst.

On the next night he walked the streets of Abriendo Avenue. There was a coating over his tongue that tasted of mold. He walked into bars and ordered drinks for people and watched them drink with a silent satisfaction. One man he fought with over a stool and on another night a fight with a man went out into the streets, nearly to the front door of Bruna's apartment. The building woke up to the sounds of thumps and screams.

Finally, he stopped working and sat in the dollar movies over at the Chief Theatre. He rode around on busses and slept in the public library. He paid the rent for half the month, then not at all, until the landlord, Mr. Archuleta, had no choice but padlock the door. At Archuleta's apartment he argued and pounded at the walls. The landlord had no choice but to call the cops and so Neto left without Bruna's clothes or photo albums.

THE DAY WAS ENDING when Bruna caught up with Neto. He had been sleeping in the backroom of The Klamm Shell, sometimes working as a dishwasher. He had just drained two doubles and felt warm and sleepy.

"You living here now?" she said.

Neto struggled to recognize her then turned away to stare at a viejito who kept calling the bartender "nurse" and laughing out loud. Neto said, "I haven't seen you."

“I tried to make you more of a grown up. I tell them all I tried, Neto.”

“For Christ’s sake.”

“You’re as dead as your brother, Neto,” she said pushing and slapping at his chest. He wouldn’t raise his hands to her. He just sat back in his favorite stool and hunched over a fresh glass.

Part Four

Pinche Murder Mysteries

18

Rudy Martinez

Three men out fishing on Minnequa Lake heard what sounded like a car backfire or some kids playing with fireworks; the sound was actually the liar Rudy Martinez being shot and killed.

At the jury trial, where Cornbread Vigil would soon be acquitted, my Tio Neto, the public defender's key witness, testified that he lived down the street from Vigil and did not hear the shots and didn't know anything about Rudy Martinez or why Ray Vigil would want to kill the man.

As for Rudy, the papers reported he was in his mechanic's overalls and because of the rigor mortis they had to cut his jacket and vest before they found the small red mark, below the center of his back.

This was Vigil's third jury trial. The first two had ended in acquittal and word spread across the old neighborhood that Vigil was charmed.

"I believe that man has to be the luckiest s.o.b. that ever walked the goddamned neighborhood," Tio Jake said the afternoon Vigil made bond and returned to his wife.

"Be careful now," the old folks would say. "Cornbread gonna come looking for you."

In those months following the murder, my Abuela stopped walking to church. She started getting rides from compadres the two blocks to St Francis of Assisi and her afternoon Masses.

The Abuela had known family members who had spent time in Cañon City prison blues and she knew men's harshness firsthand. She gave no man sympathy for hurting another. "I can't believe that man ate in my house. I should have known those Vigil boys. I know their papa and he was a borrachon and a wife beater. From the same tree," she liked to say. "I don't trust a man who would harm a woman."

And because I was young myself and didn't think that much about what I was afraid of, I didn't think twice about the story. I was pretty used to the shootings around the neighborhood. There were a total of twenty or so that summer of '87, I would later discover from my research. I wasn't much worried when this one took place two miles west from the old house on Spruce Street where my mother left me to be raised. I guess what made this different from all those instances of violence and craziness was that Vigil was one of us, a member of the steel union and one of Neto's old crew.

I don't think I would have imagined the murder of Rudy Martinez, a man I hardly knew from the old neighborhood, if I hadn't done things with alcohol and guns myself I was ashamed of. I doubt that I would have remembered the man people called Cornbread, or be haunted by the idea of the man into my thirties, if the murderer hadn't been so close to my Tio Neto. If he hadn't been so close to my father.

Perhaps the beef between Cornbread and Rudy all started in Central High School. Cornbread mocked Rudy's lisp and saw him as weak bodied and weak willed. The quality of his soft voice and the way he stopped talking to think about certain answers in Mr. Miller's earth science class got him called faggot. They wrote it on his locker and on the white t-shirt of his gym clothes with a Magic-Marker as he showered. They called it across the cafeteria and across the student parking lot. And when Rudy wrestled junior varsity they yelled it from the stands.

One afternoon Vigil waited for him out back of the high school by the trash barrels and beat him pretty good. They say Neto held the young Martinez as Cornbread bashed at his eyes and attempted to knock out some of his teeth.

Afterwards they say Rudy's mother went looking for Vigil's father and found the sister. It could've been March and pretty windy as she stood on the porch and lectured to the young sister.

"Where's your mother?" Rudy's mother might've asked. I can picture her on their front porch, straining to see into the house through a locked screen door.

"She's not home," Vigil's sister answered.

"And your father? Where is your father? My boy is hurt and I want to know what this is all about," the mother would have asked. "I won't have any of this. You hear me, girl? You hear me?"

"I hear," the sister said. "My father still ain't home."

"You tell him I could call the cops, you know. You tell him I could call the cops on him. What is keeping me from calling them?"

"Then call 'em. I don't care."

People say Rudy's mother started a campaign that day against the Vigil family. Started the rumor they were criminals and degenerates. That's what the Abuela would say, "degenerates."

I found out later, according to the Rawlings Library in Huerfano County, that Rudy was the woman's only living relative. They were all they had for one another. When Rudy married his girl Rosalie Pacheco, right out of high school, he had all of the Pacheco family for himself from

Rosalie's side. Perhaps Vigil was jealous, and like the Abuela on Spruce used to say, when an old Chicano gets something into his head you can't drag it away with a team of geldings.

So, years later, when Neto and Vigil went out for RC Colas and sausage sandwiches—or when they went out to Loco Liquor and they saw Rudy with his mother in tow—they couldn't help but give the man shit. When they saw him carrying groceries or dropping his mother off at the post office, when they saw Rudy taking his mother to the Chief downtown for a movie or when they saw him with her on Junction Avenue at Carson's Candies, they laughed and mocked poor old Rudy.

The story Neto sold to me was that every one of the old folks knew the hate that Vigil had for the young Martinez boy. They understood the narrative of it. They saw the violence as an inevitable end to the rivalry, to the "feud," as the local paper wrote of it.

"Que feud?" Tio Neto said to me as he read. "I tell you he wanted to kill the liar from way back."

WEEKS BEFORE HIS DEATH Rudy Martinez found young Bea, Cornbread's daughter, lounging in the front seat of his Bronco and asked, "Now why would you want to do something like that?" He grinned deeply for the girl.

Rudy had stayed at The Donahue pretty late past his shift when he met the young Bea in the parking lot. She was fucking Gilbert Ruiz at the time but had been stood up. She stayed in the back of the parking lot near the buzzing street lamps and the Bessemer ditch and happened to be admiring Rudy's Bronco. The windows were down and she reached right in. It was pretty much an impulse but she was drawn to jump inside. Mostly she wanted to watch Gilbert walk up and she wanted to surprise him.

“Your ass is in my seat, cabróna,” Rudy said. And with that he unzipped his jeans and parted the slit in his underwear to stream piss onto the back tire. His head went back and he moaned.

Bea watched. She rolled up the windows and locked the doors.

“I’ve got the key, cabróna,” he said. He held the keys up in front of the driver’s side window and jangled the ring for emphasis. “I gotta get home,” he repeated. “I’m fucked up. I ain’t got time for little girl’s games.”

DOWNTOWN, the young Bea asked Rudy why he drank. She asked him what it did for him. She asked him about the Ford’s idle and asked him to drop her at Mineral Palace Park. She asked him if he had anything to smoke.

“What are you, like twelve?” Rudy asked.

“Eighteen,” she lied. Rudy nearly choked and laughed out loud.

They stood out near the pavilion and the amphitheater where the church sometimes had Christmas festivals and where children sang carols. Rudy liked the feel of the parking lot and the way the willow trees could almost hide the car from the rest of the parking lot in certain spots. They walked around and smoked weed.

“I never smoked this before,” Bea said.

“That’s because you’re just a little moco,” Rudy said.

“I ain’t no little girl. I drive, don’t I? Drove your sorry drunk ass.”

“Driving don’t make you grown. Neither does smoking.”

“Well, I’ll show you,” Bea said, taking another long toke into her throat and nostrils before gagging and coughing it all up.

In the third hour of driving around town and talking to this young woman Rudy felt right and focused. Maybe it was the cocktails, the weed or the burning moon out that night, the brightest in months, according to The Chieftain that next morning. And as the two ate eggs down at Daylight Diner over on West 6th street, Bea smiled wide and ordered immense crème-filled donuts and éclairs.

"Ain't you got a home?" Rudy finally asked, after about the second round of milk and treats. He couldn't help but smile and laugh at the mustache and crème filling on her neck and chin. "Ain't you got no one to be looking out for you?"

Rudy's wife, Rosalie, would protest and argue over the man's whereabouts. A few times she sat on the porch waiting for him and later she packed all of her clothes and all of her children's clothes. She left them at the top of the stairwell so that no matter how late Rudy would be home he couldn't miss them. And he never missed them when he returned to shower and clean the deep grease and smoke stains from his face and neck with Vaseline.

"And what do we mean to you, Rudolfo Martinez?" Rosalie lectured.

Rudy had been prepared to provide for his wife and his family. He was prepared to own a home and live with his two children. He was prepared to take his mother's overbearing nature and his father's absence but he never prepared to be bored. He worried that all the married men in the neighborhood, all the old viejos he grew up with, felt this way about marriage and work. He was thirty years old that year and he was beginning to think about his life and what it all meant. His life was work and income, family and duty. Life was about his mother and now his wife. Most of these thoughts turned into confusion and the need to go out so he wouldn't have to think.

The wife frowned and put her laundry onto the ground

at the door of the garage. "All day and night in this garage, Rudy," she said. "Aren't you ever coming in?"

He might've walked in with her and sat on the edge of their bed and begun to undress. He kissed her hand and he half-hugged her then escaped into the bathroom, afraid to say a word.

That next weekend morning at the Motorist Manor Motel south of town, he sat with the naked Bea close by. There was nothing to be done. He had come inside the young girl foolishly and passionately. He didn't think of the girl's age or the trouble it could mean. He waited for sleep to overtake him and before falling away into sleep small tears came from his eyes and down his cheeks. He hadn't wanted to love this girl and he didn't mean to use her. The thoughts sweated through to the pillowcase underneath his head until the room filled up with mid-afternoon sun and warmth.

The memory of making love to the young Bea, her skin and birthmarks and her small frame as well as the smell of little-girl-styled perfume, burned inside of him every day, I imagine, as those slugs burned on the very last morning of his life.

"I'M GOING TO TELL YOU straight out whether you like it or not, Rudolfo Martinez," Rosalie said the week before his death. "And you're going to hear me."

It was the first time Rudy had ever been fully called out by the mother of his two children.

"What the hell are you talking about, mujer?"

Rudy wasn't much of a liar. He might bullshit at work to lose a shift or to friends in order to skip a night out, but when it came to his wife, Rosalie, he found he didn't have the tongue. At the news that Rosalie was pregnant with his third son, his face went flush. He couldn't speak about his worry for money and for time between the two of them.

He hurt over it and beat himself with the selfish thoughts and so he remained silent. More and more he found himself quiet and unhappy and thinking of the night with the young Bea, her body and her face. The conversation they had that first night.

"I want to hear straight from you, you bastard," Rosalie said, her eyes bright with tears.

"I don't know what the hell to tell you," Rudy said.

"Say it," Rosalie pleaded. "Say it. You so scared to tell me what already been done? Do you think I don't know, you fuck of a man? So don't expect me to believe a word from you again. Don't ask me to believe nothing you say from now on. I want to hear it from you straight. Not from the neighborhood or from this woman or that one. I want to hear it from you."

Rudy thought he had the words for her, but as she spoke and her voice rose, he dragged her to the street and beat the woman with an extension cord. He focused on the crooked teeth at the bottom of her mouth and the hair on her lip and chin. The whole neighborhood stood witness. The soon-to-be-dead liar echoed down Spruce Street: "What you want to hear, mujer?"

19

Cornbread in the Attic

Bea was old enough to keep quiet about her father, the murderer who found his way back from Cañon City to living in the small Spruce Street attic.

The girl knew if she told anyone her Abuela or Tio would pull the belt. Even at fifteen she grew to dread that belt. Once the old woman pulled it after Bea tied some firecrackers to the neighbor's door. She pulled it again when Bea crashed down on her Abuela's lazy Susan and also when she smashed a window with her cousin's baseball bat, and when she pushed toothpicks into the lock of her dead Grandfather's '59 Dodge, and in the parking lot of St Anthony's church after she cried and cried without end during Saturday night Mass. Her Tio pulled his belt at least a few times a month out of habit and rage when the construction jobs ran short of pay. Back in the day that was how the old folks kept order and quiet.

A few times that month the young girl slipped and mentioned that her father was staying with the family.

"My father stays with us plenty nights," her friend Gloria said.

Bea finally admitted, "He's a killer. I heard my Grandma talking."

She told this story again while the girls walked home and sat on the concrete porch. She made a point of mentioning the man in her attic wore chains on his feet.

"You fucking lie, Bea Otero."

Bea was sleeping when he first moved in and surprised when she saw him coming out of the bathroom and going up to the attic. She spotted him again heading outside for a smoke. She watched him from the kitchen window out back smoking cigarette after cigarette. She watched her Tio Neto cut off his jeans and underwear to free them from the chains around his legs. She watched her Tio saw at the metal chains and cut free the pant legs of his blue jeans.

Out back he smoked the Tio's cigarettes and ate her Abuela's tortillas and mashed beans. Later she would bring the houseguest food and water along with six packs of RC Cola and the man would wink at her and frighten her. Sometimes she brought fresh socks and sometimes bologna and pieces of bread. For ten days she carried bottles of liquor and also clean bedding up into the attic.

She couldn't understand but she heard the words, she knew the man was a fugitive and she knew he was her father. She knew they said the man killed her mother. She knew so much at such a young age. She knew her parents weren't married and she knew her Abuela had hated the man she called father because they warned her of him. She knew but she didn't understand.

"Is Neto working?" the folks in the neighborhood asked her. Or they would ask, "Does Neto hit you? Does he pull that belt on your Abuela too?"

Her Grandmother, Cordelia, out of everyone in the neighborhood argued the most with Neto. Mostly in the afternoons and after dinner. Mostly about the man in the attic they called Vigil.

"You could go to jail, cabrón," the Abuela said on the matter. "You don't think of these things. I have to think for you. They got a name for it."

"Leave it alone, Ma."

"You're helping him and they got a name for it."

Or they would argue outside in the garage so Cornbread wouldn't hear.

"How long is he going to be here?"

"Viola comes and stays for months. He's been here a week."

"The police are not after Viola, cabrón."

"He'll be gone soon."

"When?"

"His brother is coming with a car."

"When?" Neto didn't answer. "You're not thinking straight," she continued. "I have to do all the thinking for you. What has this Vigil ever done for you?"

"You shut up, vieja," Neto shouted. "You shut up. I can't think with your goddamn voice in my head."

"I didn't raise you to talk to me like this," the woman yelled. "If your father were alive to see the way you talk, Neto."

"Well, too bad. He's dead-meat and buried."

"I swear, Ernesto. I'll take these words to my grave."

VIGIL HAD WALKED THIRTY MILES from the exercise yard in a Cañon City prison to Huerfano and Abuela's front door. He slid out a gate with a road crew and kept moving. He covered himself in mud and brush for seven hours until the sun set and he walked the miles to the Abuela's home. I wouldn't have believed it if I hadn't read the paper myself. If Bea hadn't saved the headlines and articles along with her thoughts in her diary and if she hadn't read it all to me one night over the phone across state lines.

The Huerfano Chieftain reported:

> *Sentenced to thirteen to eighteen years in prison for murder, Vigil escaped from a Cañon City prison on January 18, 1987, walked to Huerfano and was arrest-*

ed here 16 days later.

Eventually she became curious and climbed the step-ladder into the attic. She brought him soap and water, a washbowl from her Abuela's bathroom. She held a clean shirt from the dead Grandfather's closet along with the newspaper.

"I know you're my father," the young Bea finally said.

"Is that right. Gotta know your family."

"And I ain't scared of you. Even though you had chains on you like a ghost."

"Good, darling," Cornbread said. "In your life don't be scared of nothing. That's all I got to teach you."

Later she asked him: "Did you name me or my mother?"

"I wanted to name you Connie."

"Connie?"

"You know, like Connie Francis?"

"Who's that?"

"You know," Cornbread said. "The singer."

"Never heard of no singer named Connie."

"She was your mother's favorite. One of the first albums she ever bought. You ever seen a cut like this?" The chained man pulled up the loose pant leg frayed around the edges.

His legs were thick and crusted with dried blood. She had seen her Tio's legs the time Neto fell off the ladder and her Abuela was nowhere around to help. His legs were thin and weak. This man's were powerful, like tree trunks, she thought. Bea spent the next hour or so cleaning and dressing the wound. The man told her what to do and called her love and daughter, things the girl had never heard. He kissed her forehead.

The Abuela returned home from her shift at Dundee Cleaners. She was tired from riding busses and had her head full of worry.

This man doesn't care for my family. What trouble will this bring to us? Think of the girl's poor dead mother. What could he do to poor Bea?

When she searched for the girl and found the ladder to the attic, she threw down her purse and called out Bea's name. She howled for her Neto.

She found Cornbread with his legs exposed and the bloody gauze and the young girl on her knees near the army cot. The woman thought of Bea's mother and exploded. She grabbed Bea around the waist and nearly fell down the ladder.

"You're way the fuck wrong," Vigil yelled. "Not right to keep my girl from me."

"She's no child of yours," the woman said.

"Jesus Christ. You old bitch."

When Neto returned home he was near drunk and the two men wrestled on the porch, something the two had done dozens of times. Before the police finally showed, and as Vigil and Neto tore each other down, bashed at faces and shoulders with closed fists, Bea watched from behind the Abuela. She clasped her hands to pray as she was always taught.

20

Lunch

Neto takes the bus down to Union and falls into his favorite diner, the place with the greasy floors and the faintest smell of lard.

He first went in eleven years back because of the fluorescent sign that read Coldest Beer in Town. "I had to challenge it, Manito," he told me years later when his spirit was long since broken and dead and he was more honest about his life and ways.

He is hungry and first he orders two sides, onion rings and French Fries. They are both plates of greasy mess and Neto imagines they've been sitting under heat lamps for hours but he gulps them down with ketchup. Licks at his fingers. He drains his first three drinks, RC Cola, Dr Pepper and 7-Up. He notices he has been following the segment of the menu labeled sides and drinks. He decides to finish up with an iced tea and lemonade.

"You must've been thirsty, huh?" says the waitress with the nametag that reads Salina or something like that. Next, his eyes move to the bottom of the menu and he orders breakfast. "Served all day," he repeats from the sign over the soda fountains.

Neto orders the huevos rancheros and the steak and eggs. "T-bone or chicken fried?" the red-haired waitress says.

"Yes, both please," Neto says. "And thank you kindly."

—

"You got the money for all of this?" the waitress says as he's putting it away.

Neto pulls his bankroll and places it all on the sticky counter. Next he orders the waffles and the pancakes. He finishes off a glass of milk and a glass of buttermilk. He has to wait a minute while the kid at the end of the counter is done with the maple syrup. He smothers the plates and orders another combination, this time with bacon and sausage. Next, he orders the Denver omelet and of course the veggie omelet, each with hash browns. With a belch and dirty looks from those around him he begins on the lunch specials. He orders the tuna melt and the open-faced steak strip sandwich.

"Wanted to try that steak number, Manito," Neto explained to me later.

Before the waitress has the plates cleared and more plates down, Neto has already ordered again and again. Egg salad on white with pickle. Chicken salad on wheat. The taco plate and the lunch burrito. Spaghetti and meatball with side salad. He asks for coffee from the manager who is out from his back office to follow up on the voices spreading throughout the diner. He is a fat man with a clip-on tie and comes from behind the counter to ask questions.

"Best food in town is what the sign should read, no?" Neto tells the man.

Neto is finishing off the crust from the child's order of grilled cheese and tater tots when the manager answers.

"You have money for all this?"

He belches and coughs, this time much more loudly. "I usually do not," Neto says. "But today I am flush with cash, sir."

"Well, you had better. Ever heard of a 'bilking a board'

charge?" The manager can smell the alcohol on his breath but says nothing. He chuckles and picks up the bankroll Neto leaves on the counter.

"I don't want no trouble, sir," Neto manages as he shovels the food down.

By the time the late lunch rush finishes Neto has tasted the special of fried okra and fish sticks. He finishes the lean meal of cottage cheese and pineapples and the fried pork chops with applesauce and mashed potatoes. By his fifteenth plate of food the waitress and the manager are counting the money trying to add the totals and finally the cashier lends them her calculator, pad and pencil.

"Cashed my check this morning," Neto explains. "I got more than three hundred dollars," he announces to the diner, "and I need to eat. A man can't earn a living unless he eats. I'm a working man. I got the dollar bills. Cashed my pay this morning. You all believe me, no?"

BY DINNER TIME the word has spread up and down Union Avenue. The mailman and bus driver who come in to order iced tea and French dips have mentioned on their routes about the young man at the diner who has ordered half of the menu. Neto eats a bowl of green chile and the red. He wipes at his face with his sleeve when Salina offers him a napkin. By dinner the neighborhood begins to gather around the window. They laugh and point at the frumpy man in his greasy coveralls but they can make out a leathery neck and ratty steel toe work boots.

"I'll be goddamned," they say.

Neto orders the stuffed peppers and the bowl of manager's choice chili. While he waits he grabs another RC Cola and another chocolate milk, which reminds him of his little moco days at Minnequa School. He asks for a pre-dinner glass of sweet wine and for his first beer. The waitress has to fish extra plates from the back and deep into the refrigerator for supplies to help the short order cook.

"Ain't no one ate like this in here since I been around," she says plainly to the Korean kid washing dishes. She fills a plate with rice pilaf and the last Salisbury steak in the kitchen. "The man might explode."

Next, Neto waits for his prime rib and his order of roast beef. He reluctantly orders another side salad. He asks about the freshness of the halibut and the trout.

"Ah, who gives a goddamn so bring it out anyway," Neto says.

He asks the woman at the cashier for change for the jukebox and if he can step outside. "I'm Your Puppet is my song," he says as he pushes B19 down on the machine with a cachunk. "I gotta hear it." Neto steps outside and watches the sun go down as he prepares a cigarillo to smoke. The song and baseline fills the street and enhances the dusk air and light. His stomach begins to grumble. He belches out into the late afternoon air.

"I need my dessert," Neto announces as he sits back down the counter and tugs at Salina's apron. "Something sweet." She brings cake and two different styles of pie, cherry and chocolate. "What? No apple?"

"We have ice cream," she says. "Fresh cream, too." He begins with the vanilla and the chocolate. The puddings, tapioca and the pistachio. He orders the banana split. "Goddamn it," the waitress says to herself. "I can't remember the last time a grown man comes in here and orders the banana split." Neto wants to order the shakes, strawberry and chocolate. "What kind of a man eats like this?" one patron repeats.

After Neto finishes up his last slurp of milkshake out of his straw, he belches from his gut with a roar. "I'm sorry," he says loudly to the diner crowd around him.

"Don't be a pig," Salina says.

"I said I was sorry."

Neto finds the bill to be 238 dollars and 50 cents. He tips 60 dollars to the young waitress and he adjusts his coveralls. He loses his coat and removes his handkerchief from the back pocket to wipe at his forehead and face. He loses the trucker's hat he's been wearing and Salina can see the visible tan line on his forehead. He unbuttons his shirt and removes it as he stands. As he exits he unclips and scrapes off his greasy t-shirt from under the coverall straps and stretches his shoulders out from the straps and stands bare-chested in the doorway.

"Hey, get out of here if you gonna strip down," the manager yells over the families, the husbands and wives eating their chicken fried steaks and gravy. He wipes at his chest and holds open the glass door, striking the cowbell tied at the hinge. "We fed you and now you've got to get."

Standing in the open street as traffic piles past, the evening air of summer feels warm over his chest and neck. He imagines children and fathers staring as they cross with the light onto State Street and Union. Blocks down he lights a cigarillo, his final smoke. In minutes he will check into the county jail. In hours he will be stripped and deloused and introduced to his concrete home and the consequences for perjury and aiding and abetting. As he is introduced to what the county calls breakfast, a cup of oatmeal and white toast, he will request butter and jam and of course salt. He will close his eyes to imagine his woman Salina's flawless hands.

21

Beer and Milk

Bea had been getting paid under the table at the Whitehorse Inn for about three weeks. This was after she shaved and tattooed her head and dropped out of high school, the time she defied the Abuela and moved into a squatter's house out by the old football field.

With nothing to do after her late night shifts as kitchen help, she started drinking with the boyfriend and driving around all night. She often bought weed from a friend down at the fairgrounds.

She sat in the back seat scraping off her work shirt and nametag and changing her pants while the boyfriend peered over to talk. "What the hell are you doing, B?" he said.

"I don't like lard and booze smell on my clothes no more," she said. She leaned her head against the bench seat and sighed.

The boyfriend didn't understand. "What are you, a princess or something?"

The two found a west-side diner where one of the waitresses once accused Gilbert of running out on a check.

"This creeper came in last night asking me about my age," Bea said, sipping at her iced tea.

"What creeper?"

"Some guy saying he knew my mother, and I wanted to tell you," she said. She sat up and pulled her feet up beside her in the booth.

"In the Whitehorse?"

"Yeah and he looks at my scar, right? And he says, Ah, my dear what happened to you? and so I want to tell him to fuck off, right? But he keeps sitting there at the end of the bar and asking about me."

"Uh-huh," the boyfriend said, taking a long drink of RC Cola and finishing off some cold fries.

"Well, he sits there most of the night and is staring at me. He asks me my age and I tell him. This idea comes to him that this party he's got going on with his friends should turn into like my quinces or something. Looks me right in the eye and insists."

"He told you this?"

"Not to my face but around me. He told the guys at the bar."

Gilbert nodded.

"He asked if we served milk. Then he tells them all I'm ripe. Can you believe that shit? Says it just like that, ripe. Just says it."

"Oh yeah?"

"And that's not even the shit of it. He spots my scar and asks me how I got it and if it came from my father. Everybody is staring and asking questions. Everybody is laughing. He wanted to know if it was a burn or a stab. Holds my arm like a vise and asks where I got it. He wants to know my story, you know. Then he starts passing around a plate for money. Says they all owe it to me. It's like one in the morning and the whole bar is talking about my face and exchanging dollar bills."

"Did you take the money?"

"No! The next thing you know I'm freaking out and leaving early. That fuck, right?"

"Probably he was a drunk. Don't worry about it. They

don't mean nothing."

"He said he knew my mother. Knows my people and how they are. I just wanted out of there."

"Probably he was drunk."

OUT ON THE HIGHWAY, Gilbert continued to smoke. Bea drove and for a while the day was clear and peaceful. Soon they would be in New Mexico, Bea could tell by the road signs.

"To get divorced I have to file," Gilbert admitted out past Aguilar. "I told you. I thought I told you."

"No, you didn't tell me."

"Well, yeah, that's why we have to go New Mexico. I told you she owes me money. We get my stuff out of storage down there and we're set. The thing that matters now is getting your car down there. Then we can sell it."

"It's my father's car."

"Whatever, girl."

"Was my father's car. When he went to jail for the final time they all wanted to auction it but I saved it."

"You told me but we need the money."

"I kept it since he always said it was mine. I was the one who saved it."

Somewhere around Trinidad, about thirty miles from the New Mexico and Colorado border, Gilbert began to complain.

"I swear to fucking Christ, Bea," he said.

"What," she said. She was bored and playfully blowing at the match. "I don't like you smoking and blowing on my face while I'm driving. I told you I'm trying to keep the smell off of me."

Gilbert finally cracked Bea's head back into the driver's side window, the glass fracturing into a spider web. The tears came instantly.

Gilbert lit his Camel, throwing the pack up onto the dash. "I'm sorry but I warned you. You've been fucking with me all morning and I warned you. Tell me I didn't warn you?"

At the next rest stop she pulled the monstrous car off the interstate. The top of Bea's head burned as she placed the car into park and slid over the huge seats. She crossed her arms and fixed her eyes beyond the cracks of the windshield.

"There's no place to turn around, B. We're gonna have to get gone," he said.

Gilbert opened the window to the smell of rain and snatched the key out of the ignition. The Mercury's primer-colored passenger door creaked opened and then slammed. "Stupid fucking cunt. I said I was sorry. I'll fix the damn window if you want me to."

Bea watched his long shorts and high-tops take the walk up the bricked path to the fiberglass port-a-potty.

In that moment alone she thought to pull the spare key out of her jeans' pocket and dropped back into the driver's seat. She pushed her limp Mohawk from her eyes for a second before pulling her father's gearshift into D. She turned on the lights.

Moving forward she saw other things than red: a green unreadable highway sign, a stretch of faded fence posts tied with wire. The car bumped over a thick layer of weeds and garbage up towards the green fiberglass toilet. The large Mercury fishtailed violently, pulled sideways before catching traction and the thin layer of mud that would lurch the metal beast forward.

When the Mercury cracked the foundation and the barrier that was the door, Bea slammed the brake pedal hard and laid her head on the metal steering wheel. The hood smeared with a mix of shit and blue chemical, a stream of cracked fiberglass and wet, month-old funk. Gilbert fell clear, and then he took two steps to pull up his newly muddied fatigue shorts and belt.

When the car stopped rolling ahead and Bea could make out some sort of expression on the man's face, she had the car in R and was barreling backwards towards the highway, towards the white line of Interstate 25.

She must have driven for a few miles before the wipers cleared the blueberry windshield and her view. At Cliff's Stop and Sundries, the blue and gray skies started to fall in big, cold drops again and she left the car running, wipers working overtime. She slammed the door while the engine still ran, and the door locked behind her. "Fucking shit!" she whispered through gritted teeth.

The rain fell harder now, and she moved under a small eave. She stood in Gilbert's pullover that smelled of sweat and weed. The damage she scanned was mostly to the hood, where the fiberglass structure had wrinkled the metal. The falling water slowly started to wash away the mud and stain.

All this time she kept an eye out, noticing that the Union Pacific tracks rolled through hills and gullies and spread out from the highway out into rangeland. She leaned against a bare, stucco wall and closed her eyes. The smile slowly crept up her face.

22

Hamburgers

Captain Ortega had a lean look like no other I'd ever met, thin-hipped like a dark Gene Autry. He was muscular and a foot taller than anyone in the group, always nodding his head and yelling in a crazed tone.

Out between burned buildings and twisted wrecks on the roadways, we heard a rumor about Ortega shooting a kid over the border into Bosnia, while on a patrol just like this one. I heard that the official report said a SAW machine gun, like the one I was stuck carrying most of the time, had discharged "accidentally" while Ortega's group was putting up fencing around a school in a village called Gornja Slatina.

The SAW was a real monster, a smaller version of an M-60 but using the same rounds as an M-16, a twenty-pound piece and a bitch for me to drag through the mud and to clean, that much I knew as fact. Some more reliable recounts I've heard said Ortega was drinking and some said he wasn't properly checked out on the SAW.

"Coulda got three years to his whole life but that cabrón a smooth operator, operatin correctly, you know," Romes said, his final thought on the matter.

I also heard that two sergeants major, a first sergeant, a major, a captain and two lieutenant colonels had tried to testify, but Ortega still got off of all charges and specifications. I also heard speculation that the only consequence was his transfer from the 2nd Battalion part of the German-based 1st Armored out to our little band.

We tried not to judge him, though. In fact, we held him in high regard for it. I mean he was no stranger to bodies, so later we all had questions. When I tried to nail him down on it years later, in a bar in San Antonio called Sharkey's, he told me again, "The only reason I was helping put up fences was because the air strikes and shit tore them down." He also told me the round caught the kid in the shoulder, and he bled out in less than an hour as they dragged him for help. "I did what I could but the kid was dead-meat, you know? There was nothing I could of done."

Ortega was born in Utah, somewhere near the Four Corners, and so he spoke a mix of English and Spanish slang that I could almost understand. He explained more of the Ute's creation myth to us, in one of his unguarded moments. He wore his yellow teeth and full-pack with an awkward pride, and he gave me my first taste of European weed. "Hydroponics," he said, winking.

Later, Ortega taught me Chicano slang and the importance of his Aztec tattoos as he flexed. I was nineteen that winter, and I remember asking him so many questions because it was my first time overseas. "A deployment 'virgin,'" Ortega said.

In Macedonia, near Camp Bondsteel, Romes and I ran across a muddy street that resembled a small river, and we must have stood for six or seven hours inside an old stone vestibule, pulling checkpoint duty and trying to light cigarettes while blocking the rain with our ponchos. The surrounding villages here were nothing but rubble, remnants of gas stations, remains of the Bank of Commerce and an empty marketplace. "Fuck me," Romes said, after designing our first makeshift checkpoint of tense rope and oil drums. "It's a fucking ghost country."

When I was fully awake and my homeboy was up and moving, I pretended I had a cigarette, and the cold Macedonia night air I blew was the smoke. The dry cold was the only thing familiar, like in Colorado, the only thing that felt good on my cheeks and bones.

"Don't do that," Romes said.

"Why not?" I said. "I smoked everything up last night." I mimed flicking the ashes and taking another long drag.

"Why do you do that?"

"I'm just smoking."

Romes rolled his eyes. "Why do you help them fuck with you? Like you want it?"

"ORTIZ. ORTIZ, GET YOUR ASS IN HERE," Ortega said over and over again. I heard Ortega's size-thirteen footsteps coming at me immediately on the wood floor before I saw his face. "I want you to make a run and get these guys some food." He had a brown cigarillo in his mouth and spat all around himself as he spoke. "You got a problem with that?"

The church around us smelled of wood and had been recently cleaned. The scars and dents had been varnished over and over, but I was sure they were still growing. I remember thinking the only things with a semblance of upkeep here in Macedonia were churches and bars.

I was happy to be called inside because it meant warmth. I could hear the drops from the roof pounding out of tune to the young singers and piano player that would sometimes collect for morning concerts. The drops leaked through and filled their water jugs so quickly that the old woman playing piano had to empty them twice as they practiced. My inner ear was failing from hiking through rain and the muddy streets.

"What, am I talkin to a fuckin deaf person? Ortiz," he repeated loudly. "Hey, you want a hamburger? Jesus, Ortiz.

Go get us some hamburgers, and move it."

I nodded and froze for a minute. I gave him a look and my lip must have quivered.

"You got something to say, Ortiz?"

"No. No, sir."

"Ortiz. Why are you still here?"

"Where am I going to get hamburgers?" I asked.

"Jesus, Ortiz. Were you out with this particular unit yesterday?"

"Yes, sir. I was—"

"Was the night that long for you?"

I shook my head.

"I know you were with us. But you don't act like it." He gave me a disgusted look. The Special Forces guys and the German guys were laughing. "We were in Bocinja?"

I gave a blank look.

"Do you remember the village down the hill? Do you remember the drainage we passed? They sell them there! Christ!"

"I'm not sure—"

"Jesus, Ortiz!" he screamed. "Romero knows. Go ask Romero. Ask your homeboy! He'll straighten your ass out."

WHEN ROMES AND I FINALLY DECIDED to move, the fog came thick, like smoke from a burning building. Around 10:00 we were backtracking when Romes stood still and said, "Fuck me, Manito."

"What?"

"You're the reason we're here shit-stomping through this, you know that, right? So shut the fuck up and keep that piece covered."

The M249 SAW was to be covered in the rain but I was always forgetting, dropping it to the wet ground. I fumbled with the safety and the rain cover.

"And try not to shoot me in the head, a'ight," my boy Romes said.

We had heard several stories when coming in to this place. Stories of refugees coming over the border to escape only to find more trouble. In person, I saw women disgraced and degraded. They covered themselves and their daughters coming across the border from Kosovo into Macedonia with just blankets, sheets or whatever they could find. I saw families searching for their lost children through countryside that was very much a wet and muddy mountainous wasteland. I heard stories of kids lost for days in the rough terrain interspersed with small villages and attempts at community. After my first three months in the country, I felt very much like those people I had heard about and that I had seen, completely unprotected and susceptible to the environment.

"Fuck if I know where we're at," Romes announced. He sat on a cropping of dead logs and tried to light a Marlboro in the rain. "Fuckin Ortega wants some shit then he can get off his dead ass and find it himself. Chinga Ortega and chinga this whole fucking country, Manito."

Later that afternoon, as we jogged, the mud built on our boots and our pants. I had mud crusted to my thighs from taking a shit in the surrounding empty fields. I had mud in my boots and in my goddamned shorts. We were more tired than we had ever been after a full morning hiking and pulling our feet out of the mud that gathered on the shoulder of every muddy path and miserable stretch of back road we hiked through.

In rather pitiful time, we reached a village that looked like a possibility. The second building out of eight that had a small shack attached was littered with wood and what looked like cedar and alfalfa drowning in wetness. Under the wide metal eave, two old women with moustaches were selling American-style burgers, no cheese, though, and a few random newspapers – the first commerce I had seen here.

We went crazy and spent all of our pay. We must have bought two-dozen burgers and their entire inventory of chips and warm soda. Romes was so damned happy he lent me more dollar bills. The old ladies even had Winston cigarettes. My brother leaned back and chugged two sodas himself immediately.

We collapsed on the ground near the stand and I carefully wrapped the treasure inside my coat. I hid everything from the elements. Everything except the SAW; I unstrapped that and sat it in the mud.

"Fuckin shit, Manito," Romes yelled. "I ain't cleaning that piece for you."

"I just laid it down for a minute, cabrón. It weighs a ton." I tugged my collar up towards my ears and zipped it all the way up to keep the food dry. We smiled greedily and humped it back.

And we didn't touch any of it, not one bite, but we forgot that the valleys are rough and densely wooded in some areas. I wasn't thinking, I guess, because I got behind of Romes for a few miles. The clouds darkened again and moved over. I got so far back struggling with the food and the SAW, my brother appeared as only a stick on the horizon.

THE RAIN FELL A LITTLE HARDER and Romes decided to head us straight west in a very unscientific move, since we had traveled east to the nearby village. In a small clearing that looked new and unfamiliar, I dropped to my knees with exhaustion and decided to make camp for the night. Darker clouds were moving in overhead.

I remember thinking that you can't hide from these elements when in the field. You can't get comfortable enough to sleep in the mud. You can't roll out a bed or stay down in it. You have to crouch almost in a ball and cover your body with your issued rain cover. You have to let yourself take the rain. You have to sit through it, try and smoke to pass the time. It's difficult to keep cigarettes dry or a lighter from flooding. Sleep comes an hour or two at a time without any feeling of rest.

The rain didn't stop but only got thicker, more complex. I couldn't dream or think. Everything I cared about, my letters and my notebooks I kept, were soaked through with mud and sweat. I decided to give in to the immense despair and rage I felt at that moment. Perhaps it was fatigue or madness but I just curled into some underbrush and choked on about five hours of tears while the fog rose and filled the horizon like a sunset of bright dark and gray.

During the night I thought of the girlfriend in California and my friends in Mijak, waiting for their food and their share of a large dinner that was disgusting and soggy in my coat. I watched the dark, starless sky and did not move. I have had many lonely nights like this after leaving the service, halfway house after halfway house, but all these others have been a sad imitation of this first.

I thought I saw my daughter's face in the immense darkness and I fell asleep for maybe an hour or less. I couldn't sleep but rather could only listen to the strange and compelling night sounds that somehow told me I wouldn't get home and would never be fine. There were no sounds of human presence anywhere. And the rain, always the rain—things no one should ever have to experience.

At dawn, I still sat motionless, watching my brother Romes paralyzed with sleep. With that first light, we came around full circle. Perhaps it was the little rest or the thoughts of wanting to see my wife or my nameless daughter, but with the sun on my face we both rose and made our way through the drizzly, foggy morning and made it to a clearing and a small bit of water pretending to be a stream that we remembered passing the day before. We followed the water to a small valley that comforted us and we could see the village and church walls on the horizon. We suddenly realized just how very much off course we had been.

We wandered into town, and the squad was exactly where we had left them. I saw my unit and started to run the last couple of steps. We could see on their faces their night had been cold and tiring. Everybody still ate the burgers despite the mud; despite the cold, those burgers were all they had. And they were pissed, but they still ate them. My buddies hated me and didn't talk to me for the longest time, but they ate every goddamn muddy bite of those burgers, like Christmas fucking dinner.

I KNEW I WOULD HAVE TO EXPLAIN the muddy SAW and the night out, admit to our fuck up.

"Business is business, Ortiz," Ortega told me. He got right up in my face. "And you don't own that weapon do you, you little fuck up?"

I shook my head.

"The taxpayers of the United States of America own that weapon." He got right in my face and lit a cigarette and chewed on the end. Blew smoke in my face. He took off his cover to stare at me. "And more specifically that weapon is the unit's weapon. Which means that is my weapon. Do you hear me, you fuck?"

I nodded.

"In fact, I don't think you own shit, do you, Ortiz? Maybe your pricker, uh? Uh?" He kept flicking at my crotch with his middle finger. Everyone was standing around watching and laughing. He was standing next to Romes and a kid named Watson who was a year or two younger than me and who had just lowered himself into a folding chair. They both had that "not a chance in hell you're getting out of this" look on their faces. Ortega turned to Watson and Romes and laughed, flicking his ashes.

"You fucking baby killer," I whispered. I just out and said it.

Ortega spun around, not believing what he had just heard. "What the fuck?" Ortega said and spat. He looked at Watson and then Romes. Ortega grinned, kept smiling.

Ortega grabbed at my shirt and then at my neck, quietly and hard. His thumb pushed deeper into my throat, keeping me from swallowing or breathing. I tried not to whimper.

"You should watch your fucking mouth," he said.

I shoved at him, but I was exhausted, covered in mud.

"Hey," he said. "Romero. Get your ass over here and tell your brother or boyfriend or whatever the fuck he is to you and tell him to learn how things work, uh. Tell your boy here how to take orders and take care of his self."

Romes came over and put his hand on Ortega's arm, but Ortega wasn't having any of it.

"Your boy here is stupid tryin to act smart," Ortega said. "I thought you boys from New Mexico were supposed to be tough." He watched Romes for a moment and smiled and then he slowly let loose of me. That's when the tears came.

Outside, I crossed our muddy street with orders to clean the squad's SAW. I went down about a mile into a field of weeds and broken down metal signs that used to mark the roads closed. I stayed in the field on my knees until I heard Romes calling for me, until the rain stopped, and I heard the thunder of medevac aircraft.

I turned and swung my forearm wildly at his face, bash-ing at his nose and forehead. He stutter-stepped back. He nodded, smiled, and then he clocked me perfectly along the jaw line with a hard right. I could feel the blood filling inside my mouth.

"Jesus fuckin Christ," he said. "You got to keep that shit inside of you. Hey, you hear me?" He wrenched at my collar and t-shirt and pulled me to attention.

23

Descansos

The first man I'd met while working maintenance became my friend and gave me a place to sleep in his basement out on La Vega Road. He shared posole and mashed beans with me at his dinner table and he drove me around town looking for fluorescent liquor signs out on Central, Northern and East Ninth.

This one evening, this one time, while we were drinking beer, I asked him, "How much longer you gonna fuck around with that car?"

"A man works to keep himself," he instructed.

The half-primer, half-purple Chevy was a '76 and the first beautiful thing I'd seen after the Army. At first I didn't want it, at first I didn't want the responsibility. His wife and kid landed up dead-meat in the thing out on Interstate 25 near Aguilar, Colorado, about two years back.

After we drank as much as we could, we drove out to the crash site and just pulled over, turned off the engine. Luis' eyes flooded and he doubled over with yearning. He was bulky and shaped like an ox and it was strange to see him cry. Headlights streamed by and I stared at the sad wooden cross and roses to the side of the highway, the wallet-sized photos and an old locket placed beneath.

He ended it by making the sign of the cross and saying, "Descansos por los muertos."

—

THAT MONTE CARLO was a piece of shit afterwards, mangled and smashed. But his work had an amazing effect. He dropped a new Windsor V8 and banged out all the dents to smooth the body. He lowered the suspension and fixed her up with a new set of basket rims, all chrome and clean.

"It's drivable," Luis answered. "You can drive it."

"Well, that's the point, right?"

His shoulders slumped. "It's not about selling a damn car." He wiped his long forehead with his ancient fingers, shifted his cigarette from underneath his moustache.

While I packed up my stuff, Luis airbrushed the figure of a woman. He introduced the hood of that Chevy as a vision. I didn't know Luis as an artist. I'd never been around one. I saw the woman had angel wings, but her eyes seemed gray and cold, her flawless arms crossed low at her waist.

I TOOK LUIS'S CAR and went looking for Romes and found him sitting in a squatter's house with his hair combed back and his collar up, suffering through the cold of a New Mexico night. He looked strung out and thin. I really thought he was in jail or dead.

I put my hand on Romes' thin shoulder and took the cigarette out of his mouth. "How'd you ever imagine finding me, Manito?" he asked.

He was the only one laughing. Out of everyone at the party, he was the only one laughing.

"I'm heading out to California," I told him.

"A lifetime ago, Manito. I was in Colorado a lifetime ago." He smiled widely with big, yellow teeth.

People were always fixing him drinks, rolling the fattest blunts to get him to slow down, making him talk while they quickly guzzled. The people at this particular party, this particular night, I didn't know very well, and I was confident they didn't know Romes all that well either. He told me he had just lost his house and his common law wife.

I told him, "I know the kid's out there somewhere, you know."

He shook his head furiously as if he had been there with me the whole way, every mile. "What kid is that, Manito?"

"My kid."

We started telling stories about Army days. We talked about Camp Bondsteel and the 7th Infantry. At one time my brother had tried to explain it all to me, but this night I was out of luck. I came all that way and the bastard kept it hidden.

"The Army is over for me and you," he finally told me. "I know that much."

Only the drinking and the weed came out that night. He was in high spirits after receiving his latest VA check and he showed me his wallet and the ten twenty-dollar bills he had left. At this moment, while on that disgusting little couch, as he rested the money out on his lap, I noticed how his curly hair was clean, how things were going to be all right for him for the next couple of days, until the money ran out.

"Shit happened a long time ago, Manito. Two years ago, whatever. So don't ask me no more, Manito. Jesus. Jesus. Jesus! Don't ask me," he repeated and then he laughed at himself.

Romes kept talking and sounded glorious: he told a fifteen-year-old girl that he was working in Taos as a vendor at a baseball field, and then he told another woman whose face I never saw he was living closer to the mountains and restoring old cars. He asked another girl if he could sleep at her apartment, and then he told another junky-looking girl who was fighting with her boyfriend to meet him in the narrow street out front and to forget about the little chivato she had come with, that he had a custom Monte Carlo outside.

"Just let me borrow the car, cabrón."

After a day and a half, California came like speed trials. I drove Luis' death-filled Chevy all night and stopped only to eat, then once to piss at the head of an entrance ramp. I was high on amphetamines my brother Romes gave me in New Mexico and I wasn't used to driving.

I stopped in an AM/PM for gas, gave my troubles a case of Bud Light. The woman's face behind the counter was veiled in bulletproof glass. The tattoo of an eastern sun on her neck lit the wall. Her nametag read "Lynn." "If we were in love," I asked, "would you ever leave me?"

The Chevy fell into park, and the brakes cried in front of Loretta's house that morning, our house on Cardinal Avenue. All the houses on the block were flat roofed and earth-toned and built by the same company, but this house stood out because it sat inside an immense garden. She loved the beauty and the neighbors would always admire her roses and marigolds. Once I took a shortcut through the garden in a straight line for the door, and Loretta said, "Can't you see that's disrespectful?"

I managed the steps to our home's front door. It was missing a screen, so I reached my hand through to feel the knob. The metal felt cold and reminded me of loneliness, so I rang the bell three or four times. I looked in through the living room window; there were no curtains and I saw toys on the floor: a little plastic kitchen and a spotted horse on springs.

I smashed a window.

Inside, the green carpeting in the hall to the bedrooms

was stained, and I could feel the blood pumping through me. Loretta's bedroom was cluttered and sad. The door frame had been fixed from when she locked herself in, and a queen-sized waterbed now filled the room. Two antique-looking dressers stood side by side near the closet. Work clothes were stacked neatly on her bed. A necklace rested on one of the dressers. I held the metal in my hands smelling for perfume.

I sniffed around like a dog, continuing through her jewelry. I found some photos, the faces in them all strange until the Polaroids taken just before I left for Macedonia, and a copy of one of the pictures of my daughter Belle that I had kept in my wallet.

I pocketed some money from a jewelry box, about fifty dollars folded into a small square. It took me a while to notice the man's work shirts hanging on the door to the closet, but the gray material looked pressed, with the top button done up with care. The logo over the pocket read Allied Electric.

In the photo, my daughter Belle posed in front of a large tree. Her clothes were too big for her frame, and her face was mischievously young and rosy, her perfect nose like her mother's. In another, newer photo, a young man stood in front of the house, a handsome man with a white face and a red beard, smiling wide, patiently waiting for the picture to be taken.

Around the corner from our bedroom, I edged to where our daughter slept. Toys lined the dirty carpet of the small room, and I had to clear a little path to get into the center. Her books littered the long shelf over the picture window, looking out into the back yard.

The walls up to about four feet were an institutional brown. The color reminded me of the room at the halfway house, but here brown meant a prairie and rolling hills, the sky meeting them at the level of the bookshelf and the dresser that held my daughter's clothes.

The blue horizon blended into majestic purples and turquoises, fields rolling backwards into hills and then finally mountains, and then on to amazing distances, billowing, cloud-filled horizons over the twin bed. I lost myself in view of those faultless clouds, along the tops of trees that extended on the walls and some white picket fences added for detail over the brown hills. Then I rested on my daughter's bed and the light fixture poured warm sunshine over me.

THE MAILMAN PLACED the mail. The phone rang a couple of times. I felt sick and weak and had to vomit in their bathroom. And in that lowliness I became the worst thoughts.

I held the .32 Romes had given me in case of trouble. I had the gun in my front pocket, and every once in a while I would pull it out. There were no bullets so I kept pulling back the hammer and letting myself have it. My eyes squeezed shut and warm tears cut down my face.

IF I REGRET ANYTHING from that day it's that Loretta's hair wasn't down. "Jesus. I can smell the fuckin' beer on you." She shook her head with terror.

She eyed the gun and before I could say a word she had the phone. "Can you even imagine in your stupid fuckin' head what I have to do to explain to your daughter where you have been and what the hell you have been doin'?" Her round face had no makeup whatsoever, pure as a saint. Her skin remained close to porcelain.

"Loretta, I've moved on."

"You hear me, goddamn it? Goddamn it! You see?" she said. "You fuck of a man."

I dragged her to me and my muscles began to spasm.

That's when I could feel what was alive in her, that pregnant belly. I squeezed her arm down to the bone. With those blue skies around me, I swear I wanted to hurt her. I wanted to break both her goddamned arms.

She jerked from me into the hallway. The threads tore down her shirt. I grabbed at her shoulder and then at her hair.

"Ah, please Retta," I repeated, still holding the gun. "Shit. Fuck. God."

When I saw my wife pulling away from me and running out the door in a full, short-legged sprint, still bawling, I knew our goodbyes would never be real, that they would have to stay inside.

After two or three days of me haunting around Retta's neighborhood, they hauled me out in front of a Denny's. As the officers had the cuffs on me, between parked cars, and as they draped my body over the trooper's hood, for several less-than-conscious moments, I pleaded with the woman on Luis' Monte Carlo and her naked, airbrushed frame.

24

Laundromat

An all-night Laundromat just behind the golden arches of a McDonald's and a Sinclair station stood as the only life for miles along the interstate. At first I thought the lights were a sad hallucination, but I pulled the Monte Carlo into the parking lot on 13" rims after a heavy and wet snowfall. My shirt sopped wet against my skin because the damned driver-side window wouldn't roll up. It happened to be the day before Thanksgiving, even though it felt more like Halloween, and the strange sky that night had just opened up with a small sickle cell of a moon.

For the most part, the story is that I had been out haunting parked cars and neighborhoods, looking for the men that had attacked me, who had produced the black eye and the bashed forehead.

The two kids and I had an unspoken camaraderie before I had even gone into the place, before I started my laundry, before I even met their mother. The walls of glass appeared miserable and fogged up, and I could only see their round faces. At first I was nervous about going in, but I wanted to get out of the cold, and the kids signaled to me with fingerprints and nose prints on the foggy glass.

Inside, the place smelled of floor cleaner. Washers churned. My jaw ached and my face strained to adjust to the fluorescent lighting. It signaled to me: 30lb Washers/ Save Soap/ Save Quarters.

I wanted to acknowledge the kids right away. They both had dark hair and were dressed shabbily. The crusted mucus on the little girl's nose and the boy's missing high top. The little purse she had and the boy's toy cars. It was all so familiar.

They climbed over the long stretch of white machines, dirtying their hands and the boy's white t-shirt. For a while they were just running and later they took turns locking each other in a dryer, holding the door shut on one another.

I stretched out my two pairs of jeans and the t-shirt I was wearing on the tops of the washers and lay down on the counters, not caring if I slept or if I died. I pulled out a cigarette and lit it casually. I found my shirt had blood on it. It was just after midnight when I noticed that the two little kids and their bucket of chicken belonged to someone.

THE MOTHER WAS ON THE PAY PHONE. Most of what she said was in Spanish, which I regretted, and it's taken me a while to really translate it all out in my head. "Yah. I'm with the kids. I've got 'em in the laundry with me. Yah, well, what else would I do with them, cabróna?" She shook her head and her long straight hair, half of a Camel tucked neatly behind her ear. She was a big woman of the llano, maybe in her forties, wearing tight, red jeans, and the tiniest belly shirt slit down her large front exposing a tremendous bosom. "No, I told you, I don't have a ride. Can't stay here all night," she repeated over and over again. "Can't stay here all night."

I REMEMBER I HAD A GREASY BAG of burgers and fries from the McDonald's that reminded me of the rain in Macedonia, the lonesomeness of everything you own being wet through and heavy. And they looked so sad, the kids, I mean, like a couple of saints, so I couldn't help but lean way over and drop the bag in between them.

The son had a sloppy crew cut with an awful rat's tail down his back. He had a mouth full of yellow teeth and couldn't stop smiling stupidly as he threw pennies, targeting the reflection of my smiling face in the dryer doors. After several loud screams of direction from their mother the kids finally sat and ate. The boy sat on the concrete floor eating and didn't touch any of my fries. Later, he climbed up into one of the dryers, shutting the door behind. This silent kid just smiled and stared at me from behind the closed glass.

A FEW LESS-THAN-CONSCIOUS MOMENTS LATER, the little girl shook me into sitting up and for a moment I couldn't quite tell what was memory or what was real. I was still on the washers trying to sleep.

Her dark green eyes gave me a quiet look all serious and thoughtful. She wiped her filthy hands and precious mouth along the front of her sunflower-printed dress. She handed me one of the pennies that her brother had fired towards her head. I smiled and took the greasy penny from her little flawless hands.

THE FIRST WOMAN TO TALK, the one who looked like someone's Abuelita and who had no teeth in her mouth, asked me how much time the dryers gave you per quarter. I scraped on a newly dried t-shirt over my head, and she huffed when I told her, "Years." Another woman with glasses seemed to be staring right at me, everything a reaction to me. Sometimes I was prone to forgetting. How I look, I mean. I guess I should always remember but times like these I am prone to forgetting, to dozing off.

Anyway, I did forget as I was listening to this lady. I

didn't hear right away when she told me not to smoke. When she told me to think of other people.

The other woman at the end of the long, rectangular building wasn't much better. She was wearing black stretch pants that ran down her snake-like legs into cowboy boots. The purse was just big enough for her cigarettes and Bic and her car keys.

"I hate coming down here. Wish I owned my own. I hate the element."

My mind was like a light bulb breaking.

"I asked you if you were from Fort Carson. Are you from Fort Carson?" she asked me, or someone just like her asked me. I was wearing a 7th Infantry Mountain Post t-shirt. I forgot I had that left in my life. "Are you a soldier, young man? Are you from Fort Carson?"

"I was thinkin' you could help me with some money," the mother said to me. "Husband put me out." She balanced herself on platform shoes, between the washers and the dryers.

I had no more money. Everything had already gone into the machines. I'd drunk some too and was relying on a half tank of gas and a crumpled twenty-dollar bill to make it out to California, to Culver City. I hated to think about my own story, much less anyone else's.

For a minute I didn't think there would be anything else other than those few words. I nodded and said, "Your girl's cute." The little girl at this point was sucking on her fingers and the remains of some pink nail polish. "What's her name?"

"Cinnamon."

"Sounds like a porn star name."

She was wiping her daughter's face with spit and a napkin she had pulled from an oversized bag. "Don't know me. Can't talk to me like that."

"I didn't mean to knock you. I have a car outside."

She was folding more clothes, the children's clothes, but she looked out toward the parking lot, and then she gave me a look to size me up. "Got my brother coming."

THE MOTHER TOLD ME the boy's name was Tenok and I laughed.

"It's Mayan! I wanted to name him something Mayan."

It had been a while since I mouthed the words, since I had to explain who I was to anybody. "Ortiz."

"What?"

"My name is Relles Ortiz."

She looked me straight in the eyes. "See? I could make fun or say something stupid but it's your name. And I ain't going to."

I looked at my shoes.

"Don't care what you say, do you? Can't be like that to people. No one teach you respect? You don't know me from anyone and you want me to get into a car with you when you're obviously not right in the head." She was shaking her head. "That's why you all swole up." And that's when she laughed at me.

She nodded proudly, "Tenok is Mayan." The boy suddenly ran up. "I ain't fuckin stupid."

I nodded.

"Yeah," she said. She scooped up her squirming son and held him and sort of bounced with him making him much younger than he probably was. "Little shit looks just like his old man, too. The bastard. And he used to ride down in Telmpua sometimes. That's where we used to live. They have rodeos for weeks on end down there. It's like religion." She gave a little shotglass-sized sigh.

I'd never heard of the place, but I agreed and told her it was beautiful.

"Better than this fuckin place."

"Colorado isn't so bad. I mean, is it?"

"Look around this bitch and tell me that." She just about hung her head as if she had just come to the realization herself.

"Well, that's because it's winter. The state's green in the summer, closer to the mountains, I mean."

I put the twenty-dollar bill I kept in my sock into her hands. She smiled and I thought she was going to cry.

"Hey, you got anything to smoke?" she asked tenderly before tucking her long black hair behind both ears.

AND THE MEN THAT HAD ATTACKED ME, I forgot about the men that attacked me. I never saw them coming, either. I was in a bar called the Whitehorse looking for my Tio Neto and I couldn't find that shitty place again if I tried, but I do remember trying to make time with an eighteen-year-old from Albuquerque. She was wearing a scarf around her neck printed with small hearts on it, I can remember that much. My brother Romes and his pills were long gone and by this point I felt like a stone skipped along the water.

This girl had been singing along to the jukebox for what seemed like an eternity, which is how she caught my attention, saved me, really. She wanted nothing to do with me and she obviously felt no pain because she was fucking up the easiest of lines.

"Bottle up and explode, over and over! Bottle up and explode!"

When she did finally land up talking to me, though, which was more about boredom than attraction, she couldn't stop talking about her father and how he was a Christian. She said her father told her the Devil makes us drink, that that's how he gets into our actions.

While she was in a booth across from me, she told me her name but I couldn't pronounce it as hard as I tried. And then I found out that her father was dead-meat like mine. And that's when she asked me if I believed in God. She told me how she used to think that only by believing in Him would we be saved. That's why she had a crucifix tattooed on her chest above her tits. I had no idea what she was saying because I'm not religious, but she had the deepest, most amazing green eyes like my wife. There was a small blemish on her face where her boyfriend had taken a cigarette to her about a month earlier or maybe it was a pockmark, I can't be certain, but she kept checking it in the mirror behind the bar.

"Buy me a drink. They won't sell me anymore," she told me. And I did once, and then again and then a third time. And then after the sea of rum and RC Colas, she preached to me: "God told Job that the world has to be nasty sometimes. Can't be perfect everywhere, you know? It just can't be." She was drunker than me, drunker than anyone in the place, almost in slow motion. She said, "I mean that alone leads me to think that there's got to be more going on, going on behind the scenes, you know? You know?"

"God's a fuckin' prick."

"Yes," she said. "Yes. That's my point. That's exactly the point, you know?"

But I didn't know, and this continued out into the parking lot until just before she was about to get into my Chevy and show me more of those tattoos on her chest. Until this fuck she had been dating and his crew rolled up on us. And this is the part of that night I wish I could say wasn't clear, that I can say proved anything about myself or who I was becoming. But I can't say that.

—

The story is really about the mother with the two kids. Later that night, I was out in my car with her, smoking my dog shit from New Mexico and trying to put my hand down the front of her pants. I was trying to get her to come to the Whitehorse with me, to drive all over town. She wasn't having any of it.

We smoked the last of my dog shit out of a pipe whose filter was pretty much dirtied up. Her hair smelled like peaches and her skin was becoming darker and lovelier.

She looted around her purse and finally dumped the contents out next to me. She showed me a picture of her husband Javier. He was in full Charo garb out on a llano somewhere on a pale gray and spotted horse straight out of a Clint Eastwood movie, the leather a bright red and ornate. His hat was in his hand over his head. His face wore a bearded smirk.

"The Lone Ranger," I said, serious as hell. The mother laughed and her large breasts shook. For the first time she moved in closer to me. We were just about holding each other.

I remember thinking that if someone were to see us in this Monte Carlo, if someone were walking by they would think we were happy.

"So why do you think he left?"

"Don't know."

"You can't think of even a little reason?"

"Cuz he's a pendejo, I guess."

"Really? That's what you think?" For a while I left the car running so she wasn't so cold. The window I could roll up started to fog over and gave us quite a bit of privacy. I wanted to kiss her and tell her to come with me, but I had no idea how to take care of myself, much less her. I asked her about what she remembered.

"The fuck you sayin'?" She gave me a look, like it was the first time she looked at anything. "Never heard questions like these," she said. "Shouldn't worry about the past. Should worry about you."

I couldn't make sense, make her understand.

She had a look in her eye and no emotion on her face. She was higher than high, laughing and sort of crying. She didn't care what I said or did, and then, before I tried my damnedest to kiss her, she said, "Sometimes we choose shit and it don't just happen to us, Army. I hate to tell you." My head went down and the static in my inner ear failed. I was the first one to fall asleep.

THE SKY THAT NEXT MORNING was a brilliant light blue and gray, and warm sunlight filled the car like a policeman's flashlight, the ground covered white with a fresh snow. The car was freezing and smelled of old cigarettes and pine air freshener. We were out in the parking lot, I could tell by the sound of the cars, but for a minute I wasn't sure where I was in time and space.

And then the mother screamed, and the sound sort of carved into me, cleared my head. It came to me right through the open window. It was so beautiful and definite, like the emptiness inside of me. It was about 6:45 in the morning and my last view of her was out in a southern Colorado morning, searching for my little girl and the boy.

25

House of Order

Neto rides out to a bar called The Hideaway, a dark place with a dance floor the size of a welcome mat. His beloved Freya Lynn kisses Joseph Vigil and so he drains rum and RC Cola all night. He misses curfew. His face covers in tears and he speaks soft, damning words to himself. He yells out for her and grabs for what is around him. The next morning in the smelly darkness of his third floor room, he hunches in a ball on the floor and cries. Shivering, Neto waits patiently after he drives the needle through the flesh of his arm until he hallucinates soft kisses down his spine.

His sponsor tells him that he isn't a man. That he could never be a man without respecting his family, without respecting the house rules.

"Ernesto Ortiz," Bob Wilson lectures. "We are all good men in here. We all have the power to do better."

Neto stares. His mouth drops open with boredom.

"Every hardship we live through will lead us to becoming stronger," Bob says.

This afternoon Neto is taking an especially ferocious attack because his stash has been found out. He feels sick and achy. Bob promises not to contact Neto's PO as long as Neto promises to attend "group" and not leave the property for at least three weeks other than to work.

"I am not blind, Ernesto. I am giving you every benefit

of the doubt." He looks directly at Neto. "I know what you say about these sessions. I know what you think."

"What do I think?"

Bob says, "You think I don't know why you do the things you do and say the things you say."

Neto almost laughs out loud. And so do the other men at the meeting. He tries to hold on to their names: Bob Apples, Mickey Torrez, Something Smith, and No-Named Archuleta.

"You think I don't know the pain you feel," Bob repeats. "I used to be just like you, Ernesto. I am your Christian brother. I had everything once. I had a home and a wife. I had a teaching job and I had a car. It was a Chevy. And I had money in the bank but I had nothing. More nothing than you have right now. Until I found Jesus."

Everyone at the meeting is silent, careless. No one could remember Bob revealing so much in these afternoon meetings. But after finding Neto on the floor the place is pretty shaken up. Bob's authority is pretty shaken up.

Bob continues: "I was afraid to be seen and I was afraid to get through the day. Afraid to admit what I was. And I was afraid everybody would see me. I know that's what you're afraid of, Ernesto. And I am telling you God is here for you. I see your crucifix on your neck, Ernesto. I know you know what I am talking about."

"I know what you are talking about," No-Named says. "I don't want to be seen."

"Thank you, No-Named. Today, though, we are focusing on Ernesto."

"Let him talk if he wants to talk," Neto says.

"Ernesto, I am the director of this meeting," Bob says. He can feel the meeting becoming cracked open right down the middle and a thousand baby spiders crawling out over the community room floor.

"Well, that's what we supposed to do here, ain't it?" Neto says. "We're supposed to talk."

"Yeah," someone says and a few others repeat it.

NETO TOLD ME THE RESIDENTS named the building the Highland, after the street it was built on in downtown Colorado Springs, and that later, in the 70s, some state agency changed it to Pikes Peak Health Horizons. But Neto always referred to it as the house of order. The place to get your habits straightened out. The red brick mother of a building was in poor condition, and in the past fifteen years he had lived in several halfway houses, friend's homes, and girlfriends' apartments, and for a time he lived with his cousin Tino in Denver. He lived with nieces and nephews on sofas and fold-out beds, and he had lived in five hostels since his girl Freya Lynn put him out of her house in Colorado Springs. Nothing compared to the Highland.

From his window at the Highland he looked out at the sacred power mountain of the Utes that was Pikes Peak, a mountain looming always to the west of the city, and littered with businesses and chimneys, the low roofs of hotels and residences cutting into the view of the Navajo red foothills and absolutely jagged hills and green lowlands. His window was high and his room was narrow, and from his room the stream of pigeons and the sounds of downtown trains and buses filled his inner ear and woke him at midnight and at three and again at five. His shades were frayed and tattered and did not keep out sunlight or the moonlight. The room had a single, bare light bulb and the walls were thin and could not keep out the sound of the neighbors' slamming doors, arguments, snores or hacking coughs.

Neto Ortiz had no intention of staying on at the Highland. He continued to pack his clean laundry into his duffel bag, readying for his exit date and his moving to better living conditions, readying to run from his sentences.

I FIND HIM IN DENVER, on the 5-North wing of the VA Hospital off of Colorado Boulevard resting on sheets frayed around the ends and stamped:

Department of Veteran Affairs
United States of America
Government Property
Not For Sale

"Cabrón," he says. "You just looking all over for me, huh?"

"How you feeling?"

"I'm all right, hijo," he says, slapping my hand. He keeps rubbing at his chin and his unkempt head of hair. "Nothing's wrong. Nothing. Who told you something's wrong? Who told you that?"

"You're in the hospital, Tio."

Neto laughs and winces as he shifts his weight. "This catheter pinches my verga, you know."

His hair has grown out quite a bit and makes him look like a rough old Chicano. His body has changed from the hulk of a man I remember in my youth to a sickly 140 pounds. His arms are thick and sore, a row of adhesive tape clasping the IV and the tubes to his skin. His arms look cut and bandaged and his legs look thin and weak. He is shirtless and he has a crucifix hanging around his neck.

He finally tells me he was sober for most of those years I was away and that he held jobs in New Mexico and here in Denver, Colorado, where the new wife sobered him up. The living situation worked well for Neto until he received the divorce papers. Things like that were always happening to us.

A year later Neto celebrated a third divorce with a three-week drinking binge that led to his fifth DUI, which equals felony status in Arapahoe County. He cheated going to jail for months because the county made a clerical error and lost the paperwork for two of those charges, but it turned over the whole life he had made in New Mexico. He moved right out of his girlfriend's house, into city jail for eighteen months, and then into a halfway house for six.

An elderly woman with a hearing aid, her face dark and puffy, walks into Neto's hospital room and gives him a bag of toiletries and a small Bible. Her name is Tilly Mendoza and she is patting Neto softly on the shoulder. "You a good Catholic boy, Ortiz," she says.

"You're the only one in here who talks to me decent. These damn gabacho doctors."

"They'll take care of you. They do good work in here."

"They ain't fair about the pain medication."

"Life ain't fair, hijo," she says with a seriousness. "If life was fair, the horse would ride half the time, no?" She puts her hand on his side, approximating where his kidney should be. "You in good shape," she says and I start to get the feeling she tells everyone the same story. "Just stay away from the tobacco. That tobacco will tear you down, hijo. And the wine. Stay away from the wine. My father used to drink the wine. No beer, just wine."

She looks right into my eyes and then she winks.

"I know we got a strong one here," she says, giving Neto one last pat on the shoulder.

Later, a twelve-year-old doctor comes in and goes over his entire medical file, and then Neto receives a prayer from another woman volunteer. With tears forming in his eyes, he watches as she reads the prayer. "Peace be with you," the woman tells us.

Neto is living off of Colfax Avenue and I have to make several U-turns because of the parking situation and also because Neto can't remember his own exact address. I thought we'd have to drive all over town if not for his sudden memory of the street. We go past Carter Avenue and find the place. Looks like a one-room apartment buried in a sea of one-room apartments. Neto has no car and no income except for a small social security check and even smaller VA benefits, and the place looks it. Reminds me of the old neighborhood though I don't tell Neto any of this.

As we walk to the door a young girl and boy are throwing handfuls of rocks towards the parking lots and windshields. They barely stop for a second as we pass. Neto laughs and blows smoke from a cigarette around them and throws his cigarette butt down.

He explains that months back he felt at his chest and couldn't breathe, decided to walk to the bus stop down the block. He points at the spot where they found him. The doctors told him it was a minor heart attack brought on by the many meds he takes for his one remaining kidney. They told him he needs to stop smoking and drinking. Told him to take it easy and watch his diet and meds.

"I could of called the 911," he tells me. "But no money, Manito."

"You could have died on the street, Tio."

He says, "It will all be yesteryear soon." And to this I have no idea what to say. I nod.

Neto stands in his apartment and takes off the shirt he is wearing and places it into the garbage bag, then takes another from the bag and pulls it over his head. There is a ripped pocket over his heart and a hole just near the stretched collar. I recognize a few of the collared shirts I gave him years back before a cousin's wedding when I was afraid he would wear a Denver Bronco jersey.

The living room has three sofas and the room smells of mold and cat piss, though I see no cat. I notice exactly what is missing. There is no television and no walls between the bathroom and the bedroom or the kitchen. There are no bookcases, lamps or clocks. No appliances on the counter except for a hotplate and nothing covering the bare cement floors. There are no newspapers or magazines, no bird in the birdcage. There is no telephone and no closet.

I ask him, "You got a cat, Tio?"

"Damn thing ran off."

What Neto does have are glorious photos, several large framed shots saved from the Abuelita's albums.

Abuelito Santiago and Abuelita Cordelia on their wedding day, the young man in his Army dress uniform and the young woman in a white lace dress.

Emeterio Ortiz when he is in his twenties, which looks like a black-and-white photo that's been hand colored, like they used to back in the day before there were color photos.

There is a large one of cousin Ricardo on his wedding day standing with Neto in front of the Alibi Bar and Grill in Huérfano County.

Neto introduces a photo of an old woman as his Great Grandmother from New Mexico. "Full blooded Navajo," he tells me, like he is letting me in on a secret. There is also a lone photo of my mother from back in the day. She's in a cheerleading outfit standing out front of Central High.

There is no sign of Neto's brother, my father. I double-check the apartment walls as Neto pisses into the toilet bowl across from the sofa.

Next comes one of those moments. I see a plaster figure of La Virgen de Guadalupe. The same Mary from the

Abuelitos' backyard, right from the old neighborhood. The plaster is cracking and the golden rope around her waist is frayed and fading. Her hands are clasped and a few fingers from her left hand are missing.

I ask, "What are you gonna do with her, Tio?"

"Take it. It don't mean nothing to me no more. Take it. It never did nothing for me. Take it now."

I wrap La Virgen in a blanket that smells of cigarette smoke and carry her out to my ride. I gently lower her down into the trunk on top of the spare tire.

I COULDN'T REFUSE driving him to his old haunts. He hasn't been down south or around Colorado Springs since the new wife put him out, and he needs someone to drive him to visit friends and family out on West Avenue. Needs someone to cash a disability check for him. Needs someone to pay for the gas.

Down stairs carpeted with rubber treads and past fake wood paneling, we tour a subterranean place called the Shanghai Lounge where he supposedly met a girlfriend named Miranda years before. Then he takes me to Valesco's Diner out toward Arapahoe County, where we sit down in front of a broken down counter straight out of the 1950s. We face two tired waitresses and a kid cleaning up tables.

I am introduced to Valesco, as the man flips omelet orders, fried potatoes and pancakes on the ancient looking grill. Jorge coughs and yells, shakes his finger at Neto and then slaps his hand.

"You look too damn skinny," Valesco says as he slows to talk with us. He wears pale gray fatigues and a wife-beater t-shirt underneath a greasy apron. "You'll have to sit here and eat, cabrón. Have a few beers. Put on a few pounds."

"He ain't like me," Neto says. "Little man's all grown up. Headed to state college. He's got what it takes, you know."

Valesco has three or four orders going and I am envious of how the man can speak and joke while getting food out on narrow plates and thumbing through order tickets from those two waitresses.

"I hope you keeping your Tio straight," Valesco says. "Nobody else can, pocho. But maybe you can try, no?"

In a booth near the plate-glass window that looks out on to the old highway, Neto is talkative and loud. I notice his forehead is longer and he still has his hospital ID around his wrist. My Tio Neto drains two tall drafts and gives me some of Valesco's bud wrapped in tin foil. I tell him to go easy. He points out each hole in the gums for each tooth he had removed while in jail. What teeth he has left look rotted and stained.

He hands me one of my father's dog tags. I hold the smooth metal in my hand and read the stamped letters:

ORTIZ
RELLES J
US 55874642
O POS
Catholic

"Your Relles was a good man," Neto says. "A goddamn real-life Vietnam hero."

Later I have to interrupt the old stories to say, "I'm going to have a daughter. Inez stopped taking birth control."

"Inez is the school teacher, no? With the fat ass?"

"Another kid would make two." I hold up two fingers before I slip the dog tag away and light another cigarette with the last cigarette. "I'm saying I can't stay away too long, Tio. I gotta get back to her." I get just a touch of comprehension from him, or I only imagine it. He seems to only want to talk about the past.

We pull out of the place and enter the purple Monte Carlo, bounding down Interstate 25 from Colorado Springs to drop him off in Huérfano County. We stop in almost every bar and dive Neto can remember. I have so much time with him. I don't know what to ask or how to ask him.

The owner of this one joint is turning around the open sign and we are back in the car. We both are too drunk to be driving. I admit the girlfriend doesn't want me drinking like this and he finally agrees. The engine is crying from overheating and we limp up and down those strange interstates.

I phone Neto only one other time not too many years later when college is all done and behind me, and when we speak he is quick to think I want money or a place to stay. I break down and try to tell him more about Inez and the daughter. He reminds me he is an old man, reminds me I am still young. "I don't know, Manito. All I can tell you is stay away from places like the Highland." He drunkenly tells me as the line goes dead, "Try and save all those troubles."

Part Five

Half Adult

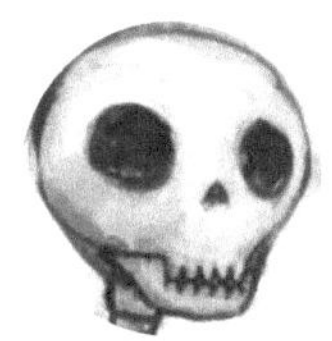

26

Dead Jefita

When the Abuela passed, I remember Tio Neto showed up with a paper sack filled with beer cans to lecture the group of old folks gathered at St Francis of Assisi Church.

At first he was in the balcony, and after the uninspiring words from the old folks, he cracked his beer and walked down. He pushed some of the compadres and Father Dwyer off of him before standing in front of the entire audience.

"I know you don't want me here," he greeted the crowd, wearing only a stained t-shirt and faded Levi's. "And I don't want to be here too much myself." He spit and scratched at himself. He sipped from one of his beers and wiped at his lips. "But I got a few words."

Tia Viola told me Neto was the one to walk in and find the dead Jefita. She had collapsed on the floor and Neto dropped down on his knees. Viola said the paramedics found them both together. And then he ran out of there. No one had heard from him until that moment he called out during the services.

Neto thought for a long minute and then he began. "What a lousy fucking family. Working and toiling away. Never taking the time to mind the house and the woman's garden. Shit. Half of the folks here I ain't seen around the woman in years. Where and the hell were you people when she was down and out? Where and the hell were you when she had all them doctor's appointments and procedures? And the other half of you here ain't even called her. I'm glad she's dead so she don't have to see this sad day. What a lousy goddamned day."

There were jeers and some of the compadres cleared out the back. Neto spat his gum out and slapped his shirt pocket for his Marlboro Reds. He lit one with a match.

"Go on and clear out of here. Run out to your pathetic lives. Nobody cares to hear from you," he seemed to call out to Tio Ben specifically. That was all there was to say to that man. "I hear Viola has sold my Mama's house. Never even talked on the matter with me. Just made the deal before the woman's even in her plot. Before the woman was at rest beside her husband or oldest boy. For Christ's sake I can't even stand to look at none of you people no more. Who the hell do you think you are? Like fucking vampires and shit. Vultures and buzzards!"

He fell to his knees and nearly vomited right out onto the carpeted riser and before Jesus on the cross and all the suffering saints watching. Someone started to shout but Neto kept interrupting with heaves and then finally hollers and yips. "I'm glad she's dead not to have to see any of this. For Christ's sake you bastards already had your trucks backed up to her back door for her furniture and her goddamn bed frame. Get your fuckin' hands off of me."

The interior of St Francis had been built before the rest of the neighborhood's history and echoed with the man's voice. The confessional booths held a façade of ornately carved wooden arches, columns and tiles, the wooden alcoves bathed in a variety of colors present in the wood, the look of endless amounts of refinishing. Neto tortured the crew of old folks for minutes before the audience overcame him and had him ushered to the side entrance and out to the rectory offices.

After the exhausting confessional, the absolution and then the penance, Neto sat on the steps of the rectory and began repeating his penance softly to himself as he gripped his mother's Rosary. He pulled his last can of warm Miller High Life from the paper sack.

On the way to the burial, Neto asked me to make a long detour onto the old highway. He had me pull up onto the shoulder of the two-lane road.

"I'm gonna stand out here in the grass," Neto said. "You want to come out here with me?"

"It's raining?"

"Come on," he told me.

I waited at the other end of the car, leaning on the fender, and didn't listen to the man. I knew he was talking and going on but I wasn't listening. What can I say about that afternoon along the highway? Neto stood and spoke to his mother. At first he paced to the mile marker and then back again. Then he threw a piss into a patch of weeds and gravel.

I'd seen Neto speaking to himself as he drank plenty of nights over the years, whenever he felt cheated or accused. That was his way of therapy, walking out onto the road under large southern Colorado skies. He had a beer can and at first he professed the importance of the aluminum can over glass bottles. He crushed his empties.

"I always told you I couldn't trust Viola," he told me.

Because of Neto's tears, I felt burnt down and tired. I suddenly wanted one of those beers. I suddenly was ready to give myself up for years and years to whatever darkness Neto spoke to.

I went to get in the Chevy, and discovered Neto had fallen to his knees and was saying, "I love you, my poor, poor mother." I couldn't get the man back in a car.

27

State Hospital

The first time I took the notorious Cornbread Vigil up to the roof, I nosed his chair over to the ledge. I lit his pipe and then tamped my pack of cigarettes.

A grouping of pigeons sprayed out over power lines and rooftops. One wore black streaked feathers, and I liked to imagine him as the leader. I imagined they shot into this one smashed out window for warmth or safety.

"Best part of this place," I said, but he didn't seem to hear.

Sometimes an orderly came in while we were in the middle of a real nasty "Code Brown" on the third floor, a glove and mask job. "I'm sure you have everything under control," they said. They never sounded like they wanted to get involved. "Of course," I said. "Be careful where you step."

Most of the time I worked with Deion. He was the bullshit type, and I did most of the heavy lifting because of his back. I talked to the nurses. This afternoon we were working on this awful explosion. A line came out of a dialysis machine, and she lost it all over the place. The resident lost it and the orderly lost it. No one wanted to go near the machine, so it pumped out onto the floor, some of the worst vile shit you can imagine.

"I've been running around with this girl," Deion told me. "Maybe soon, she tells me. Maybe. Can you believe that shit? Maybe."

"Deion, do you have to cuss so much around the orderlies?"

"I'm talking about fucking this girl."

He was a big fat-looking guy with messed up teeth, and I couldn't understand how the man kept finding these girls.

I said, "Didn't you say the wife caught on to you?"

"Oh, Jesus. I'm not talking about my wife."

Three times in the past six months he'd cheated and told me all about it, the meeting to the dating to the motel they could get into. One time his wife came home early from work while a girl of his showered in his basement. They all had it out in the living room. The girl was naked and the wife pulled a straight razor and nearly cut the girl while Deion watched. He explained to the cops over and over again what happened. I asked if the girl was at least eighteen. He slowed his mop down for a second and looked at me. "What the hell are you talking about? I told you I have to fuck this girl."

Most days I hid out in Cornbread's room. He had a hospital bed, a dresser, along with an old record player thrown to the floor. No carpet or rugs to speak of.

In Cornbread's framed photographs the younger version of the man looked bien firme. There were photos of him in a suit on his wedding day, and shots on fishing vacations, on lakeshores and sand, standing beside a rainbow trout somebody had hooked. There were pictures of a dead wife. Pictures of his daughter, Bea. Pictures of children and very young babies, grand kids, I imagine, in various junior high school pictures.

I dragged my hand over the swap meet quilt. It reminded me of my old neighborhood and my Abuelos. I told him I would take him up on the roof any day he wanted. All he had to do was find me. I promised him.

"WOULD YOU LIKE TO KNOW about the new girlfriend?" The weird longing tone to my voice surprised me. "She works at that market up the street. You can make out the top of the building. It's called Miscelanio. These old folks own it and they gave her the work, you know?" I showed him a new picture I found and he got a kick out of looking at Inez and her hair cut like a boy's. "Inez," I said. "Her name's Inez."

He put his lips together and made a sound that came close to a whistling catcall. He wore those dark glasses, and I couldn't make out too much of an expression.

"She's a cashier. I used to go in there sometimes. That's where I met her. She's the cashier." I stared out over downtown towards the Mexican restaurant on the corner and their sign that advertised Colorado's Largest Margarita.

I took a long drag. "I suppose you don't," I said.

I stopped for a few minutes. I didn't want to interrupt the steadying of his shaky hands to bring the wide blunt to his lips.

"Inez is pregnant," I continued. "And, well, I have to think about the future, you know?"

To this he took the last of his cigar and stubbed it out on the bottom of his worn slipper. He tossed the cigar end over the side of the building with a flick, smacked his lips with delight.

"Inez stopped taking her birth control," I continued. "Says she wants to have the baby. I mean what can you do in a situation like this, you know? You know? She told me on the pay phone. Just now, before I came up here."

Again, he cracked a smile.

"I've got a kid in California. From an ex-wife. Another one would make two." I slipped the picture away and lit another cigarette with the last cigarette. I held up two fingers.

I fished out a piece of receipt paper and wrote on the backside. I wrote, "You want I should take you down or what?" I handed it to him, and he took it in his large dark hands. I read it out loud to him over his shoulder as he read. He looked at my hands closely and he wiped his ashy, coarse hands over mine, my bit and ruined fingernails.

He motioned to me to pass him my pen and he took the paper with great care and leaned back into his chair. He wrote the single word "lovely."

I MISTAKENLY TOLD INEZ about my talks with the man the Colorado newspapers once called "the notorious Cornbread Vigil." She said it was pointless. Said he was less than worthless.

I told her, "The Bible says everyone who hates his brother is a murderer."

"Jesus Christ!" she said. "Why the fuck would you help him? You don't need the trouble."

In the months since getting together, she had never said the word "trouble" like that before and it surprised me. I'd come home drunk and smoked weed with her brother in the living room of her apartment. My car was repossessed and my foster-brother Romes practically moved in and she had never once mentioned the word.

"You wanted me to get steady work and that's what I did. Jesus, Inez. I just give him cigarettes," I said. "And we talk."

"What the hell do you have to say to a killer? Are you taking down notes on the guy?"

I shook my hand at her and threw her car keys. I told her I didn't care.

Inez stomped around the apartment with a look in her eyes. "Well, you better start. In a couple of months you sure and hell are gonna have something to care about, cabrón." She held her stomach tenderly.

"He had a stroke," I said. "It's not like he knows what the fuck I tell him."

I HAD MY SHARE of "incidents" in Colorado and California. Car accidents and DUIs. So much that my Uncle Neto and I made a joke out of it, over the phone. I remember I asked him, "What's going to happen next, Neto? Who is gonna fuck up next?"

"As long as we come home, Manito," he said. "As long as we come home, who gives a fuck?"

Most recently I lived in a halfway house for a while after losing the driver's license, I guess, when I finally got released and found this job. My head was pretty messed up and everyone wanted me to be making money, Inez and the people I had met since leaving the Army.

The State Hospital was where I got the job, across from the park out near the YMCA. I found out well after I was hired and watched all the risk management videos and signed all the paperwork that Cornbread had been a resident for years.

In the orientation, on my first day, Nurse Clementine gave a lecture on all the rules and regulations, leaving me numb in my seat and not wanting to talk. My shirt was half-heartedly tucked in.

"And the residents are priority," Nurse Clementine said as she finished up. "Whatever your problems are, well, theirs are worse and quite frankly you've got to keep all that home."

She was a middle-aged woman, the woman who gave us all our positions. She wore a blonde football helmet of a hairdo, and she dressed in a thick, wool sweater and athletic shoes no matter the weather.

"I say this because most of our residents," she continued, "are psychiatric hospital patients with past arrests for violent crimes and also unable to care for themselves, and they rely on us for all of their care."

She went over to the map of the building and the layout of the place, and she pointed around to where we were allowed to go and where we needed a key. She pointed out the break room and every cleaning closet, trash compactor and incinerator unit. "And you must never touch or handle any of the patient's personal belongings," Nurse Clementine said, lastly. She seemed to be looking right through me.

THE LAST TIME I spoke to the ex-wife in person was in Española, New Mexico. She was marrying the boyfriend, Stevie, in a month and hadn't yet gotten a proper divorce from me and so she drove down from Culver City for a reunion, for a signature. This was all before I met Inez.

She got a room at the Motel Six over on Northern Blvd to avoid my Uncle Neto or anyone else in my crew. She hired a notary public to drive out and meet us. I went to her room, a person visiting another person to talk and sign copies of legal paperwork. I was strung out drinking again.

My daughter Belle had these pink sneakers like her mother and I asked her how old she was and what grade she was in. I asked her how she was getting along. "Okay," she whispered.

"That's great," I said, not really knowing what I should have said. "That's really great, Belle."

The ex-wife asked me to help her with the bills, and while we were talking, she hugged me. Not much of a real one, but she hugged me. "Good to see you," she said.

Later, Belle got into bed to watch cartoons, and the ex-wife took me in to the bathroom. She stood with her short back to me, putting on her flannel pajamas. Suddenly I remembered mornings and showers, breakfasts and endless Saturday mornings staying in bed. There wasn't much space so I had to stand real close to talk. "Drinking makes you heavy," she told me as she washed her face. "Your face is all doughy and shit." The cartoons were blaring, and I was embarrassed for the two of us, ashamed for the whole disgraceful relationship.

Cornbread began giving me lists on little pieces of napkin or newspaper in almost illegible writing. I kept them in my notebook. Some read: "black licorice," "salted peanuts" or "beef jerky." I found one in the third floor maintenance closet tacked up to Nurse Clementine's assignment board: "rum." Sometimes Cornbread wrapped them around five dollar bills: "smokes."

"My Uncle Neto is in jail," I admitted to Cornbread. "You know Neto, right? He's up in Arapahoe County. Drinking and driving. I haven't even told Inez. It is so much easier to tell her that I don't have anything, and she never pushes me." I clipped the end of his cigar with the knife I kept and passed the blunt. "It's not too far from here. My foster-brother Romes called me up and told me. Told me he's in Denver. But I haven't gone to see him. I should go to see him. I don't know why I don't drive out there. Need a car first, I guess."

He wasn't looking at my lips. He was focused on that black streaked bird that led the group across the street, but I kept talking anyway.

"I mean I got my driver's license back now and Inez has this pickup. I could get up there real easy, you know? But you can't give him any money or anything for him so what's the point. I couldn't give him any food or cigarettes, or at least that's what I hear. So what's the point?" I threw the butt of my cigarette over the side of the building with a flick and watched it hit the gray sidewalk. I kind of zoned out for a second, thinking. "I mean I could go while Inez was working and she wouldn't even know." I lit another cigarette. "They've got him listed as 'indigent.' That's what the county clerk told me when I called. Can you believe that shit?"

Cornbread handed me another of his notes. This one was on a yellow Post-it note folded in half so the ends stuck together. He'd held on to this one for a while because it looked slightly crumpled.

I read "ride" and I looked at him. "The van takes folks to physical therapy. You can't go anywhere else." I wrote on the back of the Post-it until I ran out of space. I wrote, "Where do you need to go? Why don't you ask the sister to take you somewhere?"

He gently took a pair of eyeglasses from a thick brown case in his sweater pocket. He replaced the usual sunglasses he wore with reading glasses. He read the note and his smile drained from his cheeks. His bright eyes and broken teeth looked sad for a moment. He handed me another folded Post-it with an awful seriousness that stunned me for a second and scared me, really. This one had an address: "4400 Northwest Van Buren Drive Apt 117."

Later Deion and I were back on the third floor, facing another disgrace in the community shower. I kept Cornbread's note in my pocket and when the curiosity finally got to me I asked Deion about his girlfriend.

"I just had to fuck the little thing," he told me. "I never said I was a role model."

I picked up a resident's robe and threw it out of the muck. In a minute I was about to clean up shit and I cursed myself for not getting back to school.

WE DROVE THROUGH DOWNTOWN Colorado Springs in Inez's truck. Halfway past Frank Waters Park he handed me a note that read "Manitou Springs," the section of Colorado Springs closer to the foothills known as Old Colorado City.

We drove for an hour but Cornbread just sat and smiled. He cradled a bag of corn chips I had brought for him, and he smoked his pipe. Across the last city bridge, I turned and looked at him. "This should be the quickest way," I told him, but he didn't respond.

I started to miss the familiar streets of downtown, and I turned a corner and followed the directions Cornbread had written down for me until I found Colorado Boulevard and Van Buren Drive. Cornbread stared as I slowed behind a utilities truck to look for a rectangular, brownstone-type building. We drove slowly until he tapped my leg and pointed to a stoop with his pinkie.

The houses looked like they'd been recently put up. They all had new-looking paint jobs and fresh lumber on their front porches. Blue tarps protected patio furniture and the lawns all looked fresh.

I pushed Cornbread up the stoop and a man with a harsh burnt face came out. I thought for sure there was going to be some sort of shit, some sort of chingazos. I halfway expected it. The man looked about seven-foot tall and had his head shaved. I imagined this must be the place Cornbread's girlfriend lived. This must be her old man, and Cornbread came at the wrong time of day or the man was hanging around to catch who's fucking his old lady.

Then the man gave Cornbread a spleen-crushing hug that about lifted him from his chair and the two stayed in their embrace. Cornbread sat loose and happy. The man kept kissing Cornbread on the forehead and cheeks, and the tears were falling. The man gave me a look.

"I drove," I finally said.

Inside, I sat in the man's kitchen sipping on a can of soda. I could hear them crying and laughing, and later Cornbread hummed along to the radio. I could see Cornbread shaking his finger at the man, his hand moving along to some music on the stereo and coming through the walls.

Later on when the men were eating and draining their own sodas I asked, "Why doesn't he work on getting his voice back?"

"He's old. Just gave up on it, I guess. I don't know." He wore a gold chain over top his sweater, and he was darker skinned than Cornbread, with thick, white boils on his neck.

"You the brother?"

"You got it," the man said. "He's never been out here before."

I nodded.

"My sister's a bitch. Don't make it easy, you know how it is. Still the same though she's loyal as hell. No matter what the man might've done. Family's got to stay together."

I didn't know what to say or how else to end it. I walked back out to the truck and gave the men as much time as they wanted.

The next morning at work I noticed a woman sitting alongside Nurse Clementine. They were both talking with Cornbread in between them. I was pretty sure I was going to be fired. I expected that "I am sorry but things don't seem to be working out" speech. Maybe the security agent would walk me to my locker. Usually they do it at the end of the week, usually on a Friday or on a payday. They've got it all figured out.

"Oh, hello," Nurse Clementine said. "Pauline, this is

who I've been talking to you about."

Cornbread's sister was the same story as Clementine; she looked like a fucking pro. She was about fifty and didn't really look like I'd imagined. She had a thin, attractive face and looked put together, sophisticated. She said, "I hear you're from the old neighborhood in Huerfano."

I took her lotioned and braceleted hand and immediately I had a crush on her. I mean I liked her. And before I could say a thing Cornbread slipped from his chair. The coughing fit came over him and he fell onto hard tiled floor, down onto hands and knees. I moved in to grab him and held him close under his wet armpits as he fell.

When we finally had the man settled and sitting up comfortably, with his legs beneath him, Pauline kissed me and then took the care to wipe the lipstick from my face. "Thank you for serving a fellow Christian," she said to me. It all made me feel as if I had something left.

28

Segundos

Out in front of the hospital my Tio Neto's latest girlfriend stood with dark sunglasses and clove cigarettes, draining a bottle of iced tea. Later she shadowed a counselor up the big steps to the door who informed her of transplant protocol and some of the support groups available after the surgery. It was winter and the mountains of downtown Colorado Springs were all around her. The snow was deep and the plate glass windows of the lobby were cold and nearly blinding.

The girlfriend handed the paperwork with Neto's last name and his room number to the nurse on the third floor. She and the nurse went through a security door together. I wandered over from where I was hiding down in the cafeteria and found Neto's room. I told one of the nurses and the latest girlfriend my truck had broken down and needed a tow and I had to walk out to the hospital. Which was a lie. I was terrified at the idea of Neto passing on or worse needing an extended stay in the hospital. I had them convinced. This was when the girlfriend asked me for some money to help her out. Money for a cab and some drinks. She didn't seem too concerned over my truck situation and so I handed over the dollar bills.

"You the boy?" she asked me and I nodded. "You staying until this thing is all done?"

"I might have to run out and check on my truck," I said.

"They say they need a family member to sign some papers and be responsible for him. They say he's indigent."

"Indigent?"

"Yeah."

"Do you want to sit?" I said.

"I told you I needed the money to run out of here."

"Are you coming back tonight?" I asked the woman I had never met before.

"I told you I'm getting a cab."

I SAT DOWN in the waiting area and read the notices on the wall. In a couple of hours the nurse came out and said to me, "Ernesto was wild with the medication. Crying out. But he's comfortable now."

"Is he dead?"

"No, of course not."

"I was daydreaming he was," I said to her horrified look.

"I don't know what you mean."

"I mean I was wondering what I would tell the old folks if he was. The family. That's what I meant."

I went in through a glass door and found Neto sitting cross-legged on his bed. "I've got a kid's kidney," he said to me first.

"How you feeling?"

"A twenty-year-old kid's kidney. Said he crashed his motorcycle and they flew him up from Huerfano County."

"That sounds like what they do," I said.

"Medication's pretty heavy," he explained. "Heavy with rat poison."

"Poison?"

"Rat poison in the rejection medicine. So my body doesn't push it out of me or some shit."

"I can't see rat poison, Tio."

"That's what they said, Manito. Everything is all upside down and inside out here, you know."

He showed me the ten-inch incision in his lower abdomen. Pulled up his patient gown revealing all his crotch and verga for the room and the hallway to see.

The nurse said, "Hey watch the show now, Mr. Ortiz."

"Call me Neto," he winked and smiled to her and then he said to me, "I was just thinking how my kidney is younger than yours, Manito."

It was snowing outside as I stood to smoke. I thought about the kid with Neto's kidney crashing and losing control out on the blacktop. I thought about the kid never waking. Maybe the kid with Neto's kidney liked to sit way back on his crotch rocket and ride fast all day long down Highway 50 and out to the west-side housing projects where all the units looked the same and were framed by Pike's Peak. Maybe he liked to pass the semis heading out to the new Wal-Mart and brush up alongside the stream of air their massive wheels kicked up. Maybe he especially liked the bombed-out squalor that used to be the old reservoir and what they used to call Little Coyote Canyon. Maybe he also liked the old public swimming spot a little more north where the kids drank beer and fucked, liked watching high school kids scream and wail as they kicked off the forty-foot cliff.

He was in his twenties. The hospital won't let us in on any more details that that. Or maybe they don't keep the records. All we know is the kid with Neto's kidney died for Neto's second chance.

Months later my Tio Neto drank all night and in the morning he gathered up the girlfriend's possessions in a grocery cart outside his door. He had the thought to take it down to one of the second-hand shops, or segundos as he called them, out along 8th Street.

That's when Patsy Baca and Neto got into it, along with some of the kids from the other side of the complex.

First, he spotted Patsy wearing a pink camiseta the girlfriend once wore to a waitress job.

Neto watched the whole thing from behind his window. He couldn't take it. "Who and the hell told you to go through this and take that shirt," he yelled at her. "Those are my woman's clothes."

Patsy was quick to yell and laugh: "Garbage is free and clear for people to take. I ain't about to take no shit off you."

"Jesus Christ," Neto spat. He weaved in between parked cars. "People don't respect a man's property."

Later when the cops turned up to inquire about the argument and the complaints from the neighbors, Neto demanded the güero officer fill out a report for one pink blouse. The overweight officer saw the open container and asked him how much he had to drink. Asked about the knife he kept on a long chain attached to his keys. He went through my uncle's pockets.

"I am at home," Neto spat drunkenly. "I live right here. I own this place. It is my place. I'm the one who called you. I'm not some goddamn bum roaming the streets."

He stayed drunk for days after that and searched for other pieces. He found the girlfriend's jeans and one of her sweaters on a junky-looking girl over by the check-cashing place. In the Lebanese deli he swore he thought the girlfriend's housedress and slippers were walking across the street into the Christian Center. Down the block near the Dunkin' Donuts the girlfriend's corduroy pants stood at the corner market and along Colfax eating at the taco stand.

He held an open container from the 7-11 and back at home he pulled what was left of the cart into his apartment. He had the thought of burning up the clothes and killing the memories that way, even went as far as pouring lighter fluid onto the pile. He kept seeing the güero gal with her arms around him, seeing her kisses down his shoulder and chest. Her mess of hair on his shoulder and down beside him on the couch watching TV.

"Poor, Neto," the compadre Guzman said that afternoon as they bought each other shots at The Broken Arrow. "What the hell you think she's wearing now?"

"Fuck you, Guzman."

"A sight to see, travelling without no clothes."

"Why are you joking at a man's misfortunes?"

"It's a good story is all I'm saying. A good story to tell."

The two men decided to walk to the bus stop and head downtown. This helped my Uncle keep it together for the most part. He smoked and walked. Decided to stay a while in Guzman's company even though the man was a "degenerate" in Neto's mind and had no sense for ball games or dog races whatsoever, had no taste for liquor or weed. He told him to his face once down on Colfax at the Liquor Mart when they first got into it and were both arrested a year or so back.

"That Guzman will smoke anything. Knows no better," Neto would complain to people, always behind the man's back. "Fuckin' cigars from K-Mart."

He put up with the man and his stinky cigars and walked with the man to have someone to talk to. To have someone to distract him.

"Hate to see you all lonely and shit," Guzman pressed at him nearly all afternoon. "What you gonna do about rent? What you gonna do about them clothes? You gonna burn them all up?"

In the low light of afternoon the two sat in the second

bar of the day, a place called The State. They sat out front near where a huge plate glass window had been boarded up.

"Everything you say makes me want to crack your head against this bar," Neto said. He sucked at the foam of his draft.

"We gotta get out of Denver," Guzman added. "It's this goddamn city that's killing. Probably reason she moved on, you know?"

"How can a city hurt someone? That's so stupid."

"I'm just saying. Denver has been known to burn people up."

"Drop it."

"Probably no big romance neither. Bitch probably out getting religion up in Wyoming. Ain't nothing in Colorado no more for anybody but meth and hate around here. No work neither. Probably out in Wyoming. Or maybe Utah."

"What the hell do you know about women, Guzman?"

"I know women. I was married for nearly eighteen years. Couldn't get things right, though, but I was married. I tell you nothing destroys the soul more than living with a woman. Like suicide or some shit. I tell you you're better off."

"What the hell do you know anyhow?"

The two men pulled out their cards and dealt a hand. This was something the owner of the bars never liked; they broke it up no matter how much beer or shots the two men ever ordered. The girl Loraine came out and shut it down pretty quick. Told the two men to take their game out to the park.

"Jesus," she said. "How many times I gotta tell you that I get ticketed for card games. I ain't gonna lose no amount of money over you."

"Playing cards is not illegal," Guzman insisted.

"It's the money, for Christ's sake. If they come in and see your money on the table I'm out five hundred bucks in fines," she explained. She treated them as if they were children and sent them out without letting them finish their drinks.

"I'll tell you why the world's going to hell," Guzman observed as they walked.

Neto said, "I don't want to know."

"A man used to go into a bar with a stack of dollar bills and be seen as somebody."

"Oh shut up. You don't know nothing."

"I'm telling you now everyone does what the devil pleases and they write you a goddamn ticket for whatever and there's not a thing a man can do about it."

"Whatever, Guzman. You drunk. You loser."

"I tell you I got rousted from the park for falling asleep. Sleeping and resting in the shade. Ain't no kind of city for me and you."

"You were trying to live in that goddamn park if I know you, Guzman."

"Ain't right the way they treat people anymore is all I'm saying. And the problem with you is you hate people too goddamn much. You gotta love. I'm telling you, Neto."

"That's all you saying?"

"Yeah, that's all I'm saying. Ever since the steel mill died and everything went over to Japan this state has suffered. Piss poor world is what I'm saying."

"What do you know about steel?"

THAT AFTERNOON my Uncle gave Guzman a thesaurus and a collection of love poems the girlfriend picked up in Colorado Springs. This was done with a quick handshake and was something Neto immediately regretted. My Uncle had driven down to Colorado Springs with the girlfriend's sister and the girlfriend when they found a favorite bookstore closing down after dozens of years in business. The girlfriend broke down. She started to cry right out in the street and when Neto tried to console her near Palmer Park she continued, almost nonsensically explaining her love for the place when she was living in a halfway house around the block and would come in and rest and read books in the place for hours.

She cried and carried on, "I had no idea how easy it was to dissolve into oblivion."

Neto had nothing to say so he walked across the street to one of the segundos and bought her the love poems. He found it in a box out front for a few dollar bills.

LATER, GUZMAN SAID to him, "Let's get down to Lawrence Street and get some food."

"Goddamnit, Guzman. How many times do I have to tell you I ain't homeless. I have cans of food in my place right now. I came down here for a drink."

Because this was turning out to be a few of the worst days of my Uncle's life, he followed Guzman down to what the locals call Hobo Island and the 8:30 pm feeding. They stood in line at the Christian center for some hot food and a place to come out of the Denver sun. There was a woman pouring soup from a ladle that Neto swore he knew and swore he had talked to before, but Guzman ended that speculation very quickly.

"That was my wife," Guzman insisted. He started talking to old friends from sad Army days, a shirtless guy named Pat and another dressed in Army fatigues he called Ramirez. The men sat across from one another at the table and shoveled soup and bologna sandwiches.

"Is that your necklace?" Neto asked.

The bigger of the two men looked Neto in the eye and

squinted and nearly winked. "What the hell are you asking me? I'm wearing it, ain't I?" Ramirez said.

"Maybe you stole it from a woman I know?"

"What the hell are you talking about, fool? I don't even know you."

Guzman tried to ease the tension and started in on his history lessons: "Did you guys know that Playboy magazine once wrote that Colfax Avenue was the longest and most wickedest street in America?"

"This ain't no kind of a place to be calling me out. To be messing with a man while he's digesting," Ramirez said.

"Shit," Pat said. "He's drunk."

"They say no one lives on Colfax," Guzman continued. "Everyone passes through."

"I don't care where I'm at," Neto said. "To me I don't care where I'm at. If I see an injustice or something stolen from my woman I have to say something about it."

The huge barrel-chested man said nothing. He could've killed my Uncle where he sat and ate and drank his plastic cup filled with water, but instead Ramirez took a long while to slap his hand down onto the table. Ramirez shook his head and drained his soup and swallowed his sandwich in a tremendous gulp. He wiped at his mouth with his shirt and his forearm. He pulled the necklace from around his neck. It was a turquoise and silver choker job and the latch broke as he yanked. "I'm giving this to you, friend. You say it belongs to a woman you know and damn it who am I to disagree."

Guzman's belly convulsed as he held in laughs. Neto reached out his hand and took hold of it and everyone watched to see what Ramirez or his compadre Pat might do. Later Guzman would admit to Neto that the man Ramirez had lung problems and was telling folks he didn't want to live the month. He wanted to walk his last days on Colfax and Lawrence and all over Denver and Golden. When Neto accused him and called him out, he knew the thing to do was to help his fellow man.

"I'll tell people you thought that was my wife's necklace," Ramirez explained. "And the bitch ran off with my daughter and I ain't had nothing but bad luck since she did, and so it's yours."

Later the newly formed brotherhood of men rode the bus down 16th Street and watched the city from plate windows, and Neto pulled dollar bills from his sock and splurged on a round of drinks down at The Larimer Lounge.

There was no jukebox or radio to distract from Guzman's bullshit. "Wal-Mart and strip malls stole all the business and is responsible for the death of all the local businesses along West Colfax, or so reports The Denver Post," Guzman said.

"Who gives a rat fuck," someone said from along the wooden topped bar.

"And I also want to tell you Colfax runs nearly fifty miles," Guzman continued, addressing his remarks to Neto only to be ignored. "And I believe I've been born again to wander every inch of it."

29

Apartment in Oregon

Marisa likes to go to the supermarket. She sees old women searching for cantaloupes and can't help asking questions.

"Is that woman a mama?" she asks.

"Abuela," I say.

"What?"

"She's a grandma."

"Ab-well-ah," the girl mimics. "Where is the grandma?"

"Right there."

"No, my grandma?"

"Nevada."

"Where's Nevada."

"South of here."

"Why doesn't she come?"

"She has her family there and we have our family here."

"Will she send me presents?"

"Sure, mi hija. She'll send you presents. I'll make sure."

"For Christmas? And my birthday?"

"Sure."

"Where does all of this food come from?"

"Trucks. The land. All over."

"What land? What trucks?"

"Trucks from the highway."

She asks, "What are all those? They're frozen."

"Those are beers."

"When will I be in school like you?"

"Soon. Very soon."

"When will you be out of school?"

"Well, I have to write something. I have to write a thesis."

"What's that?"

"A big idea."

We walk around and finish our shopping. I don't select anything except for a six-pack. Marisa fills the basket with whatever she wishes, mostly candy and some things you couldn't eat: balloons, crayons, and a toy gun that sparks when you pull the trigger.

Marisa doesn't like the woman cashier. She gives her a serious frown. Doesn't like the way the father and the woman smile to one another.

"Hello little sweetie!" the cashier says. Her face is bright and warm. Marisa doesn't answer. I don't prompt her to. We pay our money and walk to the car.

"Mama is prettier than that woman," says Marisa.

"Yes."

"When did you meet mommy?"

"Years ago in Colorado."

"In Colorado?"

"Close to the mountains."

"Will I be close to the mountains?"

"We'll find them sometime. But we're closer to the ocean now."

"Can we go to the ocean?"

"If I can finish school."

MOSTLY I WRITE and ride the bus to class. I sit in the library reading and working at assignments. I've been given students to teach and been given a stipend for rent and for books. Late at night after returning home I listen to the rain outside the bedroom where I've set up Neto's card table. I have notebooks and try to write each day. Try to pull the family together the way I want them to.

Some nights I lose my thoughts and venture out to the bar or to the apartment of a friend. I drink and walk through campus on cool evenings waiting for the words to come to me and in the right order. I sit and talk to professors with years of experience and listen to their thoughts on failure and what to do with it. Sometimes I sit and gamble, play the poker machines at bars. That's legal in Oregon. I throw away stipend money after wandering between parked cars outside of bars and grills and I think of my Tio.

At night the girlfriend Inez and I find voices outside the window. We listen out for our neighbors. Together we listen to their lovemaking and when they argue. When voices travel through the walls and reach our inner ears, I go to their door and find myself hollering. "My daughter is trying to sleep," I yell, but mostly no one answers.

One night the little plastic phone rings and rings and I struggle to find it behind a stack of books near the window. It is my Uncle Neto, my sometimes uncle, who has gotten into the habit of getting drunk and calling long distance from a pay phone at his favorite place called the White Horse. He pays with a stack of quarters. He pays with phone cards. He tells me he got the only waitress there to dial in the numbers. He says his fingers are swollen.

"When you coming home, mi'jo," he slurs.

Usually I would have pacified him and reminded him of the dates of the three-month summer session but instead his voice makes me listen closely.

"How's the little one and the girlfriend?" Neto asks.

"They're sleeping, Tio. It's four in the morning here. I have to get up in a few hours and get to work, Tio."

"I'm sorry, mi'jo," the old man slurs. "I wanted to talk

to my boy."

THAT NIGHT the neighbors' arguments rise above the level of Inez' AM talk radio as she tries to sleep. The walls vibrate and the sound of a woman screaming shakes her. She lights a cigarette and finds me with my nose in the writing.

"You gonna call or am I?"

"Call for what?"

"They're killing one another up in that apartment. That's what."

"Let'em kill one another. Nothing to us."

"They'll wake the baby. You don't want your baby hearing all that death, do you?"

It gets me thinking and in a minute I find myself wandering up the steps and knocking on the neighbor's door. In another minute her bruised and pecked-out face greets me, and she has me standing near the couch where she settles back down. The place stinks of cat shit and mold. She wants to know if I'm a cop. Wants to know if I'm going to call the cops on Maynard.

"Who's Maynard?"

"He hits me and then runs out. That's all he knows."

"My daughter needs to rest and I can't have this screaming. I got a kid down there that needs to sleep."

"He'll kill me," she says. "He'll murder me and then the cops will have him quiet enough for you."

THAT MORNING I sit on the concrete stoop in a daze and stare into the rain and smoke my Tio's dark cigarillos while the sun spreads through the apartment.

Inez eventually comes out of the kitchen holding a milk carton in her hand. "This is what I have for our breakfast."

"We just went to the store."

"We can't eat beer or toys, Manito."

"I bought some cereal."

"And we ate it."

"Why don't you ride with the girl out there to the store."

"She wants to go with you. She only wants to go out with you. She only wants her father."

"I have to finish up some homework first."

"We can't eat your work."

"See that mouth on you? Just like your daughter's."

"Manito, just get to the store, please!" she holds the carton, balanced in the palm of her left hand. "Please! I work, too. Every little thing doesn't have to be a fight." Inez walks into the kitchen with the milk and sits down to her coffee.

I kiss my little girl goodbye and walk to the closet for my raincoat. I can't help but overhear the daughter and the mother as I search for lost keys.

"Daddy is gone," Marisa says.

"Yes, I know," Inez says.

They both sat at the kitchen table together.

"Is he coming back, mama?"

"After his school."

"He's always at school."

"It's important to him."

"Will he come home soon?"

"Yeah, the cabrón, he'll be back."

"What's a cabrón?"

"It means goat," she says and laughs. "I love him anyway."

"You love a goat?"

"Yeah," laughs Inez. "I do. I love a goat. Come here, mi'ja, on my lap."

THE NEXT NIGHT the noises begin earlier. Some pictures dive down from the walls. Inez' mother and father on their wedding day. The baby on the day of her christening. This is what sets me off. Has me away from my notebooks.

"Shut the hell up," I scream as I bang the ceiling with a mop handle.

"Shut the hell up," Marisa repeats.

"Don't you curse."

"I didn't."

"I just heard you."

"So did you."

"I can."

"Why can't I?"

"Because that's the world."

"I don't like the world."

"Me neither," I say. "But that's the way it is."

THE NEXT FEW NIGHTS are quiet until a week after the 4th of July holiday. The couple argue on the concrete stairs and the woman screams blood and murder into the parking lot. Inez pulls at me to keep me from the scene.

Maynard has his girlfriend down on the concrete and has her under his knee. He's screaming her name and slapping at her face. He drags her up the stairs into the front door before I can raise a hand to help.

"Me and that one are gonna head up in this mother before long," I tell Inez.

"You ain't gonna do nothing. They'll haul you outta here with all your street thoughts. Let them have their fights and keep out of it."

The next night the woman screams for Maynard to kill her. To take her life from her. The baby never wakes and I imagine the cops arrive too late to save anyone. And I say nothing. Stare at my notebooks and then stay warm down next to my Inez.

30

Long Distance

The first woman I drove down from Oregon to meet I happened to be in love with. At first we didn't say a word. The sun drained from the motel room and we kept the lights off.

"Twin Falls, Idaho, is where Evel Knievel made that jump," Bea started. "I thought you planned that. I thought you liked shit like that."

Her bangs shaved like Betty Paige's and her large green eyes made my heart vibrate through my neck. "No," I managed to say.

"I remember you always were around my father's motorcycle. Hell, I thought you'd show up with one."

I flipped on the television and hoped the unfamiliar voices off the screen would break the tension somehow. Finally she told me about going to school to become a community counselor. Then I told her about Inez, my daughters and college and then the move to Oregon, how I found a new beginning and was writing and reading. Seeing things through for one of the first times in my life.

"Oh, snap," she said. "Little cuz in graduate school."

"I've been talking to your old man," I interrupted.

"Who?"

"Your father."

"What are you talking about?"

"I worked at the State Hospital for a while and he got a bed there. He'd just had a stroke and I looked out for him."

"Is that what you came to tell me?"

"I'm writing him letters."

She paced the floor and lit a cigarette. She didn't say a word for a long while and I cursed, hating everything about myself. At first I thought she was leaving, getting back in her truckito and heading back out to Colorado. She put out her cigarette butt in the sink, jumped into the shower and left me on the bed.

While she toweled off and changed clothes in front of me, I finally had to ask, "The fiancé know about your father?"

"I'm not my bastard father," she finally said.

"I'm just asking, Bea."

"It's biological genealogy. Parents are a percentage of who we are, Manito. I'm something completely new."

"What?"

"It's easier to talk about this when we think of plants, you know?"

"He's a bastard but he's your father."

"He's a bastard and that's it."

She stood with her jeans and t-shirt dampening over her skin. She apologized and finished her cigarette and drank water from the tap. She told me she'd been fucking a woman.

I called to her in the bathroom. "Woman?"

"I met a friend of a friend and we sort of played around."

"That's the fiancé?"

"I can't stand to be with anyone else. Can't explain it. I wish I could make you understand."

"Christ."

"Don't hate on people like the Abuelo or Neto used to. Please."

"Jesus," I said.

"You'll meet her sometime maybe. You'll see her."

"Does she know you're here?"

"I tell her the truth and she respects me," Bea said. "She knows you're my brother and she knows we were close."

"We're cousins, Bea."

"You've got a good thing in Oregon? That's your world now."

I nodded and Bea slipped on her socks. She kept her clothes on and wiggled her small frame over to place her watch and car keys on the side table. She clicked on the light.

"So you're a lesbian now?" In a minute I asked her more questions, if she thought at all about the craziness when we were little mocos. The trouble and things we saw.

"There's only now," she said. "Time moves in only one direction."

"It just seems so much bigger to me," I told her.

"They all told me the old man was a killer and a thug. They all told me to be afraid."

"We all heard that."

"This one time he was leaving to work and he kissed me," she laughed and her eyes softened. "I was just a little moco. He leaned down and his lips were so warm. It made me think the man was just a man. No matter what they said. Or the papers said. No more of a monster than any of us."

Next I slipped up and mentioned I was on my way to meet with my mother.

She climbed beside me and I rolled into her and held her, or at least I held her the most she'd let me. "What in the hell you driving out there for?" she said.

Later on I had to ask, "Don't you remember how we climbed out the windows, and the old man dragged us to church and pinched at us—"

"Oh, Manito. Let's not tell such things. Let this be the

story right now."

My mother yelled at me at my second stop, all under endless Nevada blue skies. "Did you come here to live?" she said. "You can eat here but I don't have a bed for you."

She pushed back at her dyed auburn hair, and I noticed she looked tired and heavy.

"You can stay with your sister and her husband down the block. It's not that I don't want you here; I don't have a spare bed. You know you're welcome here. You know that?"

When I walked up she was outside on the cordless phone, stabbing at a pad of paper, getting a number down. "Your brother's here," she called into the receiver.

I could feel the heat coming off the blacktop driveway and hear the air conditioning unit buzzing up on the roof.

Three tired-looking wiener dogs ran around at her feet. She waved me inside and I used her bathroom and stayed in there a long time, staring at myself in the cabinet mirror and chain smoking.

"Don't use up all the hot water. Frank is coming home soon and needs to shower up," she said. "You'll have to move your car from the driveway."

I thought of envelopes filled with money and boxes of cookies shipped to my Abuela's on Spruce Street in Colorado. All signed, "XO, Mom."

"When I got home from work the Abuela took me down to Lena's and there you were. Just a little moco of a baby wrapped up on the kitchen table," my Tio Neto once told me. "That baby was you, Manito. You know that? That's the way people were in those days. Nothing to feel bad about."

I would sleep in the same basement as Tio Neto and my father. I would live underneath the same Abuelitos and I would dream of Neto and my father out in the front yard scrapping and clawing. I would stare at the same knots in the wood of the unfinished ceiling and I would hurt for my life in the way Neto hurt for his. Picturing Bruna from photographs and what family had told me, I imagine Neto staring at the same concrete walls.

At five the husband came home to Bruna and dinner was on the table. He had a round belly and gray hair with reading glasses up on his forehead. He told me he drove a truck in the silver mines and could find me work.

I told him I was on my way back to Oregon and school. I told him I was teaching as a graduate assistant.

"Assistant to who?" he asked.

"To professors or to the department, I guess."

"Where's this again?"

"Oregon," I answered and left it at that.

"I've been to Seattle," the husband mentioned. "That's a good looking ride you got out there."

"Belongs to a friend."

Bruna said, "You don't have your own car? I never liked borrowing."

"I meant I bought it from him. To make the drive."

"What's with all this cigarette smoke in the house? I can't even breathe. I have to open all the windows."

"I can't have you smoking in here, son," the husband said.

After plates of cheese enchiladas I found myself only wanting to smoke in the bathroom.

"What the hell are you doin' in there, kid?" the husband said at the door. "How you feelin'?"

"He's stubborn like his Neto," she said.

"Which one was he again?"

—

After Frank went to sleep, my mother sat trapped and answered most of my questions. I scratched them down in my notebook:

. . . You know I was born in a bed out in the San Luis Valley somewhere . . . Who the hell knows where? They would do that in those days. A mid-wife and a doctor would come by for a little bit . . . I don't know what you want to hear, John Relles...

I met your father working at the K & P on Evans Street. The K & P was a dance hall. He worked in the coatroom. I don't think he really worked there. I think Abuelo Ortiz worked there as a bartender or a bouncer. Maybe he was a drunk and hung around to drink. Some stories you don't tell. What else you want to know? I do remember they had slot machines in the back. I had never seen a slot machine. I didn't know what it was. Mother told me later it was illegal. In fact, mother was the one who took me down there. I sat and waited while she was with people from work. I can't remember if she was with Jeri then. She must have been. I was a little girl. Fifteen or so... What else?... Oh, I also remember he poured what was left of different beer bottles in to one bottle. I thought that was gonna make him sick but he did it anyway. This was back when we were in love.

. . . No, I don't remember Neto there. He must have been at home. I don't know. Neto was always sitting around for a disability check from someplace. I mean, not at that time but most of the time. Later on, I mean. No guidance or discipline. Never went to church . . . Yeah, Neto fought with Jeri about something but I'm

not exactly sure. People didn't need much reason to get into something in those days... After your father died, I was left with nothing and I had to scramble around for whatever I could. I had a baby to give birth to and bills and everything. Your Grandmother Montoya was not a very kind woman.

... I couldn't take a baby on the road. I couldn't raise a boy. I didn't know boys. I'm sorry but I couldn't do it. I didn't have it back then. I didn't have it. I had to give you to the Abuelos. I had to. I never told you these things. But I'm sorry. You had a family. You had the Grandparents.

Don't despise me.

My sister wore a purple maternity dress and looked like snapshots of a young Bruna. Her memory was pretty remote though she was the one to reveal to me Frank wouldn't have me moving in with them.

"Don't hate the woman too much," my sister told me. "You don't know her life."

In a minute she clicked her lamp on and we sat on her couch staring at old pictures. She kept repeating how I looked like the young man in photos that was my father.

"Not much like mama," she said. "A quiet angry look to you."

"Angry?"

"I remember a dance one time for the Grandfather," the sister said. "It was his birthday and we were all in a broom dance and you were pissed because you didn't want to be in it. You were like eight, I think. Which means I was seven, right? How old are you?"

"I don't remember that."

"The Grandparents made you hang around me," she said. "This is your sister, they kept telling you, but you didn't want to have nothing to do with me or Mama. Not raised with us. I can imagine what it was like having people telling you, This is your mama, you know. This is your sister."

"Yeah."

"They made you hang around me. I walked you out to church, remember? And you dragged your feet the whole time. They had you in cowboy boots. You remember that?"

"No," I said.

"We were in Mass and you kept fidgeting around and finally I had to walk you out of there. It's like you didn't want to have nothing to do with me."

I told her I was sorry and that a daughter had made me see things differently.

"Oh, I heard you had a baby girl," she said smiling. "You've got to bring pictures and let the poor thing write to us. Or bring her for Thanksgiving. She's got to know family."

It was 4 a.m. before my Tio Neto finally picked up the phone and at first I didn't understand him.

"Was that you calling all them damn times?" he said.

"I guess it was," I said. "I was staying up all night and wanted to see how you were keeping yourself. I wished I knew what you were doing."

"I could've killed you for calling me all them times, you know."

"Where's Mona?"

"Who?"

"The girlfriend?"

"I give her money and she disappears. You know how it is."

"When?"

"This was last week."

"She'll probably show up soon."

"A college boy with a load in your diaper."

"What?"

"When you were a little moco you walked around with a load in your diaper," Neto joked. "You don't remember? Always with a load of shit."

"I'm at Bruna's."

"Where?"

"My mother's."

"Holy hell," Neto said. "I had a mother once."

"That's where I'm calling from. Nevada."

"Sometimes I swear I think you want her shit," he said. "You drove all the way down there yourself. She didn't call looking for you? Looking for money?"

"No, Tio. I wanted to see her," I told him. "She's my mother."

"She's a whore," he said. "Poor little Manito with a load in the diapers."

Then I forgave him and explained about the university and the wife and the daughter. Nothing I hadn't talked about before.

His voice continued to slur nonsense. "I'll see you in your sad, damned dreams, Relles' boy."

A COUPLE OF MONTHS LATER I drove down with Inez and Marisa. It was Thanksgiving I think and Inez brought a vegetable dish, and we sat around and told stories. For a long while though I smoked in the driveway and listened to laughing and dinner plates clanking.

The morning we left was a Sunday and while Inez and the girl finished up in the bathroom, my mother hugged me and put some folded dollar bills into my shirt pocket before I could wave her off.

In the middle of her posing me for a picture I popped the trunk of my Chevy and unwrapped Neto's La Virgen de Guadalupe shrine. The plaster had cracked and the golden rope around her waist was frayed and fading.

In a minute I thought to carry her over near the cement foundation. "Neto had it in his apartment," I said. "It's what's left of the old folks."

"Don't want that," she said at first. She ran after me and nearly put her hands on me.

"Saved from the old neighborhood. Since the Abuela Cordelia passed," I explained. "You can move it when we leave."

Frank came out and slid in between mother and son, assuming we were arguing. We were too close to one another, just about an inch, I guess, and any other time I think we would've gotten into it. Had words. But the three of us huddled around to witness La Virgen, to point out a few missing fingers and cracks to her palms.

My mother pulled and borrowed Frank's reading glasses. She kneeled down beside me and her mouth hung wide. "Are you the one keeping the things we all throw out or what?"

Part Six

San Luis Valley

31

Trip Home

The Green Line bus cried to a stop near Alamosa, Colorado, and dropped Lena Valdez downtown still holding on to her mama's Rosary beads. She stood and grinned at her father's primer colored truckito parked alongside the ticket office.

Through the driver side window Lena threw her arms around his sunburned neck and nearly exposed shoulders. "You getting so damn old, Papa."

Lena's Jefe, Carlos Montoya, shook his head while she hugged him.

"In the last six months I've had sores and weakness in my legs," the Jefe admitted to Lena's concern.

Lena threw her suitcase into the truck bed and ran around to sit beside the old man. "What's the baby's name, Jefe?"

"We named her Bruna after your Great Abuela from Chama."

"The poor thing has to live with a name like that."

"It is a family name and Felipa thought the baby should have an old name," the old man explained. "Tranquilena has served you, girl. So don't say no more about it."

Lena watched as he rocked his legs back and forth and rubbed at their poor circulation.

"You should have me drive, Jefe."

"You got a license, did you?"

"No, Jefe."

"How are you going to drive me? I'm not near half as dead as you think I am, Lena."

"Well, you got the sugar and I'm looking out for you, Jefe."

"Shit."

On the way to the Jefe's house, which seemed to be farther out than she remembered, Lena leaned back and closed her eyes, opening them when the truckito stopped for a signal light on First Avenue, and again at the El Monte Hotel.

The Jefe had slammed the door and started unloading her suitcase before Lena noticed.

"What's this, Jefe?"

"Your stepmother wants you here, hija," the old man admitted. He wiped the sweat from his brow with remorse.

Lena's eyes played an amused game with this, and she thought she might cry and carry on. She thought she might lose all her courage right here in the middle of downtown Monte Vista.

"If this works out for you, mi'ja. This might all be for the best, no?"

THAT NIGHT LENA CALLED JERI back in Huerfano. First, she tried the apartment and the Army Depot where he worked for the Ordnance Corps. She also called The State over on Main where he drank. Lena walked from her single room on the second floor down to the lobby in between each call to ask the round woman behind the desk for change. She had to ring the bell on the front desk, and each time the woman walked through the back door as if to greet a new customer.

"Phone hasn't seen this much attention in years," she joked.

When she finally got the boyfriend on the phone, he

was at the bar and she could tell he was drunk. She heard it in his slurs and in his laughter. Her lips pursed and her eyes glowed with tears and she shook her head.

"I made it, Jeri," she said. "I'm at a hotel because the old lady don't want me."

"Hotel?"

"Yeah."

"Who the hell is paying for that?"

"I had it, Jeri."

"Jesus Christ. When do you get the baby?"

Instead of answering, she held the receiver tightly and she played with the phone cord. "If you have to go downtown to get something to eat, Jeri, do it. Go down to the lunch counter at the drugstore for a hamburger sandwich if you have to. You need to eat."

"You hear me? I said when do you get your baby?"

"I'll have her soon, Jeri. But I'm not going to see nobody 'til the morning."

"And the old man?"

"He drove me. He's gotten old, Jeri. Really old. You should see him."

"How long do I have here by myself? When you coming back, mujer?"

"Soon. I have work."

In her sleep that night she returned to Jeri and the apartment, and she woke wringing wet and looking more tired than when she first slipped between the sheets. She stared at herself in the vanity mirror and for a good long while she thought she heard voices and a baby crying in the hotel. The contents of the room felt strange and sad: the suitcase, the table and chair along with the half-made bed. Around midnight she opened her door and stared down at the empty hallway and out the window and the view over Main Street. She put her head against the cold glass and whispered her prayer.

THE NEXT MORNING the darkness broke while Lena had her cigarette. Out in front of the hotel she waited for the Jefe's truckito. A honk sent her running back inside for her suitcase and her coat. It was the Jefe who stopped the engine as Lena dropped into the dusty bench seats.

The Jefe's face was expressionless even as it began to burn in the morning sun coming through the windshield.

"What you got to say to me, Papa? What you come to say?"

"Your stepmother won't leave the room this morning and she won't stop crying."

"Well," Lena said with scorn and raised her hands. "Take me to talk to her. You're her husband. Take me to talk with her."

For an hour and a half the two drove around the barren city in silence. The Jefe stopped for coffee and cigarillos. The old man filled his rig with gasoline, bullshitting with the boys at the garage. He bought some beer. Lena never moved a muscle, but rather sat in the truckito. Again, she grabbed her mother's Rosary beads and said her words of prayer until the Jefe returned with his beer masked in a paper sack, placing it between himself and his oldest daughter.

As he fired the engine and looked over towards Chapman Street, he was half hoping it might be blocked or closed. He whistled loudly and sang a little into the deserted morning. The houses and trees passed quickly as they drove. Lena again had that sensation, as on the bus, that inertia pushed her out towards an answer to her sadness of the last six months. She stared outside. The unpaved streets, where there normally would have been trucks of men piling past, were empty.

The Jefe backed the truckito silently into his driveway and lit another cigarette before finally asking, "When does the next bus leave, Lena?"

"I don't know the time."

"I'm asking you what time the bus leaves for Huerfano County, Lena. You came and you gotta know the time for this. You've got to be quick, girl."

"9:15 I think, Jefe," Lena answered. "The bus leaves at 9:15."

"So we gotta be leaving for Alamosa by what time?"

"8:15 or so, Jefe."

"8:15 then," the Jefe answered. He looked at his knees and at his shaking hands. "I'm gonna sit here and drink one of these beers, Lena. Now get in there and get your baby, you hear? Get in there."

"Yes, Jefe," Lena said automatically. She opened her mouth and shut it again with shock. The Jefe pulled a Pabst Blue Ribbon from his sack below the seat and popped the top with an opener attached to his key ring.

Sometimes on sunny, cold mornings Lena had stood on the back porch of her apartment watching her neighbor's children and dreamt of this day. Ever since the phone call came that the Jefe wanted no part of this child's life, ever since the stepmother got on the phone and agreed quietly and happily, Lena had been thinking of this moment.

Slowly and carefully Lena unlatched the side screen door and walked into the kitchen. Ordinarily the kitchen would have been filled with the stepmother's children, but this morning it was empty. The small wood stove was quiet and the radio broke the silence with the morning weather and rancher report.

"You here for Felipa?" the stepmother's sister said in answer to the creaking screen door. She held a quiet baby in her arms.

Lena nodded and smiled. She stared across the room and tried hard to figure out the situation with her eyes. Maybe she was stunned, or maybe the lack of sleep caught her weak in the knees.

"Do you have everything you need back where you live?" The sister looked at Lena with a furrowed brow.

"No," Lena said. She cupped her hands over her mouth and her weak eyes ran over with tears. She nearly fell to one knee.

"No?" the sister yelled. "How do you expect to raise a child if you don't have what you need at home."

Lena's mouth was dry: "I didn't know I was even going to be here today. I work, you know."

The sister pulled the blankets from a small bassinet on the kitchen table around the baby and handed her over to Lena. The girl was in Lena's arms and she felt weak and nearly sick with the physical weight—the actuality of it all. They both stopped talking and started listening to the baby.

"What would you name the girl?"

"Bruna," Lena answered. "The same as Felipa named her."

"Felipa can't help crying. She doesn't seem unhappy about anything; she just can't stop crying."

"Should I talk to her?"

"Jesus Lord in heaven, no," the sister said.

Lena bolted out the door and raced over to the trucki-to and her Jefe. Lena shook her head and smiled, wiping the tears away above the bundle in her arms. Brunacita stopped the silence of the Jefe's drinking and staring with her soft cries.

The Jefe swore. He wiped his tongue over his teeth and spit out the window, "Here comes somebody, Lena," the Jefe said as he fired up the engine. "Well, you going or not?"

Lena set herself gently in the cab and slammed the rusty

door. Her chest expanded and Brunacita trembled in her arms.

"Lena!" Felipa called from outside of the truckito, beating her palms across the hood. The sound went up and up. "Lena!"

"It's over, Felipa," the Jefe yelled through the windshield. He drained his beer and wiped at his mouth. Lena's voice went on caressingly to the baby in her arms as the truckito pulled from the driveway.

"You have her and it's over now, Lena," the Jefe repeated.

"Lena!" Felipa yelled. Standing in the road, she looked tired and ragged in her housecoat, her face red and eyes anxious and wet.

As the truckito accelerated, Lena turned and watched the Jefe's wife fall to her knees in a wash of dust.

John Paul Jaramillo was born and raised in Southern Colorado. At Oregon State University he earned his MFA in creative writing (fiction) and currently works as Professor of English in the Arts and Humanities Department of Lincoln Land Community College in Springfield, Illinois. His stories and essays have appeared in numerous publications, including *The Acentos Review*, *PALABRA A Magazine of Chicano and Latino Literary Art,* and *Somos en Escrito*. In 2013 his collection *The House of Order* was named an International Latino Book Award Finalist. In 2013 *Latino Boom: An Anthology of U.S. Latino Literature* listed him as one of its Top 10 New Latino Authors to Watch and Read.

www.ingramcontent.com/pod-product-compliance
Lightning Source LLC
Chambersburg PA
CBHW030528310726
48979CB00010B/1836/J

* 9 7 8 0 9 9 8 7 0 5 7 1 2 *